BELIEVING LIES

Elizabeth Anne

Dedicated to:
Richard Husk (Poppop)
Billie Starr-Husk (Nana)
Daniel Merlo (Grandpa)

I miss you all.

Prologue

Thirty Minutes

He's dead.

My eardrums became walls of stone. Cars drove past, but the only thing I could focus on was raging thoughts gathering in my head. The violent thumping of my beating heart echoed throughout my body. Lights from the stores I was passing were flashing in different, aggravating colors, hurting my eyes. My stomach turned over, and the inside of my mouth was dry sandpaper. I could feel bile rising to the back of my throat, enough to make me stop on the sidewalk to breathe so I wouldn't throw up. I heard the chatter of people walking by me, but I couldn't make sense of anything they were saying.

A girl bumped into my shoulder. She grabbed her bicep and winced before she looked at me. "I'm so sorry," she said. She eyed the dirt and blood all over my face. "Oh my gosh, are you okay?"

I chuckled, then grazed my hand across my cheek. The blood started to spread, like an artist would do with paint. I could picture the red liquid coloring the paleness of my skin. I felt the gash across the side of my face when I touched it. The edges were hard, and it hurt like hell when I felt the open wound.

"Yeah, I just tripped. I'll be okay, though," I lied. She nodded slightly, walking away with fear written in her eyes.

Sweat dripped down my brow. I wiped away what I could, smudging the blood on my hand across my forehead. My eyelids threatened to close as I walked down the paved sidewalk. Droplets of rain fell onto my skin. I looked up at the clouds, remembering that Mom warned me of the storm that night. Within a few seconds, the rain got heavier. The way the water ran down my head made the scene from thirty minutes ago come rushing to me. I shuddered when the horrifying images appeared in my head.

The screaming, the arguing, and the blood all came hurling back to me like a nightmare you try to forget. The harder you resist, the more it refuses to leave your brain. I couldn't get the picture of him lying on the ground erased. I couldn't get any of it out of my mind. The horrific scene was taunting me.

Why won't they stop?

The look of terror in his eyes pierced through my soul. His bloody figure tormented me. Pain abused my head, pounding against my skull. I grabbed it with trembling fingers to ease the torture. The pain refused to leave, only strengthening its grip over my sanity.

The streetlights blinded me. My eyes burned and turned teary. I wanted to run and hide—far away from there, somewhere where no one could find me. But I couldn't do that. I had to keep walking. I pushed myself, neglecting the sweat running down my neck and dripping onto my shirt.

Thank god I wore black.

I knew my feet were moving, but I wasn't paying attention. My mind was elsewhere. It was like I was trapped in some sort of daze, walking around aimlessly.

Like a zombie.

My thoughts started weighing on me, and the pressure built up. The pain was unbearable; I didn't care where I was going. I wanted a break. A break from my head and my feet, but most of all from my body. My eyelids felt like weights, and I closed them for just one second.

"Get out of the road!" a raging voice screeched. I opened my eyes to find headlights staring back at me. A loud blast rang through my ears. I searched for an escape plan but came up empty. I couldn't see anything else—the lights were paralyzing me.

And I thought the streetlamps were too much.

The car swerved out of the way and down the street. It went far, but not far enough for me not to see the driver flipping me off. I stood on the road for another minute, processing everything. I had closed my eyes for just one second. It was only one second.

How did I end up on the road?

I stared at the end of the street. It was all darkness. The light from the lamps shined on a few spots, but each only covered maybe three feet of the sidewalk. People could have been hiding in the shadows, lurking, and waiting for someone. I scanned the empty road. Then my eyes saw something else. It was a shadow or a figure of another person. Seemed like a boy, but I couldn't tell. It was dark out, and he was far, but close enough for me to notice him. Goosebumps appeared all over my body. I shivered as I felt a glare from his direction. We were looking at each other, at least I thought we were. I silently debated if I should go up to him, but he walked away before I could act.

Guess that's my decision.

The road went silent. It was as if everything had just…stopped. The trees sang a still hum as the wind brushed past, but that was it. No people around, no cars, no mysterious figure at the end of the street. I was finally alone. It seemed like a good moment to do something I was waiting to do ever since I saw him on the ground bleeding.

I screamed.

1

Five Hours

I kept running. Every step I took felt like a leap. All I could see were trees passing by me as I ran. There had been nothing else for the past hour. No roads, no cars, no humans except for him. It didn't matter which way I went; I was stuck in the forest. My feet pounded against leaves; the sound of them crunching was the only thing I could hear. Every muscle in my body begged for a break which made running ten times harder. The fear of him catching me was the only reason I didn't take one. I took a sharp breath, using it as my only source of energy to sprint, which quickly faded soon after. A cramp began to develop on my right side; my kidneys felt as if they were imploding. But I pushed myself; I kept my legs moving. Heavy breathing echoed in my ear as I was reminded that his feet were in sync with mine.

The sun began to go down, fast. I turned to look at it, a bright, orange light hitting my pupils. Before I knew it, the only light I could see was shining from the few gaps in the trees that the sun stood behind. I looked ahead of me just in time to see a branch coming at my head. I ducked, but the top of my forehead still got scraped by the end of it. I could feel blood running down, falling onto the bridge of my nose. I wiped it away, pushing myself further.

Every turn I took, he took with me. I wanted to look back to get a clear image of his face, but I knew it would only have slowed me down. Not knowing who was chasing me made me feel even sicker. Did I know them? Were they a stranger to me? The only thing I knew for sure was to never stop running. My feet were aching, burning with pain. I needed to stop. Every time I caught myself slowing down, the sound of his stomping feet would remind me to go faster.

How was he not tired?

No matter how fast I ran, he was always right behind me. He was so close I could feel the heat of his breath on my shoulder. The forest was hot enough as it was, keeping my body sweating constantly. It wasn't until he grabbed me that I knew there was no chance of escaping. He threw me to the ground effortlessly. My back broke the impact of my fall when I landed on rocks and snapped twigs. The rocks were hard, and I knew I'd end up with bruises. The ends of the branches poked at my skin, drawing blood. I looked up at the figure that was chasing me. His face was disguised with blood, dirt, and tears. Even with the night that had fallen upon us, I could easily tell who it was.

"Nick!" I called out.

My eyes launched opened to see that I wasn't in the hands of Nick Walter. I took a deep breath, trying to relax, but it resulted in me choking. I guess I was holding my breath, but I don't know for how long. Darkness crept around me, bringing an anxious feeling along. I quickly turned to my side to turn my lamp on. My room became bright as I checked my surroundings. Posters of old punk rock bands hanging on my navy-blue walls made me feel safe. I hadn't realized how much comfort they gave me until that moment. I wasn't being chased by a bloody Nick in the middle of a forest. It was a nightmare. That felt real. Almost like a memory. But I was safe and alone.

Am I?

I was searching for air. I sat on my mattress, waiting for my lungs to be filled. It made me feel like I was six again when I used to wake up screaming for help. Mom would hold me until I felt safe. I wanted to run to her, for her to hold me. But I thought about what she would think if she knew what I had done. I thought of Nick, and his image came back to me. Watching him bleed out of his head made me feel sick to my stomach. The thick red blood was gushing out of his head, and I stood there and watched. His eyes were focused on me; emptiness stood behind them. At least they were, until his eyes were blocked by the blood pouring from his head.

My heart started beating out of my chest. It felt like my stomach was tearing to shreds. I took deep breaths to calm myself down. I looked around to check again to make sure I was safe. My head was pounding from the fear slowly building up, waiting to pop. I stood up and felt all the blood rush to my head. Heat rose to my face while I checked the time.

3:07 a.m.

The air in my room felt thick as if someone had put a sauna

in there. Sweat stuck to my body, making me feel sticky. I grabbed a towel that was lying on my floor and tried to wipe it off, but it didn't work. The heat started to make me light-headed. I walked over to my bathroom. Turning the sink on and letting the water fall down the drain reminded me of the blood from the night before. I closed my eyes and let the darkness surround me. I splashed cold water on my face and let the water flow down on its own. I wiped my eyes, then stared into the mirror. My black hair had gotten wet and slicked to the side of my forehead. It started to drip water, making a clinging sound when it hit the bottom of the sink. Shivers ran up my back, and I suddenly felt like I wasn't alone.

What the hell?

A figure stood behind me. Not close enough for me to feel it. There was no face, no distinctive body either. Just a black shadow. Standing there. If it had eyes, they would've been staring into mine. I took in a shaky breath, feeling my fingers quiver. I closed my eyes and told myself it was nothing, a mere shadow. When I opened my eyes again, it was closer. Almost breathing on me. I could feel the heat radiating from whatever it was. My heartbeat was so fast I thought it was about to break my rib cage. My entire body was trembling with fear. I quickly turned around to find nothing but my shower. There was no weird figure. I looked back in the mirror and just saw my plain, white wall.

I must be seeing things.

I rinsed my face again, hoping to wash away whatever that was. Rubbing my eyes created pressure behind them. The strain crawled up to my head to form a migraine. I winced at the sudden pain and grabbed a cloth. I patted myself dry before looking in the mirror again.

I didn't see the shadow man, but I saw something else. My gash from the night before was wide open, and blood was pouring from it. It oozed out, radiating a smell that I could only describe as metallic. My eyes were bloodshot instead of their normal ocean blue, and my upper lip was cut open. The swelling from my eyes started to block parts of my vision. It was like blowing up a bouncy house or an air mattress. I was watching my face puff up. I looked at my arms and noticed dark bruises all over them. Each one seemed to have climbed up my arms, dragging an intolerable pain with them. I watched as the blood dripped from my face and fell on my shirt.

Oh my god.

I fell backward at the sight. I had no idea where all the blood and bruises had come from. I didn't remember getting cut up that bad or bleeding that much. I didn't even feel the pain until I saw it. I started backing up when a sharp and sudden pain reached the back of my head from hitting the wall. I sat on my bathroom floor and waited as the darkness crept over me. Then there was nothing.

There was only darkness for what seemed like minutes. Slowly, the pain in my head worsened. My eyes slowly opened, and they drifted around the room. That's when the yelling began.

"Kyle! Time to get up!" There was banging on my door, which created a loud echo in my head from the migraine.

Wow, it's like I have a hangover.

But worse.

I stared blankly at the tiled floor for a few moments.

Why did I sleep on the bathroom floor?

I thought about it for a few minutes, trying to remember what happened last night. Flashes of what he looked like pierced through my brain. I pushed them away to remember the rest of my night.

I was bleeding.

I jumped up and peered into the mirror. The blood dripping from my face had completely disappeared. Even the wound across my cheek seemed to have healed a bit. There was no blood gushing from it. I checked my shirt, and it was clean besides some patches of dirt from the forest.

I forgot to change.

I looked at my arms, and the purple bruises that were there last night were gone. I checked all over, and there was nothing. I even poked at them to see if they were just faded, but no. There was no pain. I was fine. I looked back at the mirror. The glass showed my reflection. I seemed fine. Besides the huge cut on my face, you wouldn't think there was anything wrong with me. The mirror shimmered in the light.

Why did I see things that weren't there?

"Kyle!" a high-pitched voice screamed from downstairs. Before I left my room, I took one more peek at the glass that seemed to make me see things. No one was there except me. That pissed me off even more. I closed my fists as tight as I could to stop myself from punching it. I made my way down the stairs to find Mom packing things up, getting ready to leave for work.

She's the chief of surgery at the Concord General Hospital. She used to tell me all about her surgeries when I was little, back before she became chief. Now she says all she does is watch over others to make sure they don't kill anybody. She also deals with lawsuits and cases. I don't know what that means. Why would a hospital have a lawsuit filed against it? They are supposed to help people.

"There is this big case at work, and I am extremely late to meet with the patients. They must be a wreck thinking about the surgery with no answers," she rambled while making her coffee. While it was brewing, she grabbed a scrunchie and started putting up her silky brown hair. "I mean, who wouldn't be?"

I stood in the doorway, waiting to see if she would notice me before she left. If she would even look at me. I had watched her walk out that door without even giving me a thought for years. She was always so busy. When she was just a surgeon, we rarely saw her. Then she got promoted, and she practically disappeared. She was never home unless it was midnight to six a.m.

"And I am going to stay at the hospital tonight. The surgery is going to take at least seventeen hours, and we don't start for another six," she said while grabbing her to-go mug. "What am I missing? Oh! Have you seen my big folder with all of my work papers?"

I shook my head, and she frowned. Her nose crinkled up whenever she did that, causing a crease between her eyebrows. She sighed and just kept collecting items around the living room. She placed her mug down to put some things into her bag.

"Can I not go to school today?" I pleaded, finally speaking up.

She stopped for a second and looked at me. She opened her

mouth to answer, then she noticed the gash across my cheek. She gasped and dropped her purse. Her heels clicked against the floor as she made her way over to me.

"Sweetie, what happened?" She held my face, placing her fingers alongside the gash. "It looks like you need stitches."

"No, I'm fine." I pushed her away. "I just fell yesterday." She looked at me as if she didn't believe me. It was the truth, just not the whole truth. I didn't tell her where I fell and why I fell. I didn't tell her a lot of things that happened. I didn't know most of the things that happened myself.

"Well, you have to be more careful. And don't forget to clean it out. And no, you cannot skip school. You need to go." She grabbed her bags and coffee, then reached for the door. "Ask Henry for a ride. He's going to work this morning so he can bring you. Okay, bye. I love you!"

She kissed me on my other cheek before leaving and shutting the door behind her. I heard her engine turn on and listened as the tires screeched down the driveway. The sound of her car faded with every second.

Why's she in a rush?

I looked over at the basement door. There was a sign on the door that he'd had since we were little that read, Keep Out, Kyle. Made me feel like I was just this thing he couldn't get off the bottom of his shoe. Henry was my older brother, who looked after me until I was eight. That's when he decided he wanted nothing to do with me. He shut himself in and locked everyone else out. He didn't leave the basement for months. Mom finally decided to let him move his room down there. Three years later, and he's still there.

I made my way to our expensive kitchen. At least it looked like it was. Everything was new and clean. I didn't care all that much. Sure, it looked nice, but no one used it. Our marble top counters were always clean because no one used them. None of our cabinets were broken or chipped because there was no food in the house. We've grown up on takeout and paper plates. It is nice not to do dishes, though. I opened the fridge to peek inside when I heard footsteps coming up from the basement. Henry walked in, running his fingers through his hair. His deep brown hair was just a mixture of Mom's and Dad's genes and one of the things he tormented me about. He used to tease me, saying how I wasn't even Mom's kid, considering I looked nothing like her. I know better now, but it was the worst thing you could possibly hear when you're in elementary. I would stare into the mirror for hours, trying to find a similarity between Mom and me. She has deep brown eyes that match her hair. I have these oceanic, bright blue eyes with black hair that are just like my dad's.

For some reason, Henry started to flex his arms as if trying to threaten me with how much he had been working out. I rolled my eyes, looking back into the fridge. Out of the corner of my eye, I watched as he slipped his red uniform on over the tank top he was wearing.

He didn't have a respectable job like Mom and Dad. He worked for a small hardware store in town. The owner was generous and paid Henry a little more than minimum wage. Henry lucked out with the job, but he never seemed to be that appreciative of the guy.

"Mom said you have to drive me to school," I told him, closing the fridge door. We had nothing in there besides milk and some old hotdogs. No one ever went grocery shopping for the house.

"You can walk. I'll be late to work if I drop you off." He grunted, fixing his hair in the mirror that was hanging on the wall.

"I can't walk!" I argued. "I'll be late and sweaty!"

He smirked at me while he grabbed a mug of coffee. "Too bad. I have to go."

He left, slamming the door shut. It rang in my ears, slowly fading away. The sound reminded me of something. Like I'd heard it before, but it was followed by a feeling of fear.

I ran outside in my dirty clothes to see Henry getting in the car. His smirk remained, which made me see red. I could feel the anger boiling inside of me. I wanted to punch him in his stupid face. I pictured myself hitting him, his jaw being knocked out of place, and him falling to the ground. The sound of his head banging against the driveway, his blood pouring out of his skull. His life leaving his unmoving body.

Like Nick.

Except I wouldn't feel guilty if it was Henry.

He climbed into the driver's seat, glaring at me. I marched

up to his window. His face peered through it, but he wasn't paying attention to me. My fists automatically started to bang on the glass. His head snapped to face mine, and he rolled down the window.

"What the hell's wrong with you?" He cursed. "You are gonna break the damn window!"

"Dude! You can't just leave; I need a ride!"

He rolled it back up, ignoring me. His eyes pierced ahead, and he drove out of the driveway. I watched as his crappy, old car rumbled down the street. I stood there and listened until his car couldn't be heard any more.

Guess I am going to be late.

I banged the door closed when I made it back into the house. The sun was just starting to come up. It shined through the windows. My body in front of the window grew a shadow on the floor. Reminded me of the figure from last night. I raised my hand and watched my shadow do the same. I started curling my fingers into a fist; the shadow copied.

I control it.

I walked down the hallway of my house. Picture frames lined the walls; the reflections from the glass blinded me. I looked at a picture frame that was sitting on a bookcase. It was an old picture. The edges were a bit rough, and it looked wrinkled. I was confused why Mom would put a picture like that in a frame. She always talked about making sure everything looked nice and new. The picture had been taken at a beach. Henry, Nick, and I were all sitting at the edge of the water. Henry was messing with my hair, and I was in the middle of laughing, which was something I haven't done in a while. Nick's light brown hair was golden at the time, perfectly matching his tan in the photo. I could almost see his piercing green eyes as if he were actually in front of me. I noticed that Nick had a goofy smile on his face, covered in what looked like ice cream.

"Kyle!" Nick screeched out. The wind blew against my face, bringing sand with it. The smell of salt filled my nose, and I took a big whiff before running to Nick. We loved going to the beach together; it was our favorite thing to do back then.

"Nick!" I yelled, watching him tread water. I laughed at him,

sprinting to get nearer. I was always obsessed with water, no matter what it was: rain, baths, pools, or oceans. I loved swimming; it became my life.

Nick wasn't like me, though. He didn't love the ocean. He loved the sand. Well, staying on the sand and looking at the sky. So, when I saw him in the water, I knew I had to go play with him. I swam by him and jumped onto his shoulders, pushing him under.

I had to keep pressure on him to keep him under. He fought back, his hands coming above the surface to hit me. I loosened my grip on him so I could give him a chance. A few seconds passed, and he jumped up, splashing around. I started laughing at him.

"Hey!" He chuckled, wiping his hair from his eyes. He looked at me and shoved me back. I dramatically fell backward and into the water with a big splash. The water flew up around me and splashed Nick. "Was that necessary?"

"Absolutely!" I beamed at him. The sun was shining down on us, creating an effect in the water that made it crystal clear. "What are you doing in the water? And not in your chair, staring at the clouds?"

He looked at me and smiled. He started swishing the top of the water with his hand. "I wanted to see why you like it so much. And I get it now. I feel…invincible." He lay down on his back to float on the water and stared up at the sun.

"Why do you like staring at the sky?" I asked when he tilted his head to look at me. I've always wanted to ask him, but I never wanted to push. I know it's not that he prefers the daylight sky because he looks at it at night as well.

"It's not about the sky," he answered, still focused above. "Or space. It's about what's above it all. I like to think about what could be out there. Where my dad is."

I felt bad about asking him. I didn't think it would have anything to do with his dad. I should've known, but I didn't. It made me sad; Nick knew what I was going to say before even I knew. And I couldn't even figure out why he liked looking at the sky.

"Boys! I want to get a picture." I heard Mom calling from shore. I looked up to see Henry waving us over. He had a big grin on his face, and I smiled back. I turned to face Nick, who was already looking at me. I watched as his grin turned to a smirk.

"Wanna race?"

2

Eight Hours

I raced down the street and saw the huge building in front of me. The sign in front read, Concord High School. It had everything I hated. School, students, and people of authority. It had a grand concrete staircase leading up to the rows of red doors to enter the school. Parts of the exterior were run-down. Edges of the rectangular building were chipped, badly. Graffiti on brick walls surrounded it. I groaned while dragging my feet along, trying to make my way into the school on time. I had to walk through the parking lot to get into the actual school. Which meant I had to pass the students standing by their cars and hanging out with their friends.

"Kyle!" a high-pitched voice called out to me. I turned to see Noelle waving her arm back and forth at me. Noelle's high cheekbones were one of my favorite features about her, besides her long ink-black hair that ran to just below her shoulders and her bright green eyes. She stood with her group of friends, who I have never once talked to in my life. I had no interest in them. They were the type of girls who posted on social media of themselves crying for attention. Noelle never did that. I watched as she made her way through her friends, slowly making her way toward me.

She's trying to come and talk to me.

I don't want her to.

I shook my head at her and pointed at my wrist as if I was wearing a watch. I wanted to mentally slap myself in the head for doing that. For some reason, she realized what I meant. Her face dropped, and she nodded. Guilt sat in my stomach, just swirling around. She gave me a small smile before going back to her friends. My heart rate started to speed up as I let her walk away.

I walked away to make it into the school ahead of the other

students, but before I could reach the steps of the building, someone grabbed my shoulder. Anger fueled my body the second I felt their fingers grab me. Before I turned around, I could already tell who it was.

"Where's your little boyfriend?" a voice snickered behind me. I turned around to face Mark Evans. Mark used to be friends with Nick and me. He was our best friend; we stood by him even when he started doing weed and drinking. Even once he went for the harder drugs. But he did something we couldn't forgive him for, so we kicked him out of our group. He had never forgiven us for that.

I looked Mark in the eyes, and I gave him nothing. No emotion, response, or anything. I planted my feet on the ground and shifted my backpack to my left arm. Mark looked back at me, baffled that I didn't say anything. His blueish-gray eyes narrowed, and his upper lip curled into a smirk.

"Aw, is Kyle upset because his boyfriend didn't come to school?" His friends laughed with him.

What an idiot.

Mark looked to me for a reaction. I wouldn't give him that. He wasn't going to get the satisfaction of getting me mad. Mark shifted his attention to his friends, and they were all just staring at me. Moving their heads to the side, puzzled that there wasn't a fight.

"What the hell, Davis!?" Mark got right in my face. I could smell mint from his mouth. His nose was practically on top of mine. I didn't flinch; I just stood there. I watched as he huffed out his frustration.

We grew a crowd at this point. I couldn't exactly see who was watching, but I knew Luke was among the audience from the voice that came next.

"Dude! Just leave him alone!"

That was Luke. Always stopping a fight, never in one. He was too fragile and delicate to ever throw a punch, even being six foot three. His mom was a firm believer in World Peace and No Guns protests, which automatically made him one. He would constantly tell me about protests and charity events that he would go to with his mom.

Mark's eyes screamed rage at this point, but he didn't move. "Shut it, Cloud, or you're next!" He stayed focused on me. His nostrils started to flare, and I could tell I wasn't going to be standing for much longer. Mark was always the one who started fights. Nick and I were the ones to finish them.

I'm not finishing anything today.

The crowd had gotten bigger, and I was sure a teacher would've noticed at this point, but there wasn't one in sight. Just a bunch of high school kids wishing for a beating to happen. I looked to my right to see Noelle standing there with her friends, staring at me. Her hand was covering her mouth as her eyes peered into mine with concern.

"Maybe I should kill you. Then when Nick comes here alone tomorrow, I'll do the same to him," Mark muttered into my ears. An empty threat for sure; Mark knows he wouldn't be able to harm me unless I let him. But the thought of Nick dying pierced into my skull once again. My head snapped to him; hints of anger glowed in my pupils. He grinned, knowing it bothered me.

If only he knew why…

I wanted to fight him at that moment. I wanted to grab him by his amber hair and smash him against my kneecap. Or throat punch him and watch him fall. To watch his eyes roll into the back of his head. To wait for everyone to be quiet when they saw what I had done. Then I looked at Noelle. She had her eyes closed tightly, waiting for me to break Mark's neck. She expected my anger to take over. I already saw myself as a monster; I couldn't let her see me like that too.

Whatever expression I had on my face before, I wiped it off. Mark's grin fell, and his eyes glared into mine. I took my anger out on my hands as I closed them into tight fists. I felt the nails cut into my skin, and the blood started to drip. By the time I realized I was bleeding, Mark's fist came flying at me. The impact landed right into my eye. I let my body fall backward, and my head smacked into the pavement.

"Hey!" Luke complained. "Let him be! He didn't do anything!"

"Oh, quit it, Cloud. Otherwise, I'll show you what a real punch looks like." Mark snickered back. He laughed with his friends before Luke spoke again.

"Don't tempt me." Luke scowled. "You really wanna test it to see if I can fight back?"

He couldn't. Luke didn't know how to fight or the first thing about self-defense. He only talked like he knew what he was doing when Nick and I were in trouble. No one was going to fight the giant towering over them.

I didn't know whether Mark said anything or not. My ears were ringing. I could hear faint whispers from the people watching. I assumed Mark and his friends left because I heard footsteps right by my ears. I saw Noelle's face peek over mine. Her hair fell in front of her face, casting a shadow that blocked the sun's glare.

"No, Noelle, you should get to class," Luke ordered. "I got him."

No.

No, you don't.

Then it all went black.

~

"I think he's waking up. I should get back to work," a voice announced. The voice was whispering, but it sounded loud in my head. I heard a grunt, then footsteps, and a door closing. I opened my eyes to a light shining above me. I sat up and looked around. I was in the nurse's office. The nurse, Ms. Jones, smiled at me before grabbing some things from her desk. I watched as she opened a bunch of drawers and took things from each one. The ringing in my ears was still present, but it only muffled everything.

"Mr. Davis," she scolded, "you have been costing me a lot of bandages this year." She laughed as she made her way to me, looking at my very painful eye. "What happened this time?"

"Nothing," I muttered. I didn't care if Mark got in trouble or not; he wasn't even a thought in my mind. He was nothing to me. He didn't matter.

"Doesn't look like nothing," she responded, grabbing my hand. I winced while she turned my hand over, exposing the cuts. She eyed me while she cleaned it up.

"I did that," I assured her.

"On purpose?" she questioned, not looking at me. She cleaned up all the dried blood and put a liquid on it. It was cold, but it didn't hurt.

I defended myself. "Of course not." I watched as she bandaged both my hands before looking at my eye. She handed me some ice. The coldness sent chills up my arms. I didn't hear the phone ring, but I could see it shaking on the wall. She answered it and talked for a moment; then she hung up. She told me she would be right back, then closed the door. I watched her through the windows as she walked down the hallways.

I looked down at my hands. I clenched them, bringing pain to my palms. I shifted in my seat when I heard a wrinkled paper sound coming from the end of the room. I moved my gaze to the right and saw a pair of shoes hanging out over a bed. It was another kid, just lying down. The curtain covered up his body and face, so I couldn't see who it was.

"Hey," I babbled weakly, "what happened to you?"

No response.

Maybe he's just sleeping.

I thought about it and realized that Ms. Jones wouldn't have left a kid unconscious in her office.

"Dude—" I spoke again. "—you alright?"

Again, he stayed silent. I decided to make sure he was still alive. I walked down past the many empty beds before I reached his. My hands trembled as I pulled back the curtain to reveal a boy. His head was smashed in, and blood was dripping to the floor. There was dirt and mud all over his body and clothes. His eyes stared into mine, and I realized who it was.

"Nick!" I screamed out. I threw the curtains back as I raced toward my bed. I watched as Nick's bloody, misconfigured hand pulled the curtain back, revealing his face. I jumped onto my bed and started crying. My entire body started to vibrate as his eyes stared at me. His blood looked fresh and was dripping into his eyes. Even though he was moving, his eyes still looked lifeless. His legs swung over the side of the bed, sitting straight up. He was like a doll. A bloody, dirty, dead doll. I covered my face and started yelling for help.

I heard footsteps running toward me, and the door swung open. Ms. Jones appeared with Dad. I stopped yelling, and I wiped the tears from my face. I accidentally hit my black eye, which caused the pain to burst. I whimpered as I reached up to touch it.

"No, don't touch it," Ms. Jones warned me. "You'll make it worse." I retracted my hand from my face. I could feel the glare my father was giving me. Ms. Jones walked over to me and replaced my ice. "Why were you screaming?"

"Because of—" I started to say, pointing at the moving corpse. But when I looked, there was nothing there. There wasn't even a kid. Which terrified me even more.

I guess it's not just my mirror that's tricking me.

I racked my brain, trying to come up with an excuse as to why I was screaming.

"Because the pain just hit me."

Ms. Jones gave me a sympathetic look while writing on her pad. "I think you should go home for the day. Relax and heal." She handed Dad a note from her pad. He peeked at it and nodded. He stuffed the note in his pocket, patting me on the back.

"Let's take you home, kid."

I'd rather just die.

~

"Wanna talk about it?" Dad was driving me home from school. He was bragging about how he left work to come and get me, which made him a good father. He said that he had a big case, and he'd left his assistant alone to do most of the work until he got back.

"Not really," I answered. I knew my dad was proud of himself for leaving work early to get his son from school. My dad was always at the office when I was younger, and not much had changed. So, him coming to get me was a big deal to him. It made my blood boil. I wanted to take the driving wheel and turn it until the car smashed into the rails on the side of the road.

"Okay—" My dad clicked his tongue. "—but can you tell me what happened?" He peeked over at me, and I refused to skip a beat.

"Nothing happened."

I looked out the window to give myself something to do other than answer my dad's never-ending questions. I just watched my reflection in the glass, staring into my own eyes.

We came off the highway, and I noticed a familiar patch of the forest ahead of us. I quickly sat up and stared at the swaying trees.

"Dude, just let it be!" I barked at Nick. "It's not a big deal!" I stomped off into the forest, hoping he would stay back. I heard footsteps crunching leaves behind me, so I picked up my pace. "Drop it!"

Nick was never the type of guy to let go of things. He held grudges for as long as he could. He remembered every little thing that Mark did to both of us. It was as if he had a journal where he wrote down every wrong someone did to him.

"No!" Nick argued. "I won't drop it. What did you say to Noelle?" I kept walking, going deeper into the woods. Kicking leaves and branches out of my way. There weren't any animals, from what I heard, except there was an occasional rustle from bushes we were passing. He kept following me. "Answer me, Kyle!"

I whipped around and faced Nick. He was fuming. His face was red, and the vein in his neck was turning purple. His eyes stared back, trying to threaten me. He knew that he would never beat me in a fight. My anger always got the best of me, taking total control of my body so he would never try it.

But the look in his eyes screamed that he wanted to. He wanted to hit me.

"I just told her that I would never argue with her like you guys do," I admitted. His face dropped, and he stood there. "That's all! She was upset with you guys fighting, and she came to talk to me." He edged closer to me, listening intently. I tried to back up, but my back hit the trunk of a tree. I moved a little to the side, getting ready to flee if something happened.

I sighed. "She was crying, and I felt bad, and I was just trying to make her feel better."

Before I knew it, his fist came swinging at me. I quickly ducked to get out of his way. I heard his knuckle smash against the bark. I caught his shoulder and looked into his eyes. Anger boiled in him. I could tell that he came here for blood. I knew I would lose control, and I didn't want to hit Nick. I pushed him back and yelled, "Hey, man, get away from me!"

I hadn't realized a tear escaped my eye. I wiped it away,

pushing against my black eye again. I quietly winced at the pain, but not loud enough for my dad to notice. I held the tear droplet on my pointer finger. It ran alongside it before dropping to my pants.

"How's Nick?" he asked. It was a simple question with a basic answer. I could've lied. I could've just said that everything was fine, and Nick was good. Hearing his name out loud after what I had done. It broke me. Guilt and anger fueled me. I had no right to be mad, but I was. Flashes of his lifeless body entered my mind, and I just had it.

"I don't want to talk to you!"

Dad's smile dropped, and I felt the energy shift. I knew I messed up, but my dad wasn't going to do anything. He knew about my anger problems. He was proud of me for them. The number of times he had taken me out of school for getting in a fight then bringing me to get ice cream afterward proved that. He once said he was proud of me for it.

He kept his eyes on the road. I just stared at my shoes. They were the same shoes I wore the night before when I was with Nick. Dirt was covering the sides of them. I knew that the dried blood was stuck to the bottom. After a few moments of silence, we pulled into our driveway.

"Dad, I'm sorry. I'm tired, and my eye started to really hurt," I explained. It wasn't a complete lie. I was very tired, and my eye did hurt.

"I understand," he told me, patting my back. "Go get some sleep."

I opened the car door and shut it when I got out. Dad waved at me before pulling out of the driveway. I watched as he drove down the street and back to the main roads. I turned around and noticed that Henry's car was there.

Crap.

I stepped into my house to hear loud music blasting from downstairs. I shut the door to muffle it, but it only worked a bit. The song was still screeching in my ears. My phone immediately started ringing. I saw that Mom was calling, so I picked it up.

"Hello?" I answered. I plopped down on a dining room chair. I put the phone on speaker so I could rest my head in my hands. It was too heavy for me to hold it up on its own.

"Hi, sweetie!" Mom piped through the phone. "Are you okay? Your dad told me what happened."

I thought about telling the truth. The whole truth. Everything that happened and just come clean. If anyone knew what to do, it would be her. She would be able to make everything okay.

But what if she doesn't believe me?

What if she sees me as a monster?

"Yeah, I'm fine," I lied. "Do you still have to work tonight?"

There was silence on the other line. I heard nothing; I thought it disconnected. I heard the music slowly die down from the basement, and footsteps traveled up the stairs. I took the phone off the speaker and placed it by my ear.

"No, I'll be home tonight. Go take a nap." I told her okay and goodbye before hanging up. Henry appeared at the top of the stairs and smirked at me. He leaned against the door frame, crossing his arms.

"What are you doing home?" Henry poked. I rubbed my eyes, keeping them closed as long as I possibly could. I didn't want to get into anything with him. We would scream at each other for hours at a time about nothing, but only because we were both too stubborn to give up. I didn't feel like screaming. All I wanted was to fall asleep and never wake up. I looked over at Henry and knew he wanted something from me. Just like Mark. They wanted a reaction. They wanted to see me mad.

"Nothing," I answered.

Don't push it, Henry.

"Where'd you get that black eye? Nick finally punched you?"

I felt dizzy. It was sort of a blur. Henry's stupid grin was the only thing I could see clearly, and it set me off. I threw my phone across the room and heard it shatter against the wall. Henry's face dropped, and he looked over at my broken phone. It was in pieces on the floor, but I didn't care.

"Shut the hell up, Henry!" I exploded. There was no other way to describe it. I saw red. I saw the moment I just snapped his neck. His head would look like a broken action figure. Just hanging on by one simple bone. I wanted to wrap my hands so badly around his throat and do just that. "You don't know what you're talking about, so shut up!"

"Kyle, I—"

"No! No!" I raged. "You don't get to talk. Not any more! All I've let you do was talk for years. I get it, okay? I get that you hate me, and you blame me for everything that has happened to this family, but I'm done! I'm done listening to you!" I stormed up to Henry and got in his face like Mark did mine. He stumbled back a bit but stood his ground. Planted his feet and stuck out his chest. I poked it with my finger. His eyes narrowed down on me, clenching his jaw.

Here's where it starts.

"Stop hating me for things I can't control. Get over yourself. You're nineteen years old, living in your parents' basement, working at a hardware store. You aren't better than me. I still have a chance at not screwing up my future!"

It was harsh, I know. Henry watched my eyes. I think he was searching for something, an emotion other than rage and anger. Anything else to show what I was really feeling. But there was no other emotion. Hatred was coursing through my body. I wanted to smack him in the head.

I was waiting for his response. For him to call me names and to yell back. Henry wouldn't stand down. In all my sixteen years of living, he had never once let me win an argument. He would push and push until I gave up. I scanned his eyes, not finding any emotion within him.

He waited a few more seconds before turning around and going back downstairs. I backed up out of instinct. I thought he was just trying to trick me. That he was going to come running up those stairs and at me. The music started back up again, making me jump. I didn't believe him. I didn't think that it was going to be the end of the argument. I stood there, ready for a fight for ten minutes.

He's not coming back.

I caught my breath. A million thoughts were running through my mind per second. I couldn't figure out why he decided now was the best time to stop arguing with me. Every fight ended with me leaving and him smirking. That was the way it worked. Why was it any different then?

Does he know?

I made my way to my couch, groaning loudly. My eye was

throbbing, and it felt like someone shoved sand down my throat. I lay down, my back cracking as I fell to the soft cushions. My eyelids were as heavy as bricks. I closed them to see nothing. I slowly drifted off to sleep, praying that I wouldn't have to deal with nightmares. The one from the night before replayed in my mind, making me wonder what it meant.

Nick killed me in my dreams.

But I killed him.

I gulped, moving over to my side. I prayed for one more thing. I begged for it. I wished upon a star. I did everything I could have.

I asked that I wouldn't wake up at all.

3

Thirteen Hours

When I woke up, I knew it was coming. I knew people were going to notice, and soon they were going to ask me about it. I knew how I was supposed to act and behave, but I didn't know if I could pull it off.

A noise rang out, startling me, even though I knew it was coming. I walked toward the ringing, my footsteps sounding loud through the empty house. The sun was shining brightly through the window and highlighted the dust on the floor. I stared outside into the swaying trees that circled my royal-blue-colored house. My hand skimmed against the cold telephone hanging on the wall. The ringing continued to echo through the house.

"Hello?" My voice cracked ever so slightly. Not a lot for it to seem like I was scared, but just enough for someone on the other line to hear it. I heard a deep breath come from the other line. Before the person spoke, I knew who they were looking for.

"Hello, is Kyle home?" the male voice asked. It was deep, so it wasn't a teenager. I figured he was at least thirty, maybe forty. There was a bit of a grumble in his voice to show he did not want to do what he was about to do.

"Speaking," I replied, trying to stay as quiet as I could during this phone call.

Don't give up any information; that's what Dad always says.

"Ah, good. Now, I'm Mr. Harris," he informed me. "I work with the Crime Investigation Program as a detective. We train students who want to be working in criminal law as an occupation. But that's not why I'm calling you today, Kyle."

"Alright." I knew they weren't calling me about that. Why would they? I had no interest in joining their stupid program.

"I'm calling about Nick Walter."

I nodded as if he could see me. Realizing my mistake, I spoke. "Okay."

"Now, Kyle, do you know Nick Walter?" His grumpy voice spoke into my ear as if he were right next to me. I could feel his breathing on my shoulder, causing me to shudder. I had to pull the phone away to get the feeling to subside.

I took a deep breath before speaking. "Yes."

"Kyle, Nick Walter is missing."

Missing?

I dropped the phone in my hands, causing an intense sound. I could hear Mr. Harris on the other side asking about me. There were no thoughts in my head; there was nothing. All I kept thinking was the word. That word hung over me, taunting my mistakes. I carefully picked the phone up and spoke. "I'm sorry; I just dropped the phone. How could he be missing?"

"I understand, Kyle. I heard you two are really good friends. His mom called us two nights ago, but we couldn't do anything about a missing person report within twenty-four hours in hopes he would show up today. You didn't happen to see him, did you?"

"No-o," I stuttered. We weren't far into the woods when it happened; they should've found him.

Unless they aren't looking for a body.

They are looking for a boy on the run.

"Yeah, we figured. I don't want you to get concerned or upset about it. We will find him, and we will bring him home." Mr. Harris tried to assure me.

"Mr. Harris," I whispered. "What if he's dead?"

There was silence. I heard nothing from the other line. I kept the phone to my ear; the sound of cars passing my house was the only thing I heard. A small breeze swept in from the kitchen window and blew against my face.

"Let's not think that way, Kyle." he finally responded. "Now, if you can try to remember when was the last time—"

"Mr. Harris—" I cut him off, not wanting to hear about Nick any more. "—can you call back another time? I really need time to think right now."

"Of course," he said. "I am so sorry."

I answered him with a small, "It's okay" before slamming

the phone back on the wall, causing the remaining dust to float up into the air. My head was pounding; it was like my thoughts were trying to break free.

But I wouldn't let them.

I let the conversation sink into my brain while I sat down. I stared at my TV screen, remembering the words that Mr. Harris just told me. Nick was missing. Not dead.

But you know he is dead.

Isn't he?

I painfully remembered the night, retracing the images through my mind. Seeing if there was any way Nick could have survived. What if he wasn't the one bleeding? What if he fell onto an animal and crushed it?

That's stupid.

What if once I left, he got up and ran to get help?

You would've heard him.

I decided to distract myself by turning on the TV. I switched the channels for a bit till I found something I liked. After a few moments of watching it, there was a break, and a screen title came up with big letters that said *Breaking News!*

I rolled my eyes and turn the channel, but every single one had the same thing. I threw the remote down in frustration and stood up. I ran my fingers through my hair, unknotting it. I looked back to the screen and waited patiently for the news. A news anchor girl popped up with a microphone in the middle of her office.

"Nick Walter, age sixteen, a student at Concord High School, was reported missing two nights ago. His mother is very worried about him. He was last seen with a teenage girl who we cannot name at this time, but she is being questioned as we speak."

I clenched my jaw. He was with Noelle before me? Is that why Noelle wanted to talk to me today because Nick told her something? I grabbed the remote off the coffee table and chucked it as hard as I could at the TV. The sound of it hitting the screen was music to my ears. I stared at the big hole in the middle of the TV.

I have great aim.

I then remembered Noelle. What could Nick have told her? I clenched my fists and felt the wounds reopen on my palm.

The blood dripped down my hands and onto the floor. I looked at my cuts and noticed how they were defined around the edges. I tried picking at them, but it just made the bleeding worse.

Flashbacks of Nick's body when I left came rushing back to me. I groaned at the sudden pain of my head aching. My heart was pounding, and my hands were clammy. My stomach was doing backflips while my brain tried to keep up with it. My vision started to blur while I made careful steps toward the bathroom. The floor creaking with each step I took. Saliva filled my mouth before my throat started to burn up. I raced toward the toilet, almost tripping on my brother's bag on the ground. I lifted the lid before my lunch came back up from my stomach and fell into the toilet. I groaned before I heard the door opening, and the sound of my mother's soft voice filled the air.

"Kyle, where are you?" The door shut while I heard Mom place her bags down. "Your father is going to be a bit late. He said his assistant messed something up with a case."

I tried to speak out to her but just ended up throwing up instead. Mom heard my retching, and her heels rapidly clicked throughout the house before she reached the bathroom door.

"Oh, Kyle, I didn't know you were this sick." She bent down and rubbed my back. I felt guilty for her being this concerned about me. If only she knew what I did, she wouldn't be helping me.

I threw up a third time before my stomach finally settled. I turned to look at Mom, and she grabbed a cloth to clean up my face. I pushed her hand away while grabbing the cloth to clean it myself. She smiled before speaking. "I'll call your father and ask him to get some medicine. Do you know if it was something you ate?"

I shook my head and she frowned. I could tell she wanted to know what was wrong. Mom liked to be in control of everything. She wanted to know everything. I heard stomping from the basement, and Henry appeared in front of the bathroom door.

"Woah, what happened to him?" He snorted. Mom gave him a look, and he threw his hands up in the air before turning away. "Just asking."

"Wait, Henry. I need to talk to you," Mom announced before standing up. She patted my back one more time before turning on her heels to leave. I watched as she left the bathroom. My head still felt a bit heavy, but I stood up anyway. My vision got better, but my hands were still shaking, and my stomach still felt like it was flipping upside down. I heard my mother whispering as she was talking to Henry. Her voice was so low that I could barely make out what she was saying.

"No, I don't think he knows," she whispered.

Knows what?

"Well, he is going to find out. You can't keep it from him forever," Henry argued back. I heard him walking away. He walked past me sitting on the bathroom floor. He stopped for a moment to stare at me with his empty eyes before walking downstairs.

They were talking about Nick.

~

Dad came home around nine that night. He brought medicine with him that tasted like moldy grapes. He tried to joke about the fight to distract me, but it didn't work.

"Hey, we should see the other guy, right?" He laughed, pushing at my arm. I just looked at him and waited for the laughter to stop. He slowly calmed down, seeing my expression not change.

"Kyle?" Mom called from the living room. Dad and I were sitting at the dining table when she came walking in. "What happened to your phone?" She held up my shattered phone.

The screen was hanging off by a wire. Henry walked into the room and grinned while staring at the ground, knowing what happened.

"I dropped it."

Henry's head snapped up to mine, and I just shrugged. Mom looked at the two of us before nodding her head. "Well, I guess I'll have to get you a new one." Henry groaned out loud, causing everyone to look at him. He refused to say anything, though. He grabbed a drink from the fridge and went back downstairs.

"Should we go pick up a pizza?" Mom asked Dad. He nodded and grabbed the keys. Before they left, Dad ruffled my hair like I was a little kid. I pushed him away, hurting my arm in the process. I wasn't sure why, but it was sore.

Probably from you pushing Nick.

I shook the thought from my head, mad at myself for even thinking it. I got up to go sit in the living room, but when I walked into the doorway, I fell face first. I held my hands out to catch me and my right arm got the brunt of the fall, but my face still landed on the floor. My eye had a stinging, stabbing ache when I got my breath back. I turned around to see what made me fall.

Henry's bag.

Bet he left it here on purpose.

I looked toward Henry's room and noticed the music was on and playing. He wasn't watching me fall just to laugh at me. I stood up and grabbed the bag, about to throw it at him, when I noticed something. It was shiny and reflecting one of the lights in our hallway. I reached into the bag and fumbled around a bit. My hand grazed against something sharp, and it brought stinging pain to my palm. I yanked it out of the bag and stared in awe.

Dark, warm blood dripped from my hand. The blood kept getting darker the more I stared at it. It dripped onto the floor, creating a pool of blood.

A lot of people think that blood is bright red—but it's more of a purple-red shade. That's what Nick's blood looked like.

The cut was deep and bleeding a lot. I stared into the bag and noticed the shining object again. This time, I carefully reached into the bag to pull it out. It was a knife, dripping with blood.

Henry had a knife in his bag. I dropped it, the metal creating a sharp and loud noise. I started to back away from it, bringing my bloody hand with me. I tried to be careful enough not to drip blood onto the floor.

"Ahhhhh!" I giggled, running around the kitchen. I was about five or six at the time. Henry and I were playing monsters. He, of course, was the monster.

"Boys! Be careful!" Mom warned. She was sitting in the living room with Dad, talking about some surgery she did.

I remember because he kept saying, "That's nice, dear."

I found an empty cabinet to hide in, thinking he wouldn't look in there. I got the door to close, and he crept into the kitchen. I knew he had a grin on his face because there was a crack in the wood where Henry chipped it. I watched as he looked around the kitchen before looking at my cabinet. I couldn't help laughing at him.

He tore the cabinet door open and screamed, "Got you!" He grabbed me by the waist and brought me to the ground. He tickled me until I was breathless. We sat on the floor for a few moments before Henry decided to make the game more fun. "Let's give the monster a tool to use to find you," he added.

"Oo, like what?" I asked.

Henry walked over to the knife block sitting on the counter. He stared at it for a bit before looking back at me, wiggling his eyebrows. At first, I thought he was joking. But he kept his stare on me, waiting for my response.

"No!" I screamed. "That's dangerous!"

He laughed at me before arguing. "No! I'll be safe. It's just to make the game more fun!" He turned around and reached for a knife. I felt my heart beating in my throat. I watched as he slowly slid the sharp object out of its holder and held it in his hand.

I think that was the moment I realized Henry lost his mind.

I stood there, thinking back to that moment. I peered into the bag again. I reached my hand in there and felt around. I felt another object too. It was cold, and it felt like metal. I wrapped my hand around the end of it, and I realized I was touching a cold barrel.

Is that a gun?

The sound of a car pulling into our driveway pulled my attention from Henry's bag. My parents were home. I hid the knife back in the bag and left it where it was. I grabbed a towel and quickly cleaned up the blood. There were a few spots left, but they weren't going to notice. I ran into the bathroom to scrub my hands clean of blood.

Reminds me of another night I was cleaning off blood.

"Kyle! Henry! We're home!"

I wish they weren't.

We ate dinner in silence that night. Henry didn't join us; he stayed in his room. He came upstairs for a minute to grab his bag and gave me a cold glare. Other than that, it was an uneventful meal. Afterward, when my parents went upstairs to bed, the phone rang. I figured it was one of their co-workers, but I answered it anyway. I held the phone in my hands, feeling the chilled metal in my grasp.

"Hello?" I croaked through the phone. I coughed to clear my voice, irritating my swollen throat. I didn't realize the burning until I talked just then. It was like someone had a lighter in my throat.

"Hey, Kyle, it's Noelle." Noelle breathed through the phone. "Can we talk?"

Soon, it felt like inchworms were crawling up and down my throat. "Sure." I coughed.

"I tried to call your cell phone, but it didn't seem to go through."

"Oh yeah—" I paused to keep my voice from straining out. "It broke." My stomach started to get the same burning feeling from my throat. It was as if someone decided to set fire to my whole body.

"Oh well, I wanted to talk about Nick," she stated.

Of course you do.

I hummed in response because, at that point, I couldn't breathe. Something was stopping my lungs from working. It felt like someone grabbed my throat and was choking me, squeezing tighter with each second that passed.

"I'm sure you know that he's missing." She started to cry. My heart started to ache; not because of anything physical. But because she was crying, because of something I did. I wanted to reach out to her and hold her, but I couldn't. "I just want you to know I had nothing to do with it. I was the last person to be with him, but I swear. I had nothing to do with this."

My head started spinning like a bicycle, which made me want to vomit. I looked down at my arms and saw that a strange rash appeared. My dinner was trying to crawl out of my throat, but I kept it down for Noelle.

"They just kept questioning me." Noelle sobbed. "Asking what we did, and I was like, 'Trust me, officers, you don't want me to go into detail about what we did.' But they wouldn't stop!"

My heart was ripped from my chest, and I watched it fall to the floor. Broken in a million pieces. "What?" I gulped. I didn't want her to say it again.

"Oh, well, you know, what most couples do when they are together. If I knew what was going to happen after, then I would have—"

My heart stopped. The phone fell out of my hands and dangled inches above the floor. I could hear a faint, concerned voice before I passed out completely.

"Hello? Kyle, are you there?"

4

Day Two

My head was throbbing. Lights above me were shining in my eyes, and I could see it even with them closed. There were faint whispers around me and the sound of a heart monitor going off. It started to beep louder as my brain jumbled and footsteps shuffled in the room. I tried to look around, to even open my eyes, but I was stuck. I couldn't do it. I was too weak. I was trapped in my mind with my taunting thoughts. I took a breath in, building the strength I needed.

I blinked open to find myself in bed. The room was white. Two windows sat behind a counter, letting sunlight in through the slightly opened shutters. It cast a shadow on everything in the room. I wanted to test my shadow. To make sure I still controlled it, but I was too tired to even lift my hand.

I turned to the left, where there were two chairs. My parents sat, whispering to each other. To my right were machines; one had a line going up and down with numbers. There was a pole that sort of looked like a coat rack, and it had an IV bag hanging on it.

I'm in a hospital?

Was I sleeping the whole time?

Is Nick alive?

A doctor walked into the room, and I wanted to growl at him. He had a stethoscope around his neck and a beard that went from his nose to the end of his chin. He carried a clipboard with him and was writing when he walked into the room. His head slowly went up to look at me.

"Hello." The doctor smiled. "Glad to see you are awake."

Mom shifted in her seat to face me, smoothing down her skirt. Dad just turned his head and gave me a nod. I was sitting in a hospital bed, in pain, and all I got from the man was a nod. The dizziness made me feel claustrophobic as the doctor started poking at my chart.

"Alright, kid, do you know where you are?" the doctor quizzed. A loud alarm went off at that moment. My head swung to the side of the room where the loud sound was coming from. Pain shot up from my shoulder blade to the top of my neck. The doctor didn't seem concerned with this, and neither did Mom. Dad furrowed his eyebrows together, but he wasn't scared of the noise. The doctor was standing still. I watched as he stared at the ceiling, waiting for it to stop. "New security set. Sets off when someone enters the building through an exit door. Nurses come and go through that door, so it's okay."

I looked at my parents, and Mom confirmed this for me.

"Every five hours it goes off. That's the schedule change. Except at night, there are no changes at night," she assured me.

The doctor nodded along with her before focusing on me again, waiting for me to answer.

"The hospital," I muttered. It was clear where I was. The people dressed in scrubs walking past my door. The grunts I heard from behind my wall. The faint screams from dying people in the hallway. And the smell, the very obvious hospital smell. It's a mix of medicine and death.

I hate it here.

"Good, now what is your name?" I groaned at the stupid questions. The doctor took note of my hesitation and disinterest. "I need to make sure you are fully responsive. Then I can explain what's happened to you."

"Kyle Davis," I grunted at him. He smiled, looking toward his clipboard. He flipped a couple of pages, making Mom concerned. She looked at him, impatiently waiting for him to tell us what happened to me.

"Dr. Jones, if you don't know your patient—" My mother started, standing up. She stared him in the eye before finishing. "—maybe you shouldn't be on this case."

He looked up from the papers. He chuckled, rubbing the back of his neck. I watched as sweat formed on his face. I never saw Mom as an authority figure, or at least not a harsh one. Her tone shocked me. I was a little scared myself. Dr. Jones apologized before looking at me.

"Kyle, you went through an anaphylactic allergic reaction.

We think it was because of the bismuth subsalicylate that was in the stomach medicine you took." He grabbed my arm and flicked the IV that was sticking out of my wrist. "We had to give you epinephrine to reduce your body's reaction to the medicine and give you oxygen. Your levels seem stable now, but we would like to keep you overnight to keep an eye on it."

Before he left the room, he looked over to Mom as if he were asking her for permission to leave. She just smiled at him. He took it as a yes because he wandered out of the room, looking dazed. Dad followed him, saying something about getting coffee. I rolled my head, stretching my neck out, trying to ease the pain. I squinted with the sudden stabbing feeling in my skull.

"They all act like that," Mom whispered to me. My eyes flew open and looked at her. "Scared as if I am going to fire them."

"Where is Nick?" I asked. Mom was taken aback; it looked like she almost fell. Her eyes fluttered as she thought about what to say. He needs to be alive. All I wanted to hear was, "On his way." That's what I wanted from her. The next words that came out of her mouth were not the ones I wanted. They were the ones I expected.

"Nick's missing."

It was like a ton of bricks just fell on me. The weight of them held me down to my bed, and I couldn't get up. I could feel the pressure building. My heart was slamming itself against my rib cage as if it were trying to break free. I tried to breathe in, but there was nothing. The deeper I breathed in, the harder my lungs had to work.

So, he's really gone.

You did this to him.

"But they will find him." She tried to assure me. I didn't want to talk about it any more; I got my answer. This wasn't all a bad dream. This was real. The flashes of the forest and Nick's dead body were real.

It really happened.

I am a murderer.

~

Dad came back with coffee a few minutes later. He didn't say much until he got a phone call. He walked out of the room, leaving the door open. We heard him groaning and growling. He came back livid. Mom and I both turned to look at him, waiting for an explanation.

"My damn assistant mixed up the case files for today. I had her put some in my briefcase so I could stay here and work, but she put the wrong ones in," he complained, snatching his bag. "I'll be right back. I'm sorry."

He left in a hurry, pushing doctors out of the way. Mom just chuckled at him before turning to me. "He's crazy."

"Where's Henry?" I questioned. I felt bad for cutting her off, but I needed to know. If your brother is in the hospital, you go, right? I would go if it were him. Even after our fight, I thought he would've been there. I was lying in a hospital bed and had to be given oxygen because I couldn't breathe. Yet Henry was nowhere to be seen.

She looked guilty. She must've felt bad about Nick or not having Henry here. "You know how he gets in hospitals." She stood up before announcing that she had to go. "I'll be right back; I need to check in with some of the nurses."

I did remember Henry didn't like hospitals, but no one does. I was still his brother, and he was still not here.

"Is he going to be okay?" I asked, gazing up at the big man in a white coat. Mom was in scrubs because she was already at the hospital working when we arrived. She started yelling when she saw him, screaming that he was her baby. Other people had to come and hold her back. I watched Dad grab her and hold her. She let out loud sobs into his shirt, and he just rubbed her back.

Tears slipped out of my eyes, but I wiped them away before anyone could see. I looked at the little boy in the bed, drained of color. I couldn't understand what the doctor was saying. He mentioned water in his lungs and how it was too late. Mom bawled into her hands, kneeling by the bed. She lay her head onto the sheets, grabbing the hand of the dying kid in front of us.

I heard a sniffle behind me, and I turned to see Dad. He was crying. I never saw Dad cry before, watching the tears slip down his face, turning his eyes puffy and red as he rubbed them away. I looked back to Mom, and I felt empty. Footsteps shuffled behind me, and the door slammed shut. I raced after him, grabbing his shoulder to pull him back.

"Henry, wait!"

He turned to face me, tears streaking down his face. His nose was all runny, and he wiped away everything he could from his face. Doctors passed us, walking with nurses, but no one paid attention to the eleven- and seven-year-olds in the middle of the hallway.

"No! This is your fault!" he cried. He pushed my hand away, making me fall to the ground. "You did this to him!"

I was on my hands and knees looking up to Henry. His tears kept falling. I faced the ground because I didn't want to see him like that any more. I watched as my tears pooled on the floor. He grabbed me by the neck and pulled my ear to his mouth.

"You killed Max! You're a murderer! Never talk to me again."

With that, he ran down the hallway. My vision became blurry from the crying, so I couldn't see much. His figure became smaller by the second; the lights were shining down on me in the very bare and white hallway. I could still hear the sobs from his hospital room. The crying that I caused.

History does repeat itself, I guess.

"Honey, I have a surprise for you," Mom sang as she walked through the door. Luke appeared, grinning from ear to ear. The top of his black hair bouncing with each step he took. He was always so happy, never a sad moment with him. He and I were complete opposites; I remember thinking we were never going to be friends.

It was after Nick and I weren't friends with Mark any more. Nick told me he found a new friend; he just moved to town. He used to be homeschooled but decided to go to public school for the rest of his high school years.

He walked in wearing the biggest smile ever, hippie pants, and a T-shirt that said *Peace for all*. I wanted to slap him right then and there. One thing led to another, and we became close. I did have to teach him how to properly dress for high school, though.

"Hey!" He beamed. "How are you feeling?" I gave him a slight smile as he made his way to me. He grabbed a chair and slid it across the floor, creating this awful sound. It felt as if he were trying to pierce my eardrums.

"Oops, sorry." He apologized, redness taking over his face. He always got embarrassed easily—must be the homeschool.

"Anyways, you won't believe what happened to Mark." I sat up eagerly. For the first time in forty-eight hours, Nick wasn't a thought in my head.

"What?" I egged him on. I figured he got in trouble for what happened, considering the number of people that watched.

"He got expelled," Luke squealed. I wanted so badly to make fun of the way he squeaked when saying that, but the only thought on my mind was the fact that Mark was expelled. I didn't want him to get into that much trouble. That would go on his permanent record. It would ruin his life.

"But he only got into a fight," I murmured. "It was one punch."

"Yeah, but I guess they had enough of his crap," he said. His eyes widened as he turned to Mom. "Sorry for my language!"

She just laughed and called him "wholesome" before leaving the room. I asked where she was going, and she said to get another surprise. I was confused, considering the only friend I had left alive was in the room.

Oh god, Nick.

Luke noticed my emotion change, and he knew immediately what I was thinking about.

"They told you?"

I nodded. My eyes brimmed with tears, but I wouldn't let them fall. It was my fault. I didn't deserve to cry or to be upset. I didn't deserve anything.

I don't deserve to be alive.

He placed a hand on my shoulder. I'm sure if he didn't know any better, he would've hugged me. Even the hand was pushing it.

A beeping sound came from the huge monitor to the side of me; I watched as the lines went crazy. Luke's eyes widened as if he broke me. Two nurses came running in and started checking me. One checked my heart while the other tried to calm me.

How am I supposed to be calm when two strangers are touching me and telling me to relax?

"He will come home," Luke said. He didn't even realize he was lying.

I did some breathing to make the loud alarm go away; once it did, the nurses left. Luke and I were alone.

We sat there in silence. He didn't even know why I was upset. About the images that haunted me throughout the day. How I saw him, lying there, lifeless. How his blood spilled because of me.

"Kyle!" a new voice intruded. I turned and saw Noelle with Mom. Mom walked inside my room, but Noelle stood there, her black hair in a ponytail. Her emerald-green eyes stared into my blue ones. She smiled at me before taking in my injuries. All my cuts, bruises, and bandages.

I look awful.

"Hey, Noelle!" Luke waved, sat up, and offered her the chair. He gave me a look that I couldn't read. I stared at him in confusion, and he just sighed before leaving. Mom followed him out the door, talking about food in the cafeteria.

Looking at Noelle made me angry and confused and most of all, guilty. I took her boyfriend away from her. She would hate me if she knew. She wouldn't be here if she knew the truth.

"Kyle, look at me, please," she begged. My heart ached as she pleaded. If Nick knew what I was thinking, he would never trust me again. He would hate me.

I looked toward her, but I couldn't look her in the eye. It would torture me. Thoughts ran through my mind, and thinking clearly wasn't an option. A pounding headache was making me nauseous.

I felt her hand on mine. The warmth of her fingertips traced the back of my palm. I stopped, and so did everything else that was going on with my body. And I looked at her.

She was looking at me.

Everything was okay.

5

Day Five

It had been three days since Nick was reported missing and three days I had been stuck in the hospital. Every moment I spent alone, I kept thinking of Nick. The guilt made me sick to my stomach, which caused me to eject my dinner at night. Another reason why the doctors wouldn't let me leave.

Noelle and Luke had been visiting me since I got to the hospital. They came every day; Luke even brought me flowers. Noelle brought me herself, and that was better than anything.

"When can I go home?" I pleaded when Dr. Jones walked through the door. He chuckled at my impatience before grabbing my clipboard. "You already know what's wrong with me, now can I go home or not?"

His eyes moved to mine before going back to the clipboard. Raged filled up in my body, and I had to bite down on my tongue to not scream at this guy. Whenever Mom wasn't there, he didn't do his job. Never answered any questions, barely stopped by, and mostly sent an intern to check on me.

"Nick Walter, a sixteen-year-old boy, is still missing," I heard from the TV. I turned my head to see the same news anchor from a few nights ago. "He was reported last seen in a navy-blue T-shirt and gray sweatpants. His girlfriend, Noelle Seong-Hun, was being questioned a few nights ago." The news anchor was gone, and soon enough Noelle appeared on the screen. The sun was shining in her face, and she was squinting. Her hair was down and wavy as if she just got up. I sat up in my bed and turned up the volume.

Dr. Jones faced the television as well. He held his pencil up to Noelle. "Isn't that the same girl who comes in here all the—"

"Shhh!" I hushed him. He widened his eyes at me before turning away. I didn't care what he did, though. I was only focused on Noelle.

"Noelle," the interviewer started, "why were you being questioned?"

Noelle's ears were bright red, and she kept looking at the camera. I watched as her fragile, tiny body shook. "They wanted more information; I was the last one with him."

She wasn't.

I was.

"Did they think you were responsible for him going missing?"

Wow, that was harsh.

"Um, no." She shook her head. Her hair bouncing as she moved. "I don't think so. I think they thought I knew something about it, but I didn't. Nick didn't tell me anything."

She crossed her arms and slid her hands on her biceps. She tried warming herself up by rubbing. She was only wearing a vest and a long-sleeve T-shirt—no wonder she was so cold.

"Is this something Nick would do? Just leave? Was there anything that would've caused this absence?"

What!?

"What!?" Noelle gasped, dropping her arms. "Of course not! Nick would never leave like this! He would've told someone! And no, nothing happened to make him want to leave!"

Dr. Jones was now staring at the TV with me, more invested in the news than my health. Nurses walking past my door kept peeking in. I figured my mother scared them half to death about me because each time they passed my door without looking, they came running back.

"Do you know who Nick would've told? Or someone who knows Nick well, better than you even?" The voice echoed in my ear.

Don't tell them.

Noelle, please! Do not say my name!

She nodded her head. "Yeah, his best friend, Kyle Davis. They have known each other since they were kids. Never been separated until now."

Crap.

Dr. Jones appeared at the foot of my bed, still looking at the TV. "Wow, kid, you're famous!" He chuckled at his joke. I stared at him in disbelief. "You're right, bad timing. Sorry, kid."

I rolled my eyes and shut off the TV. I couldn't believe that now my name was out there. Most kids knew about Nick and how close we were, but now the whole state was aware. The black TV screen seemed to taunt me. The wind rushed through the windows, picking up the papers from the counter. The bottom of the papers flew up but stayed to the counter because of the clipboard. I hadn't noticed him place it down.

"Okay, now that I have your attention"—Dr. Jones deadpanned, his eyes shifting between my face and the door— "let's talk about going home."

"I'm going home?" I pled with him. He had given hope like this before, making me want to drive my fist across his face when he took it away.

Like how you took Nick's life away?

I tried to push the thoughts away, but they came rushing toward me. Like a stampede, in a hurdle, and all at once. I started wincing at the pain, and it didn't take long for Dr. Jones to notice. He moved closer and held a flashlight against my pupils. The light was blazing, and my eyes became teary. He put the flashlight away and watched me. Just stood there and watched me.

Like I watched Nick die.

"Hey, man, get away from me!" I screamed at Nick. His eyes followed me, red with anger. I could see the steam coming from his ears, and I knew I was in trouble.

"No! Why would you say that to her?" He barked at me, pushing my chest. I felt his fist and my temper run out of patience. I looked at his hand before looking him in the eyes. His were focused on mine, and I knew we were in a fight.

I must've fallen asleep because when I opened my eyes next, Mom and Dad were next to me. Dr. Jones was nowhere to be seen. There was a small breeze coming through the slightly opened window. The sun beamed through the shutters and cast a light onto the floor. I noticed a plant in my room, a small tree. A small tree sitting on a table.

"Get that out of here," I grumbled. I couldn't take my eyes off it. It beckoned for me to get mad.

"What was that, sweetie?" Mom asked, standing up beside me. She ran her fingers through my hair like she did when I got mad. She knew it was the only way to calm me down. Dad was still sitting, reading the newspaper.

"Get that stupid tree out of here," I ordered, louder than before. I heard Dad crinkle his paper, setting it down. His eyes were on me; Mom's were on his. My eyes were on that branchy devil.

"Sweetie, I brought it to add to your room," she coaxed. "To make it less like a hospital."

"Well, I am in a hospital," I hissed through my teeth. "And I don't want that tree here."

I felt my brain shut down; every other emotion was erased from my mind. I could only feel anger and only see red. Nothing else. That stupid tree seemed like it was the root of all my problems, but it wasn't. I didn't care, though; I wanted it gone.

"Honey, I—"

"Get it out!" I grabbed the nearest thing to me—a lamp—and chucked it across the room. The wires attached to me made it difficult to throw it, but I made it work. Anger burned through my body, and I had third-degree burns from it. I watched as the lamp flew across the room, and Mom gasped as it slammed against the pot the tree was sitting in. It fell over, breaking into a million pieces.

Dad stood up, staring at the broken tree pot. His newspaper was now folded in his chair, and his arms were crossed. A couple of silent moments later, his glare burned through the back of my head, and I was only focused on one thing.

Look at that tree; it's dead now.

Just like Nick.

"Oh god." Mom sniffled, walking away from me. Dad held a hand to her, but she waved him away. "I can't." I heard her footsteps race out of the room and down the hall.

She's realized you're a monster.

And she doesn't even know all the things you've killed.

~

"Okay, we will be back in the morning to get you." Mom kissed my forehead. Dad came back a few hours later, in between shifts. The alarming sound made him fall and drop all his papers. He spent the rest of the time trying to organize them and put them back in his briefcase.

Noelle left a little bit before that. We turned on the news only to be reminded that he was missing. She excused herself to go to the bathroom after that and came back all teary-eyed. She stayed, though and held my hand. Her soft, gentle palm on my scraped one.

After she left, Luke came back. I could tell he wanted to ask what happened between us, but he stayed quiet. Then he went on a tangent about the protest his mom was planning next. Something about the ocean or an ocean animal. I'm not sure; I wasn't listening.

Luke, Mom, and Dad all left my room when visiting hours were over. Mom, however, didn't leave. She was going to stay the night and work. She just wanted me to have a little bit of alone time.

"I'll be right upstairs. Need anything, tell them to come and get me. Also, try to get some sleep; the alarms won't go off until 10:00 a.m." She lectured me before leaving the room.

I was alone in the hospital room with my thoughts. The last place I wanted to be.

You deserve this.

My room was poorly lit with a lamp on a nightstand a couple of inches away from my bed. The rails were up and blocking my sides. I finally had a moment to realize how uncomfortable I was. The IV in my arm started to sting; the heart monitor was getting annoying, beeping every second. There was no way I could sleep.

I lay there for hours. I watched the clock turn every minute until it was 2:54 a.m. I groaned, rolling over. I was sick of watching the clock, so I faced the windows. The stars glistened in the dark sky. There was a ridiculously small sliver of the crescent moon. I failed astronomy, though, so I'm not sure. It was beautiful, though. Almost distracted me from the bedsprings pricking at my back. I looked back at the clock, and the time was now 3:00 a.m.

I'm not getting any sleep tonight, am I?

Suddenly, this loud, obnoxious alarm started blasting through my room and out the halls. I covered my ears at the piercing noise. After a few minutes, it stopped. At first, I figured it was another shift change.

But they weren't supposed to have one.

Something was wrong; I felt it in my bones. Every inch of me was screaming danger. I turned to my side to press the nurse button. It clicked, but no one came. The button didn't even light up. I waited for a few minutes, and no one came. I pushed on the sidebar that was keeping me blocked in. I grabbed ahold of the machine attached to me with an IV but tore off everything else. The heart monitor machine slowly stopped.

I hate needles, so I knew pulling it out would be hard for me to watch. I held the IV in my hand and closed my eyes. I yanked it out as quickly as I could, stinging me along the way. I winced quietly, biting on my lower lip.

"Ouch," I muttered. Blood dripped down my hand like a stream. I stood up from my bed and made my way to the door. The hallways were empty, not a single person in sight. The only movement was a flashing light down the hall. I heard faint screams from a couple of doors down.

Walking down the hallway of what seemed like an abandoned hospital was one of the scariest times of my life. My legs shook the whole way, and I lost my balance about halfway through. The light flickering above me created a headache. I pushed myself to stand up and continued walking. The screams were getting louder. It was a boy. A teenager.

It sounds like he's really in pain.

I came across a door where the angered yells were from. I turned the knob to the door, but it wouldn't move. It was locked. The screams continued from inside, and I tried to calm them down.

"It's okay!" I tried to convince the boy. "It's locked, but I'll try to get in."

The boy started begging for his life. Pleading with me as if I was God. As if I was the one taking his life away from him. He started banging on the door as if it was the door of life. I noticed there was a small glass window above my head in the door. I looked around and luckily spotted a chair. I grabbed it before placing it against the door as the boy suffered. The glass window was inlaid to the door, and I realized I only had one option.

Punch the damn thing.

I started swinging. My fists were bruised from the first punch, but I kept going. I saw a small crack and found its weak spot. My fists begged me to stop, but my head told me to keep going.

If you can kill a boy, you can save one.

I didn't stop punching until the glass shattered. The glass cut my hands, but I didn't feel it. I peeled away the rest of the glass and looked in the room. There was silence. The boy stopped screaming. It was dark, so I couldn't see anything.

Moments passed, and there was nothing. I started banging on the door to get his attention. "Are you okay!? Dude!"

I heard shuffling on the other side. I stuck my head through the broken window. A hand suddenly grabbed my throat. Another one closed around my neck and started squeezing. All the air escaped from my body. I tried to pull away, but his grip tightened. I tried to swallow, but it felt like a boulder trying to go through a straw. It numbed my throat. He started to lift me. Pulling me inside the room while I gasped for air.

"Now you know how it feels to be murdered."

My face, bright red, started turning purple. I could feel the veins trying to pop out of my body. The voice sounded familiar; the haunting-ness of it wasn't. A face appeared from the darkness. Nick was bloody, cut up, and drained of color. I stared at him in shock.

I did that.

I tried to scream, but nothing came out. Nick's dead, lifeless eyes stared into mine. Watching me as I lost oxygen. I heard footsteps bolting down the hall. Nick let go, and I fell to the ground. My back hit the hard, cold, laminated floor. I heard a crack, and I screamed out in pain. I crawled away from the door, leaving traces of blood around me. I wasn't even sure where I was bleeding.

People came rushing down the hallway and kneeled around me. They started doing doctor things, checking my throat, oxygen, broken bones, and all sorts of things. I saw Mom running down the hallway, and I felt safe. She engulfed me in a hug, and I wrapped my arms around her waist and started sobbing. She held me tighter. I felt my breath leave my body, and I struggled to get it back. I was sure my lungs were broken forever.

No, no, no, no!

I pushed her away. Surprised, Mom held my head back and saw my throat. I heard her gasp before she glared at everyone.

"Who choked my baby!?" she demanded. I tried to speak, but I couldn't. No words formed, even though I knew what I wanted to say.

Nick.

It was Nick.

The doctors stared at me, confused and concerned. Mom started screaming again, demanding answers this time. I held up my shaking hand and pointed to the door. A doctor walked in there and came out a few moments later.

"No one is in there," he announced. All eyes were back on the trembling, crying, bloody teenage boy sitting on the floor in his mom's arms.

Oh wait, that's me.

6

Day Eight

Eight days since Nick died. Three days since I saw him last. Three days since he held my life in his hands and wanted to crush it. Two days since I was prescribed anxiety medication. Two days since I took the medication. They wouldn't let me leave the hospital until I was fully examined and diagnosed. Mom agreed with them and made me stay more days.

"I'm fine, Mom," I informed her three days ago. "They examined me and said it was just anxiety." She stood in my room on the psych floor. They made me stay there while checking the scene and room where I was attacked. They claimed it was a panic attack, and I only thought someone was choking me. They diagnosed me with panic disorder. Told me that I need to take medicine to stop the attacks. I didn't believe them; I knew someone hurt me. And I knew exactly who it was. But Dad told me to just agree with them to get out of the ward. Mom wouldn't believe it either though; she knew that something must've happened to me. She took me to another doctor in the building to get a second opinion.

"No, it wasn't just a panic attack!" She disagreed with the psychiatrist. "He had handprints on his neck! Someone attacked my son!"

The psychiatrist, Dr. Brown, looked at me and lifted my head. He checked my throat. It was sore and scratchy. He poked at a few of the bruises before asking me some questions.

"Did you see this person?"

I nodded.

"Can you tell me what he looked like?"

"For the most part, yeah," I answered. Mom walked over to me, and she wasn't smiling.

"My son gave his report to the police. What is the point of this?" She grabbed my shoulders and held me. "He has suffered enough. Why does he have to go through this again?"

I have never seen Mom so assertive; I was so used to her being pushed around. I guess, when she became chief, she realized that she had to be tough. She even tried enforcing rules with Henry at home. It didn't work, but she made a valid effort.

"Maybe we should talk outside," Dr. Brown suggested. He held his clipboard close to his chest as if I were going to steal it from him. I almost laughed.

What an idiot.

"No, my son has the right to know what happened." Mom was stern. Her cold eyes stared at Dr. Brown, breaking him down. I watched as he trembled at her glare. He sighed before placing the clipboard on the counter behind him.

"Kyle." He looked at me. My attention shifted away from the papers and to him, fully invested in what this guy had to say about what happened. "You told us about your migraines and your inability to sleep at night. We believe that these two things have caused major hallucinations. Migraines and sleep deprivation can both cause minor hallucinations, but since you are experiencing both, we think that it advances the—"

"So, you mean to tell me—" Mom cut him off. "—that my son just thought he was being choked? What about the hand marks?"

"Well," Dr. Brown started before clearing his throat, "we believe that Kyle wasn't aware of his own self-harming."

I snapped my head to Mom, thinking I was going to have to defend myself. Nick was the one who choked me, I wanted to yell. Knowing that he was "just missing" to them, it would've been confusing, and if I told them he was dead, I would be stuck in the looney bin forever.

"My son choked himself?" she challenged. She was beginning to walk toward the doctor like a predator stalking her prey. Dr. Brown looked like he was about to be attacked. "He wrapped his own hands around his throat and squeezed on purpose?"

"Not on purpose, but subconsciously." He seemed weary. Bouncing on the balls of his feet, clenching his hands, and wiping them on his uniform.

Mom assigned me to another doctor. Everyone obliged

because she's the chief of the surgery department, so I guess that gets you some respect around here. However, they made me stay on the psych floor for another three days. For three days, I was known as the semi-subconscious self-harming boy. I talked with a girl who tried to kill herself about it. She was a delight.

Our first ever conversation was her going into detail about how she wanted to go out. She said something about jumping out of a plane with blades and snakes attached to her hair so people would think she was Medusa. That was the moment I knew she was crazy. And yet I still wanted to talk to her.

Her name is Marie Sparrow, although I'm quite sure she made up her last name. She has this wild curly mess of hair that she claims she has a tough time taming. Her skin is dark with rosy undertones, brightening her aqua-colored eyes.

She was the only one that actually understood me. The only one I really liked. There was a boy there I tried to befriend, but he threatened to kill me. Then he got transferred to a more secure facility for assaulting a nurse. So, Marie was the next best choice.

"That gets rid of the whole point!" she blurted out. I was startled at her sudden volume. We sat at the lunch table with a bunch of other weirdos, but we never talked to them. And they didn't care enough about us to listen.

"What?" I asked, confused. Marie always kept me on my toes, so unpredictable.

"To feel the pain or want it," she explained as if it was something everyone knew.

"No, but—" I quickly checked around us to make sure no one was listening. "—I know exactly who did this to me."

"Don't go all crazy on me." Then she laughed and started choking on her food.

Karma.

She coughed and drank some water. I just patted her back, which got me a glare from the male nurse that was supervising us. I threw my hands in the air and just watched Marie turn red. Eventually, she calmed down, looking back at me for my response.

"I'm not, Marie! He looked me right in the eyes!" I tried to convince her, but she just stared at me blankly. "I know who it was."

"Then just tell the police," she stated simply before grabbing her water and starting to gulp. I watched as her sleeve slid up her arm a little and revealed scars.

Oh.

I shifted in my seat. She didn't seem uncomfortable about it. I felt weird, seeing the scars on her. My head got dizzy from picturing her hurting herself. For some reason, the image was clear. Her sitting in a bathroom with razors in her hand. Blood dripping from her wrists as she pulled her knees closer together. Her mind was hazy with thoughts, causing her to cry. But I couldn't picture tears streaming down Marie's face. I pushed the scene away and focused on the Marie that was in front of me, stuffing her face with food.

"I can't tell the police, then I'd be here forever," I reasoned, pushing away my thoughts. She eyed me, tilting her head to the side. I leaned into her ear. "He's dead."

I drifted back to see her facial expression. Her eyes were widened, showcasing the light blue in them, and her jaw dropped to the floor. She grabbed the collar of my shirt and pulled me closer to her.

"You killed the guy who choked you?"

"No!" I pushed her away.

Technically, yeah.

I looked at her face. She was thinking about how any of that made sense. Before I said anything else, I thought about how this could affect me. She lived in town, but she'd been in here for a while. She probably had no idea who Nick was.

You could tell her that Nick is dead.

Just don't tell her that it's because of you.

"He was pronounced dead a couple of days ago. They found his body in the woods," I whispered, staring at the white table. I bit my lip and closed my eyes to keep it down. The scene replayed in my mind. I heard her breathing right by my ear.

"Who was?" she whispered back.

I opened my eyes and stared right at her. The sound of my heart beating drowned out all other sounds. The taste of bile was sitting in my throat, waiting for a moment to escape. My hands shook the whole table. I concentrated on just Marie, to answer her.

"My best friend."

~

Three pills. They prescribed me three different pills to take, and I could not tell you what they were supposed to do. A nurse comes in every morning to make sure I take my pills. She watches me as I place them in my mouth and swallow them; then she checks my mouth to make sure I'm not hiding them.

"Open up," she muttered. She looked in my mouth and left without another word. She stomped away down the hall. I sat on my bed for a few more minutes before there was a knock on my door.

Mom managed to get me a private room, which wasn't what I wanted. I figured if I had a roommate, my thoughts wouldn't have a chance to seep through the back of my mind. However, Mom thought if I were alone, I would have more time to heal, and because I'm her son, my privileges wouldn't be taken for granted. But so far, the only privileges I've gotten were this room and extra fries on Wednesday.

"Knock, knock," Marie chirped. She strutted her way into my room and sat on my chair. She grabbed a magazine Mom gave me and started flipping through it.

"You aren't supposed to be in here," I reminded her. She scrunched her face up and waved me off.

She responded to me without taking her eyes off the page she was on. "The nurse said she didn't care as long as I sat in this chair, and you stayed over there." She sat up while raising her eyebrow. "Ooh, scrunchies are making a comeback. I think my hair color would look good with the bright green one. I bet your Mom has loads of them. Maybe I'll ask her to bring me some. Chloe was wearing one yesterday."

I rolled my eyes at her. Marie is normally more like a guy, at least with me. But she has her girly moments. Yesterday, her grandma brought her a new top, and she actually squealed. I watched as her blue eyes lit up as she took it out of the box.

"I think we should talk, though," she said, still looking at the magazine. "About the thing."

I didn't want her to bring it up. I wished that we would just never speak of it again.

She noticed my disinterest. "About Nick?"

My head snapped to her, and she just eyed me. I gulped, pushing it down my throat. I could feel the sweat running down my back.

How did she—

"Google. Nurses don't watch you all the time. Nick Walter, age sixteen, your best friend. Also dating that gorgeous girl that keeps coming here for you," she recited before putting the magazine down. "Although, there is one thing the internet didn't tell me."

Crap. Crap. Crap.

A sharp, stabbing pain pierced through my head, making its way around my whole body. My thoughts started attacking me, slapping my mind around like a ball. I couldn't think for a moment. I couldn't breathe for a moment.

"It didn't tell me Nick was dead. It told me he was missing."

It felt like a stake to the heart. Someone was grabbing my heart and closing their fingers around it. Tightly. I didn't show her, though; I wouldn't show her how much pain I was in. I stared at her, closing off all emotions I could. Lies that I could say passed by my mind.

"But you told me he was dead."

I sighed. I was weak at this point. My mind shut down, and I was about to pass out from all the sudden pain. She caught me. This was going to be it.

That was it. It was time for the truth. I was honest with her before in the cafeteria, and now I was paying the price. I was done with the lies and the constant guilt that was eating me alive. I was done with it all.

"It was an accident."

"An accident?" She walked toward me. "So, you did kill him?"

Those words, those five words, held the fate of my life in their hands. What I answered would decide if I would spend my life in prison or not. Marie wasn't backing down; her arms were folded across her chest, and her eyes were narrowed down on me.

"I pushed him, and he fell."

Guilt weighed me down but saying the words aloud relieved some of the weight. I didn't feel so sick to my stomach any more. The bitterness that was sitting in the back of my throat washed away. I felt okay again.

Except for the fact that you just admitted to murder.

Marie looked at me. She stared for a long time, silently standing there. She was inspecting me, waiting to see if I would take it back. But there was no use; it was out there. My breathing started to hitch again; the feeling of uneasiness settled in my stomach.

"Then what happened?" she asked. "Did you stab him?"

What?

I was taken aback. "No! Why would I stab him if he fell?"

"Wait," she muttered, rubbing her forehead as if I caused her headaches. If anyone caused anyone headaches in this room, it was her. With her constant talk about random crap that no one cares about.

Like scrunchies.

"So, you mean to tell me," she started again, pulling me away from my thoughts, "that you pushed him and thought you killed him?"

I know I killed him. I watched him die right in front of me. I watched the blood drain from his head and life disappear from his eyes. I nodded to answer her because I was fuming at this point. My knuckles were white, and I was biting my tongue to stop myself from beating the crap out of her.

"Dude!" She threw her hands up in the air then placed them beside her hips. "You didn't kill him! You pushed him, and he probably just hit his head!"

"I watched him die!" I screamed at her, jumping from my bed. "I watched as the blood came out of his head and onto the ground!"

Her eyes pierced into mine. "You sound crazy."

I huffed, squatting back onto my bed. I ran my fingers through my hair, pulling on some strands. I didn't think I would have to convince someone that I killed him.

"I'm not crazy," I muttered. "I pushed him, and he died."

"People don't just die from being pushed, Kyle!" she lectured. "Something else must've happened to actually kill him!" She emphasized "actually" to make her point.

She paced around the room, continuing her thoughts. "And no, falling doesn't kill people either."

What she was saying made sense; it did. People don't just die from falling. But I saw him. I knew he was dead.

"I think he hit a rock when he fell. That's what caused him to bleed."

I was remembering the night. Seeing him there, lying on the cold, dirty ground. Me leaving him there. Running through the forest, the wind blowing against my face, screaming for me to turn back. To go get him and save him. Tears formed in my eyes. I wiped them away before Marie could see.

"Hitting your head on a rock doesn't make a lot of blood. He could've gotten a concussion. Or he could've just passed out. He might still be alive but confused," she guessed. "He could still be alive, Kyle."

I looked up to her, her eyes warm and forgiving. She didn't see me as a monster. She saw me as me. She knew the truth and didn't hate me. Something took over me then. I'm not sure if it was the state I was in or the fact that she helped me.

I stood up and wrapped my arms around her. She hesitantly hugged back. I burrowed my face into her neck, tears brimming in my eyes again.

"So, I'm not a monster?"

She shook her head. "You're not a monster."

7

Day Nine

They let me leave the next morning. They said I was doing better, and I could go home. And the truth was that I was doing better. Marie helped me realize that Nick could still be alive. Although, it didn't help that the thoughts still tormented me.

Yeah, and what if he is dead?

Then you are a murderer.

You killed your best friend.

Marie tried to comfort me about it, but they kicked her out of my room. She was muttering something about how she hates it there when she left. When I left my room the next morning to go get breakfast before leaving, she was right there waiting for me.

"Hey, Marie." She looked up from the floor, waved, and bounced over to me.

"A little birdie told me that you are leaving after breakfast," she began. We walked down the hallways together to get to the cafeteria. Well, it's not called a cafeteria because this one is specifically for psych patients. We weren't allowed in the hospital one.

I nodded. "Yep, they are letting me go today." I felt a tug on my sleeve, and I stopped walking. I turned to face Marie, who had dropped the smile on her face.

"Are you sure you're ready for that? With everything with Nick?" I rolled my eyes and pulled my sleeve out of her grasp. She pushed her black curly hair out of her eyes, staring intensely into mine.

"Yes, so stop giving me that look." I groaned. "It creeps me out."

I continued walking, passing random doctors along the way. Most ignored me until I bumped into one certain doctor.

"Kyle," Dr. Jones babbled, "great to see you, son!"

Oh god.

I placed my hands in my pockets and nodded. Marie came up behind me and scoffed at Dr. Jones. He didn't seem to notice either of our annoyed faces because he kept talking.

"I heard you are getting released today," he pointed out.

"Yep." I cleared my throat to end the awkward silence. "I was just about to go eat."

"Oh well, I don't want to keep you two." He turned to face Marie. "And I heard you are getting better every day, Marie!"

"Bite me," she barked back.

Dr. Jones didn't seem fazed by this statement. He kept his stupid smile on his face before trotting off. We both turned to watch him pass us before cracking up. Marie held her hands up and flipped him off.

"I hate that guy," she muttered. "He doesn't do his job!"

I chuckled. "Yeah, why is he on this floor, anyways?"

"Probably trying to find any excuse not to help patients." She shrugged. After a few more minutes of walking and poking fun at Dr. Jones, we arrived at the cafeteria. Our meals were preplanned, so we just grabbed our trays and headed toward our table.

"When you get out of here, promise me you'll come to visit and break me out of here," she begged. I sat across from her, placing my tray down.

"Honestly, I wish—" I cackled. "—but I would get sent back. Both of us being here isn't any use."

She reluctantly agreed with me before tackling her food. She always ate so quickly. I watched as she scoffed down her whole bagel before moving on to her eggs.

"You are gonna throw up eating that fast," I warned her, slowly taking bites of my oatmeal.

"Boo-hoo, shut up, and eat your damn food."

After we finished eating, I went to go pack. Marie came with me. She said it was to say goodbye, but I'm fairly sure she just wanted my room. As we were packing, I noticed something under my bed. I bent down to pick it up.

"What are you doing? There aren't any monsters under your bed."

"Haha, very funny," I replied sarcastically. "There's something under here."

I reached under without looking; I felt around and didn't

find anything. When I tried to pull my hand out, a razor-sharp pain shot through my palm. I winced, pulling it out. Blood started rushing out of my palm, dripping to the floor. It wasn't in a pool just splatters.

"What the heck?" I questioned aloud. I peeked under the bed and noticed a long, shiny object. It was now a little bloody, but I recognized it.

A knife?

"What happened?" Marie rushed over and gasped when she saw my bloody hand. She grabbed ahold of it. "Why did you—"

"I didn't!" I fought back before she even finished her question. "There's a knife under the bed!"

She crouched down to look under the bed. She was looking for a good two minutes before she responded. "Kyle, there's nothing under here."

"What?" I pushed her out of the way. But when I looked under, the knife that cut me was now gone. I triple-checked my mistake before staring down at my hand.

Why is this happening?

"Dude, they are never gonna let you leave now." She sighed. I stood up and started wiping the blood off my hand.

"Yes, they will because they aren't going to know about this." I walked to the bathroom and started rinsing my hands off. The clear water turned red as it fell down the drain.

Like the night Nick died.

Or didn't die.

Marie stepped into the doorway of my bathroom. "But isn't this your subconscious self-harming problem?" she tried to point out.

"No! Because that doesn't exist. I'm not crazy, and I don't hurt myself, so just keep quiet and back off." She stared at me for a few seconds before returning to my room. I shut my eyes, trying to figure out my plan. I felt bad for getting mad at her, but she is just so pushy at times. Something must've cut me. I know it.

I walked out of the bathroom and started cleaning off the floor. She sat on my bed, watching over me as I wiped away my blood. Her hair was in her fingers as she played with it.

"So, you're just going to pretend like nothing happened?"

She grunted. "Got it."

"Do you even realize how much longer I'd be stuck here for?" I argued, throwing away my shirt and covering it with a bunch of tissues.

"Yes, but because it seems like you need the help, Kyle!" she countered. "Also, that won't work; just bring the shirt with you."

I grabbed the shirt covered in red stains again and buried it in my bag. I zipped it up, placing it on my bed. There was a lot less light that day; it was cloudy, so there was no more sun shining through the windows. The bare walls made me shudder from the emptiness of the room. I groaned, pulling on my hair.

"Kyle, you saw your best friend almost die, and you thought it was your fault for nine days," she pointed out. "If anyone needs help, it's you."

"It is my fault!" I growled. "I am the reason he is hurt, and now I have to live with it! I am not allowed to get help any more; I don't deserve it."

Her eyes turned soft. She looked to the ground, unsure of what to say next. We stood there in silence. Neither one of us knew what to say. I only knew one thing; she knew about Nick. And she knew what I did, which would be a big mistake if he turns up dead. Marie had to keep her mouth shut; my life was at stake here.

You don't deserve a life.

I grunted at the thought that escaped from the back of my mind. Marie noticed the noise and huffed. "You can't live each day blaming yourself, Kyle."

Her words hit me. But they didn't stay. "I have to."

Just then, Mom walked in, knocking on the door. She stared at Marie and me for a few seconds, noticing the tension between us. Soon, she locked eyes with me and smiled.

"You ready to go home?"

Mom and I left, and she wouldn't stop talking about Marie. I spent the whole car ride trying to convince her that Marie was just a friend.

"I don't know," she insisted, "you guys seemed a lot closer than just friends."

I groaned, closing my eyes. "No, we are just friends, Mom.

Can we stop talking about this?"

She shrugged and didn't say anything else. She just kept glancing at me from the driver's seat and giggling. We arrived home about twenty minutes later, and I noticed Henry's car was missing. I asked Mom, and she thought about it for a second.

"Oh!" She realized. "He went camping. He was so excited about it; he packed all his stuff weeks in advance. Remember that bag that was sitting in the hallway?"

I stood up and grabbed the bag, about to throw it at him, when I noticed something. It was a shiny object, and it was reflecting off one of the lights in our hallway. I reached into the bag and fumbled around a bit. My hand grazed against something sharp, and it brought stinging pain to my hand. I yanked my hand out of the bag and stared in awe.

Dark, warm blood dripped from my hand. The blood kept getting darker the more I stared at it. It dripped onto the floor, creating a pool of dark blood.

"Yeah, I do," I muttered back, grabbing my things from the trunk.

I guess that's why he had the knife.

But what about the gun?

Who needs a gun on a camping trip?

The wind blew, creating a whistle effect in my ears. The trees swayed back and forth, almost dancing with the song the wind sang. I closed my eyes and let myself enjoy it. I decided there was no point in getting worked up about Henry since he wasn't there for me to confront him.

Wow, I'm not mad?

These pills must be working.

Mom and I made our way into the house, carrying some bags. I didn't bring much to begin with, but Mom brought me new clothes every day. I kept telling her that I wasn't staying long. She didn't care. Everyone hated me on the floor because of Mom. Besides Marie, that is. They all thought I was getting special treatment, and maybe I was.

The house was the same as it always was. I don't know why I expected it to look different; it was the same house I've always lived in. I guess I expected it to feel different. It was still empty and dusty. The sun even peeked through the windows the same way.

After an hour of putting stuff away, Mom came into my room.

"Hey, hun, the hospital just called me. They need me to go to do surgery. Are you okay on your own?"

I told her I was and continued to unpack. She reminded me to take my medication at seven thirty. I finished putting my things away before walking around the house. I'm not sure why, but I was drawn to the hallway with all the pictures. I stared long and hard at this one frame. It was Nick and me with Max. Nick was holding Max up like a prize, and I was laughing beside them.

I lost two of my best friends.
And they're both my fault.

I slid down the wall, slowly pushing my feet out. An aching pain appeared in my head and chest. I hated this feeling. I had to start taking deep breaths to calm myself down, but it wasn't working. I sat there, rocking back and forth for what seemed like hours.

It's all your fault.
All your fault.
You did this to them.

They wouldn't leave me alone. My thoughts kept charging at me like a lion, beating me down until I was nothing. Until there was nothing, except bones. I rubbed my eyes frantically, trying to make them stop. They kept coming until I heard a ring.

The phone.

I stood up, shaking the thoughts out of my head before answering the phone. I picked it up and pressed it to my ear, feeling the coolness of it on my cartilage.

"Hello?" I answered, still trying to push away what was going on in my mind.

"Hey!" Luke chirped on the other side. "How are you doing?"

A car raced past the house, distracting me. The high-pitched whine of the speeding car was hurting my ears, making my headache worse. I groaned out loud.

"Fine, I just have this bad headache," I replied, shifting the phone to the other side so I was now facing the kitchen. "Or migraine. That's what the doctors call it."

"That sucks; I'm sorry, Kyle."

Luke was always apologizing, even for stuff that wasn't his fault. He's just that kind of guy. Which is why I hated him at first.

"Not your fault, dude," I croaked. "Just my life at the moment."

"Still—" I heard a faint sigh before he continued talking. "—okay, so you don't have to go, considering you just got out of the hospital—"

"Psych ward." I corrected him.

He paused for a moment. I could imagine his exact facial expression. Eyebrows furrowed together, mouth open, and eyes squinted down at me.

"Same thing," he muttered. I laughed aloud before letting him finish. "Anyways, there is going to be a search party for Nick tonight. And you don't have to come—"

I tuned out what he was saying. There was going to be a search party for Nick. I could see if he was still alive. If his body wasn't there, then he's alive. Just lost or confused.

It would mean I'm not a murderer.

The thought of his body still there made my legs weak. I didn't know if I could handle seeing him like that again. It had been nine days; he would look worse. Animals would've eaten parts of him or bugs infesting in his corpse.

The image of Nick's body going through all that made me regurgitate into my trashcan. I pulled the phone as far away from me as I could, but I heard Luke asking if I was okay. I wiped my mouth clean and flicked the vomit into the trash. I held the phone up to my ear again and told him I would be there.

"You don't have to come if you aren't feeling up to it." Luke faltered.

I chuckled. "Kind of sounds like you don't want me there."

Luke gave a soft laugh, but not a Luke laugh. It almost sounded fake. "Well, Noelle is going to be there."

I was caught off guard by that. I wasn't sure what he meant, so I asked him, clenching the phone in my hands tightly.

"Nothing. It's just that you and Noelle have been hanging out a lot more recently."

"Luke, she's like one of my closest friends," I argued.

I looked at the white walls of my kitchen and focused on a spot so I could try and control my anger. I looked to where I threw my phone when it broke.

"Yeah, but you still have feelings for her, don't you? This *would* be a perfect time to swoop in and steal his girl."

My mouth fell to the floor. I stared at the spot until it meant nothing to me. The rage that was building up inside me boiled over and spewed at Luke.

"Okay, listen," I barked. "Noelle would never do that to Nick, and neither would I. We have only been hanging out together more because Nick isn't here to spend time with her. I'm not trying to take his girl or whatever else you think is going on. Screw you for even thinking of me like that."

I slammed the phone back on its holder. The holder cracked, and the phone dangled inches from the ground. I watched as it bounced around for a bit. The broken holder soon fell off the wall, leaving only a thin wire connecting it to the power socket. The phone crashed onto the ground with a loud rattle. I found it funny how Luke and I were in a fight about Noelle. It reminded me of a time when Nick and I were fighting over her too.

She was starting to seem like the root of all my problems.

8

Day Twelve

The next morning, I woke up to an empty house. I walked to the kitchen and read the note that was left for me.

—Hi, hon! I had to go to work early, don't forget to take your medicine! Also, Henry will be arriving home today. Please don't fight! Your father and I will be home before it gets too late. Love you!—

I took the note and placed it on the counter. I looked at it for a while before deciding that it was strange. Mom was never the type to leave notes.

You were also never the type to get put into a psych ward, so a lot has changed.

I went to open the fridge when a ringing went off in the house. I looked at the broken phone hanging there, but the sound was further away. I traveled around the house until I heard the ringing from behind a door. It was in my mom's office.

I could take a message for her.

I opened her door and looked around her office. She had bookcases lined up against the walls, filled with medical cases. Her desk had a lot of locked drawers, but most of the papers were on her desk, anyways.

What's the point of the drawers, then?

I pushed the papers around and finally found the phone. I answered it with a swift, "Hello."

"Hi! My name is Katherine Agnes. I work with the local news station. Is Kyle Davis there?"

I was confused. Why would they call Mom's work phone to talk to me?

"Speaking."

"Kyle, you are one tough guy to get in contact with." The woman almost scolded me over the phone. I realized why they were calling me.

Noelle gave them my name.

"We wanted to see if you would do an interview with us about Nick Walter."

No.

"No," I gritted out. She was silent; I could hear faint whispers in the background. I rolled my eyes at the room of grown-ups who were unaware of how to talk to a sixteen-year-old.

"May I ask why?" She spluttered. Laughter tried to escape from my mouth, but I covered it with my hand to stop myself.

"Listen," I commanded, "I think it's sick that you people are trying to get a story on a missing person for views or money. Nick is a person, a human being. Not some inside scoop that you guys can earn promotions from. You have pictures of what he looks like, and you know what he was wearing. Why don't you tell people that information so we can get him home instead of asking me to tell you what he was like?"

I slammed the phone down, causing the desk to tremble. Some papers flew to the floor, but I didn't care. I left the office and shut the door behind me. The house seemed to have rocked when the door closed. The way the house shook reminded me I had to take my pills.

I hate taking the pills.

I went to the kitchen and grabbed a glass of water. I took out my bottles and started taking them. One by one, I swallowed each pill. Pushing them down my throat. I've never had problems swallowing pills before, but it was hard after I was choked. The way the pills blocked my airway for a split second while swallowing them terrified me. The sound of a car pulling into my driveway distracted me from the thought. I realized who came home.

Henry.

The door swung open, and Henry came inside, carrying two bags. One of which I recognized from a couple of nights ago. Henry didn't notice me in the kitchen at first. I watched as he left his bags in the hallway and walked into the dining room. He looked up and faced me. He jumped back a bit and did a double-take.

"Oh," he muttered. "You're home. How was the hospital?"

Is he serious?

"It's a hospital," I blatantly replied, staring him down. He walked to the fridge and grabbed a water bottle from it. He nodded and took a swig of his water. I didn't break eye contact with him, and he raised his eyebrows at me.

"What?" he raged. "Why are you looking at me like that?"

"Why was there a gun in your bag?"

His face turned red, and he grunted. He started choking on the water. He ran to the sink and spit it up. He wiped it off his face, and I turned to face his back. He was still hanging over the sink. In between his coughing fits, he said, "I don't have a gun."

"You looked caught off guard just a minute ago," I pointed out. "Suspicious."

He turned around and faced me. His jaw clamped shut, and his eyes turned dark. His fists were opening and closing as if he was deciding whether he should punch me or not.

I really hope he won't.

My eye still hasn't healed from Mark.

"Why would I own a gun?" he rebutted. "Do you actually think Mom would let me have a gun?"

I thought about it for a moment, with Henry's eyes staring me down. Mom wouldn't let him have a gun. And she would find it at some point.

"But I felt it!" I argued. "I felt it in your bag!"

"Why were you in my bag?" he bellowed.

Crap.

"I tripped, okay? I fell and cut my hand on your knife in your bag. I went back in to find it, and I felt a gun," I explained. He edged closer to me, and he suddenly got taller. I relaxed my feet as he hunched over me like he was about to kill me.

Henry took a step forward, bending down to meet my height. He gritted his teeth while speaking. "That doesn't mean you get to go through my bag."

I took a few steps back so I wouldn't have to smell his breath any more. "That doesn't matter. I felt the gun!"

He walked over to his bags and grabbed them. He threw the one that I went through at me. "Go ahead and check." I held it in my hands. I could feel his anger toward me. The bag didn't feel heavy. I opened it up and placed my hand inside. Carefully, this time. I felt the prick of the top of the knife, but no metal. No gun.

"I have a question for you, Kyle." He grabbed two of my pill bottles and shook them in the air. The rattle sound of it echoed throughout the house. "Did you feel the gun before or after you went crazy?"

I clamped down on the bag as hard as I could to stop myself from doing anything stupid. His smirk burned through my head, and I lost control. I shook the bag empty till I found the knife. I held it up; the metal part shined with the sun coming through the windows. I watched Henry's eyes widen, and he took a few steps back.

"You're crazy!" he screamed at me.

I'm not crazy.

I'm just a monster.

I took the knife and raised it above my shoulder slowly. Henry stepped back, watching my every move. I threw the knife to the floor, just missing his feet. It stuck to the wood like a magnet to a piece of metal with a quick, sharp noise. Henry flinched at the sudden noise, almost dropping to the ground.

He's scared of me.

Good.

~

Dad came home later that night. He said Mom was still stuck in surgery. I told him about the search party for Nick before I was about to leave.

"Alright, but I picked up something for you," he told me, reaching into a plastic bag and throwing a phone at me. "Since your old one broke."

I thanked him and left the house. I decided to bring a drawstring bag with me, filled with some necessities. The sun was just setting. The blue sky was turning darker as the sun sank into the ground. It left waves of orange and red in the sky, but they were following the sun. There were many cars out on the street, but I didn't mind. The headlights lit up the sidewalks for me. I pulled out my new phone and texted Noelle.

Sadly, her number is one of those I memorized.

To: Noelle
   Hey, it's Kyle. I'm on my way to the search party. Want me to stop and get you?

I was looking down at my phone and wasn't paying attention. I felt someone bump into me. My phone fell to the ground with a clang. I looked up, but the girl was already bending down to pick up my phone.

"I'm so sorry!" the girl exclaimed. She stood up and handed me my phone. I checked to make sure it wasn't cracked. She spoke again while I was looking at my phone. "Do I know you? You look really familiar."

I looked up at her. Her eyes were dark, almost black it seemed. I scanned her features before I realized where she was from.

A girl bumped into my shoulder. She grabbed her bicep and winced before she looked at me. "I'm so sorry," she said. She eyed the dirt and blood all over my face. "Oh my gosh, are you okay?"

I chuckled, grazing my hand across my cheek. The blood started to spread, like an artist would do with paint. I could picture the red liquid coloring the paleness of my skin. I felt the gash across the side of my face when I touched it. The edges were hard, and it hurt like hell when I touched the open wound.

"Yeah, I just tripped. I'll be okay, though," I lied. She nodded slightly, walking away with fear written in her eyes.

"No, I don't think so," I replied. "It's alright, though." I walked away before she had the chance to say anything else. I could feel her eyes still on me as I made my way down the street. My phone vibrated in my hands, so I held it up. The bright light blinded me for a second until my eyes readjusted.

From: Noelle
   Sure! Glad you got a new phone :)

I walked down the many streets it took to get to Noelle's house. I arrived there and saw her waiting for me. She was wearing blue jeans, a sweater, and a coat. Her hair was down, flowing with the wind. I noticed she wasn't wearing any makeup.

She doesn't need it.

She saw me immediately and grinned. My heart warmed at the sight of her beaming to see me. She grabbed the bag that was next to her and ran up to me. I was shocked when she hugged me. Her arms wrapped around my waist. I stood there for a moment, unsure of what to do. Her chin was sitting on my shoulder as she whispered, "I'm so glad I have you here to go through this with me."

I smiled slightly. My eyes closed as I let the sound of the wind fill my eardrums. The sound of trees ruffling was also there. I placed my arms on her back and patted. She pulled away, still smiling at me.

"Let's find our boy."

Noelle didn't say anything for a while after that. We continued walking; I was making small talk as best as I could. After a few minutes, I got her talking again and chatting about random things.

"Nope." I answered Noelle. We were already near the park where the search party was going to be held. "I don't think it's weird at all."

"You don't think it's weird they call it a search *party*!" she said, emphasizing the word. She skipped ahead to face me. "It's not weird at all?"

I shook my head and walked past her. I heard her feet click against the concrete. She appeared next to me before muttering, "I think it's weird."

We walked silently for a few minutes. I kept peeking at her, the lights from the stores highlighting unique features of her face. If there was blue, her nose stood out to me. Red, it was her eyes. Yellow, it was her thick lips. Green, her freckles. When there was white light, she stood out.

"So, Luke called me this morning," she began. I hummed in response, letting her continue. "He told me you guys got into a fight. Wanna talk about it?"

"Nope," I replied, harsher than I meant to. It didn't daunt her, though. She strutted alongside me, clicking her tongue.

"Okay. But it might be better if you do."

I stopped walking and looked at her. She paused too and

stared at me in confusion. I grabbed her by the shoulders and forced her to stand still.

"I would, but right now, this is about Nick." She nodded, and we kept going. The group was already there when we turned the corner. It was a good amount of people too.

All I need to do is see if Nick is still there.

This will decide my fate.

I almost gagged; my stomach started doing flips. My throat burned with vomit as we approached the group. Butterflies swarmed in my stomach as I realized that this was it.

"Alright! Time to get started, people! This area of woods is small, so we need you to pair up. One of you will get a flashlight, and we will point you to the direction you need to go to."

I looked around the woods, trying to figure out where I was when I was with Nick. I noticed an awfully familiar bench in front of the trees.

That's it.

"Can we be partners, Kyle?" Noelle's sweet voice asked me. I turned to look at her. Her eyes were big, staring up into mine. The moon reflected the blueness in them. Before I could answer, footsteps were coming to us.

"Kyle, can we be partners?" Luke asked. I whipped my head to face him, and I rolled my eyes. I was about to tell him I already had a partner when Noelle spoke up.

"He's all yours! I'm going to go with Macy over there," she told me before running off to her friend that was waving her down. I groaned and stared at Luke.

It was silent between us for a few moments before the officer yelled at us to grab a flashlight.

"Why is the search party starting at night, anyways?" I muttered to myself while walking toward the officer. I guess not quietly enough because Luke answered me.

"Oh! It's because we are tracking someone, and we can use flashlights because flashlights are closer to the ground than the sun, and it makes it much easier to see footprints and tire tracks." I stopped in my tracks and stared at him. "I was wondering the same thing earlier, so I googled it."

"Go get the flashlight," I ordered.

The night was cold, and it was dark. The only light that

helped us was the moon and flashlight. There were no other light sources in the forest; it was a lot easier to see during the day. I stepped into the spot where Nick started fighting with me. Luke was standing by a tree.

"Why the hell would you even be with her?" Nick fumed. I was standing in front of him, my back to the woods. Nick never got mad at me before. He was the sensitive one, the one that would walk away to get you to stop yelling at him. He was never angry at anyone.
"Because she asked me to, Nick!" I informed him. "She was upset about your fight and wanted to talk to me about it!" Nick groaned loudly and started clenching his fists. His eyes scorched with rage. I watched as he made his way over to the bench and stomped his foot right through it. The wood snapped in half; his leg now stuck in the hole he created.
"What the hell, Nick!?"

I stared at the hole in the bench. Luke pointed a flashlight at it; he walked over there and started looking behind the bench. I couldn't move; I didn't think I could do this. If I entered those woods and saw Nick, I wouldn't leave him.

Bile bit the back of my throat. I took a breath in to relax my stomach, but it didn't work. It was as if the butterflies in my stomach were now congregated in my whole body. I could feel them under every inch of my skin, trying to claw their way out.

"Let's go." Luke interrupted my thoughts. He held the flashlight in his hand and headed into the woods. I followed suit. The leaves and branches tickled my body as we pushed our way through. We were following a hiking trail, but Nick and I went off course when we were here.

"This way, Luke," I called out to him. He snapped his head, and I waved him over to the patch of grass that I recognized.

"But we are supposed to stay on the path," Luke declared. I rolled my eyes at him and just went in my direction. I heard him following me by the sound of his feet crushing leaves beneath them.

"How do you know we should go this way?"

"Dude! I didn't say anything that was that big of a deal! It's not like I told her to break up with you!" I yelled at Nick. I was walking on

the hiking trail with Nick exploding at me from behind. I stopped walking and turned to face him. He was yelling about how I ruined his relationship.

"I didn't ruin anything!" I reminded him.

He scoffed at me. "You did! You don't even realize it, though!" I stood there, listening to all the reasons why I was at fault for him thinking Noelle was going to break up with him. I turned to my left and saw a patch of grass that led into another trail. I looked at Nick, who was still fuming, and I took off in the direction of the new trail.

"Kyle! Get back here!"

"I just have a feeling," I responded to Luke. He started waving the flashlight all around. Small movements were heard throughout the woods, like faint whispers of other searches and small animals. The leaves crunching, branches moving, rustle of bushes.

"Kyle, I just want to say I'm sorry."

We were close. I took note of a tree that had chips in the bark.

"Dude, just let it be!" I barked at Nick. "It's not a big deal!" I stomped off into the forest, hoping he would stay back. I heard footsteps crunching leaves behind me, so I picked up my pace. "Drop it!"

"No!" Nick argued. "I won't drop it. What did you say to Noelle?" I kept walking, going deeper into the woods. He kept following me. "Answer me, Kyle!"

I whipped around and faced Nick. He was fuming. His face was red, and the vein in his neck was turning purple. His eyes stared back into mine, trying to threaten me. He knew that he would never beat me in a fight; my anger always got the best of me. So he would never try it.

"I just told her that I would never argue with her like you do," I admitted. His face dropped, and he stood there. "That's all! She was upset with you guys fighting, and she came to talk to me." He edged closer to me, listening intensively. "She was crying, and I felt bad, and I was just trying to make her feel better."

Before I knew it, his fist came swinging at me. I quickly ducked to get out of the way. I caught his shoulder and looked into his eyes. They were filled with rage, and I could tell that he was here for blood. I knew I would lose control, and I didn't want to hurt Nick. I pushed

him back and walked away.
"Hey, man, get away from me!"

I took another right, my stomach dropping with each step I got closer to where it happened. Luke followed me, stomping along.
"You aren't even going to say anything?" Luke grumbled.
I kept my speed, trying to get it over with as fast as I could. "Now isn't the time, Luke."
The bitterness of my dinner was sitting in my throat. I turned over to a bush and let it out. I groaned, letting every piece out of my body. Luke gasped and started patting my back, trying to help.
"Maybe we should stop," he offered.
I wiped my mouth clean. "No."
We were so close.

"Hey, man, get away from me!" I screamed at Nick. His eyes followed me, red with anger. I could see the steam coming from his ears, and I knew I was in trouble.
"No! Why would you say that to her?" he barked at me, pushing my chest. I felt his fist and my temper run out of patience. I looked at his hand before looking him in the eyes. His were focused on mine, and I knew we were in a fight.
"She deserved the truth," I said.

I started to feel light-headed. My stomach ached from the vomiting, but I couldn't stop. I wouldn't stop. I pushed myself to take each step, Luke trailing behind me. He was talking to me, but I couldn't understand him. It felt like my ears were plugged. I couldn't even hear myself breathing. I wasn't sure if I was.

"BS!" he fumed. "You told her lies!"
I don't know what happened next. Calling me a liar triggered something within me. I used my hands and placed them on both of his pecs and pushed him as hard as I could. I watched as he lost his balance and fell backward. Before his head hit the ground, there was this loud noise. A gunshot. It blasted through my ears, and I had to cover them, or else I would've gone deaf. I looked around me and saw

no one.
"Damn hunters," I muttered under my breath.

I crumbled to the floor. Luke ran and bent down beside me. I held my head in my hands, and I tried hitting myself. The pain was getting too much for me. I vomited again.

We were so close.

I looked at Nick and watched as the blood came pouring out of his skull.

What the hell?

I ran over to him and watched as his eyes followed me. He knew he was dying. I saw that his head landed on a rock. The top part of the stone couldn't be seen, so it must be lodged in his head. I watched the thick blood come rushing out, and I tried to cover it with my hands, but there was nothing I could do.

I killed him…

His eyes stared into mine before the blood from his head came pouring down his forehead and covered his eyes. I tried to wipe it away, but it was no use. It was all coming down, and it was coming fast. I watched as his lifeless body lay there; no Nick left any more. I knew what I had to do.

I ran.

My eyes turned to the spot where Nick's body was when I ran. When I ran like a coward. Luke's eyes were concentrated on me and probably the spit that was coming out of my mouth. I kept my head straight and stared at the spot.

There it is.

The blood surrounded the area. It was everywhere. It was as if the leaves flew and wiped the blood across trees and bushes. A big gush of it surrounded a rock, dripping down from the peak of it. You could see a bloody handprint placed along the side of the rock. Luke's attention shifted to where I was looking.

"Oh my god," he whispered. He stood up and started screaming. He took the flashlight and was waving it back and forth. "Help! We found—"

I tuned him out; I was focused on the spot. The leaves were still covered in blood. The rock was splattered with it. I could hear Nick's voice ringing in my ears, calling me a liar. Footsteps raced by me as I sat there stunned, staring ahead of me. Everything was the same; everything was still there.

Except for Nick's body.

9

Day Thirteen

Waking up the next morning was nerve-racking. My head was buried with all these thoughts about the night before. I couldn't figure out if they were real or not. My mind had been so messed up; there was no telling if it happened to me.

Was Nick's body not there?

Is he really alive?

Am I not a monster?

I jumped out of bed and tried to remember what happened. I looked around for the new phone Dad got me. If I had the phone, then Nick could be alive. It's a weird concept, but it's true. If I had the phone, then I did go to the search party, and we didn't find Nick's body where it should've been. I threw my pillows off my bed, looking for the phone. It wasn't there.

I could feel my heart sink. The thoughts and voices came rushing back to me, overtaking my entire mind. The search party flashed in my head. It felt real; it had to be real. Luke calling out to the people in front of us. Seeing his blood everywhere.

Please be real.

There was knocking on my door. I looked to the door, waiting for someone to pop their head inside my room. The pounding repeated when I didn't say anything. I walked over to the door to reveal Dad. He was leaning against the wall when I opened it.

"Hey, kid, I'm about to head out for work. I wanted to check on you before I left," he drawled. He tried to give me a warm smile, but it just turned into a smirk. I don't think he knows how to show emotion.

"I'm okay," I answered, truthfully for once. Before he left, I asked him about the phone. "Hey, have you seen the phone you got me yesterday?"

Come on, Dad, please say you remember.

"Kyle," he scolded, "you lost it already?"

Yes!

I chuckled, hiding my relief. "No, I just forgot where I put it. I'll find it."

This means that Nick is alive.

I need to tell Marie.

I quickly got dressed and raced for the door. I bumped into Mom on her way out. Her hair was all messy, and she was still buttoning up her blazer. She was whipping her head around, collecting items as she turned. She finally noticed me when she grabbed her bag and hit me in the head with it. I winced, grabbing the side of my temple.

"Oh! Kyle! I'm so sorry, sweetie. I didn't notice you there!" She turned me around and started checking my head. I pushed her away.

"Mom, I'm fine. What's wrong? Why are you in such a rush?"

She groaned and started running her fingers through her hair, getting them stuck in knots. She forcefully kept combing through with her hand. "I was going to sleep in, but a big trauma case came in. It's a little girl. I think she's twelve. Her parents requested me."

I nodded and watched her run around for a little bit. She went and grabbed a coffee, banana, her bag. After a few minutes of getting things, she stood by the door. Her mouth moved, counting off the stuff she had. After a few seconds, she smiled, opening the door. I followed her to her car so I could ask if I could see Marie.

She was shoving her mug into the cup holder when she answered me. "Yes, of course."

I thanked her then waved goodbye. I waited on the grass to watch her drive away. The wet grass stuck to my bare feet. The frigid air froze my toes. She pulled up right next to me and rolled down the window.

"Don't forget to take your pills!" she reminded me as she left. I gave her a thumbs-up and a very fake smile before heading into the house. I made my way to the kitchen counter and grabbed my pills.

Wait, I don't need these any more.

Nick's alive.

I'm okay.

I left the pills where they were and grabbed my shoes. The sun was up and glowing inside the house. It was bright for a February day. It was the first time in a long time I was okay, and I believed myself. That I didn't have a wave of guilt holding me down all the time. It was like I was attached to a chain before. The remorse I had been feeling was that chain, reminding me that I was a monster. But it was gone. I wasn't constantly berating myself for what I thought I did.

I'm okay.

I left the house and started making my way to the hospital. It then dawned on me I could've asked Mom for a ride, but she was leaving in a rush, anyways. It wasn't a far walk either, so I didn't mind. The sidewalks were narrow down the main roads.

"Kyle!" I heard from behind me. I turned around to be faced with Noelle. Her hair was in a messy bun, and she had sweatpants on. She was holding a brown paper bag filled with a bunch of different food. Her eyes were red and puffy.

Was she just crying?

"Hey, Noelle." I breathed, stunned at how great she looked. "Are you okay?"

She nodded, sniffling a bit. "The news came on in the market talking about what you found yesterday in the woods." She paused for a moment, catching up to stand next to me. "Do you think it's Nick's blood?"

I swallowed. My mind went blank for a moment; I just stared into her green, hopeful eyes. The wind whistled around us. The sound of a car honking brought me out of my trance.

"I don't know," I lied. "But if it is his, it means he got away."

She nodded. "He got away from whatever monster would do that to him."

Monster.

I turned around and kept walking. Unsure if she followed me, not caring if she did at that moment. I realized that if Noelle ever found out what I did, even if Nick was still alive, I would be a monster to her.

Nick is alive, and if he remembers everything, Noelle will hate me.

"Hey, Kyle." Noelle spoke hesitantly. I shook myself away

from my thoughts and stopped walking. "Do you wanna hang out?"

"Yeah, except do you think we can hang out later?" I asked her. "I'm going to go visit my friend at the hospital."

She gasped. "Luke's in the hospital?"

Ouch.

Luke isn't my only friend.

"No," I uttered. "Her name is Marie. I met her in the ward."

Her face dropped. I watched her eyes as she started to shift them around. She bounced on the balls of her feet, and her face grew red.

"Oh." She spoke blankly. "Well, I can't hang out later. Family thing. Speaking of which, they are waiting for me, so I have to go." I watched as she scurried off without another word and took a right down the street. I stood there, trying to figure out what just happened.

Why was she so cold to me just then?

I went to grab my phone so I could text her, asking about it. When my hand reached my pocket, I realized I left it at home.

Crap.

~

I made it to the hospital, and before I went to see Marie, I stopped by Mom's office to tell her about my phone. I figured she would try to call me at some point, so I wanted her to know. A nice lady in scrubs directed me to it. She told me to wait a few minutes to see if she was out of surgery.

I sat in her office and looked around. It looked just like the one at home, except this one was a lot bigger. It also had a leather couch by the window. I waited a few minutes before an alarm went off. It wasn't the security one like before; this one flashed a blue light in her office and a loud stinging ring. I looked around to see if I could shut it off. My head started to ache, slowly. Each time the light flashed, the more the pain grew.

"Code blue!" I heard from down the hall. I've heard a lot of codes before from Mom, but I'd never heard that one. The lady that helped me before went sprinting down the hall. Mom's office had a lot of windows, showing both the outside and the hospital. I watched as people ran by the windows. You could see the sweat glistening on them.

Soon, I heard footsteps making their way toward me. Mom walked in, wearing a long white coat and holding a folder. She was too invested in the papers to notice me. She walked to her desk and pushed something, which turned the alarms off. I coughed to make her aware that I was sitting on her couch.

She looked at me, not startled by my appearance. I thought she would have jumped or at least gasped. She just smiled at me. "Hi, honey."

"Hey, Mom," I replied. "What's a code blue?"

She threw the folder to the desk. "Cardiac arrest, also known as coding. Means someone's heart stopped beating."

Oh.

I guess she noticed me staring at the ground because she said, "I don't talk about it much for a reason. It's sad, and we try our best to help them, but sometimes it's no use."

I nodded. I didn't want to say what I felt. I knew she would've gotten mad at me, but I don't like hospitals. Some doctors are great, like Mom, and others suck. Like the one Max had when he died.

"Well, I just wanted to tell you that I'm going to be home late. I want to stay with Marie until they kick me out. But I forgot to bring my phone so…" I explained.

"Alright, don't be too late, though. Use the phone in my office here to let me know when you leave." She walked out of the room and was met by a girl who was waving her hands around frantically and yelling. I couldn't hear what she said, but Mom's face dropped, and she huffed. Her arms fell to her side while the girl looked like she was on the verge of tears. Mom grabbed her shoulder, and they took off walking.

She's in trouble.

I left the office and made my way to the psych ward. I signed in and went into the visitors' lounge. It was nice to be in the lounge and not be the one getting the visit.

"Touch me one more time, and I'll beat the crap out of you, Tyler!" a voice threatened someone.

Marie!

I stood up and waited to see her big curly dark hair walk through the door.

"Who is here anyway?" I heard her complain.

She was so loud, I heard her from down the hall. I heard her shriek and footsteps slapped against the ground until I heard them right in front of the door. I was the only one in the room, so I opened my arms out, waiting for her. I bet I looked like an idiot.

"Open it right now, or I'll sue you!"

The door swung open, and Marie stood there with a huge stupid smile on her face. She screamed when she saw me and came sprinting. I almost thought she was going to push me over; that's how hard she ran into me. Her hair bounced along with her before she lunged at me.

"Relax!" I told her. Her arms wrapped around me while she yelled at me.

"I'm not a dog; you don't get to command me."

God, I missed her.

We laughed and sat down on the chairs that were in the room. The nurse that let her in stood in the far corner on his phone. My eyes rolled to the back of my head.

"Are you here to get me the hell out of here?" she hinted. Which made the nurse snap his head up. "Just kidding!" she declared. She elbowed me in the stomach and winked when the nurse looked away.

"I'm not, but I have some interesting news," I informed her. I watched her squirm in her seat for a bit before looking at me to continue. "Well, let's say that when I went to see if he was there, he wasn't."

I tried to be as vague as possible. I didn't want a nurse or anyone else for that matter to catch on. After I said that, though, I think it was more suspicious. Marie looked at me and raised her eyebrows.

"Okay, so that's good," she pointed out. I hummed in response. We sat there for a while like that, looking toward the door as if someone was going to break in and arrest me.

"Who's Tyler?" I teased. She groaned loudly, which made me laugh. She grabbed her hair and covered her eyes with it, grunting dramatically.

"I hate him! He is so annoying!" She turned and faced me. Her eyes trailed to mine. "He keeps hitting on me, and I'm like, gross!"

"I don't know, Marie." I pondered. "Sounds like you like

him."

She stared at me for a while, making me think I was right. I couldn't read her facial expression, though; she wasn't embarrassed. But she also wasn't denying it. After a few moments, she corrected me.

"Nope." She was quiet for a few more minutes. "You do know I'm gay, right?"

"I can't believe you didn't know!" Marie cackled while we walked down the hallways of the ward. The nurse said that we could go anywhere we wanted as long as we stayed within the area. We were walking to her room so I could meet her new roommate, Tyler.

I laughed. "Well, how was I supposed to know? I don't have a gaydar!"

"Hm, maybe because all of my roommates are guys?" she sarcastically replied.

I thought about how that would've worked because, at first, they must've not noticed that she was into girls. Which means they must've found out the hard way. Plus, all the paperwork to get her a male roommate.

Is that legal?

"Also, I apologize if Tyler is a complete jerk, which he will be. And if he's not there," she noted, whispering in my ear, "we can talk about Nick."

Hearing his name and not being hit with a wave of guilt was a pleasant change. We made our way to her room, which had changed three times since I left. She was telling me about it as we passed by her old rooms. Most of the reasons were because she was yelling out the windows begging people to come and save her.

We stood by the door when she told me to wait. I watched her open the door and look around as if we were spies on a mission. She turned back around and waved me to follow her in.

"He's not here right now, but he probably will be soon," she informed me, jumping on her bed. Their beds were separated, one was in one corner, and the other was on the other side of the room. Marie's bed was the one in the corner. She had a plaid throw blanket and a pillow that had a middle finger on it. Tyler's bed was still the original all white.

"When did Tyler get here?" I asked, sitting at the foot of her bed. I lay down and closed my eyes because the light was shining right into them, and it brought pain to my head. I heard her shuffling around before responding.

"Um, two nights ago. His dad was murdered, and Tyler murdered the murderer. Huh, that's hard to say. Try it."

I sat up and looked at her. "Really?"

"Yeah, the ERs are hard to say with—"

"I meant with his dad being murdered, Marie." I cut her off. I sat facing her. Her legs were crossed, and she was playing with her pillow.

"Oh yeah, but I don't think he actually did it. He said he didn't, but he was found guilty. They said 'cause his dad was murdered, it triggered something, and then they just put him here instead. He also has a history with like PTSD and other stuff," she explained. I nodded, standing up and running my fingers through my hair.

"How are you able to be in a room with him?" I asked. Being found guilty of murder shouldn't allow you to have roommates.

She looked at me. "You really think this hospital cares? And we are also watched heavily at night." She pointed to a chair in the corner. "That's where a nurse sits and watches us while we sleep. Or whenever we are in the same room."

I nodded, standing up and walking around her room. I went over to the windows and noticed that they were locked with a metal pole. I tried to push it up, but it wouldn't budge.

An image crept into my mind. If the window was unlocked, I could open it. Feel the wind brushing against my face. The window was big enough for me to fit through. I could lean on the edge, looking down at the drop. The people passing by wouldn't have even known until after I jumped. My body splattering on the ground, bones breaking, and blood gushing from me.

"So," she said, dragging out the word. I looked back at her, giving my brain a rest from that thought. "About Nick." I looked at her, and she was moving her hair out of her face. Her eyes met mine, and they had a dark vibe to them.

"Nick's alive," I told her. "I know he is; he has to be."

She placed her pillow to the side and stood up, a few feet away from me. "I hope so, Kyle, I really do. And if he is alive, what are you going to do?" I turned my head to the side, wondering what she meant.

"What do you mean?" I asked her. Her mouth opened slightly. She walked over to me and grabbed my hands, moving me over to the bed. She pushed me back so I was sitting down.

"I mean, what if he remembers that you pushed him? He is going to know you hurt him and then left him."

All the guilt and fear came rushing back to me like a tsunami. I was drowning in a wave of terror. I felt my lungs fill up with panic, and I wanted to scream. I'm not sure, but I think my body started shaking. Marie looked at me with wide eyes before sitting down next to me. She was talking, I think. Her hands moved to my shoulder and pulled me in close. I kept trying to breathe, but it wasn't working. My head got heavy, and tears were falling out of my eyes.

Am I dying?

I left the ward shortly after that. I didn't feel safe staying there because I thought they would try to make me stay and put me back in the psych ward. Marie was scared to let me go as well, but I assured her I was going to be fine. I stopped in the office to call home to tell them I was leaving. No one picked up, so I just left a message. While in the hospital, I decided to give someone else a call. After a few rings, I heard someone on the other side.

"Hello?" Luke yawned. I looked at the clock and realized it was later than I thought.

Almost midnight.

Why would they let me stay till midnight?

I looked outside the windows leading into the hospital and noticed that everything was the same as it was during the day. Nothing changed; it just got dark. But not in the hospital; they were all still running around and working hard.

"Hey, Luke, it's Kyle." I peeped. I heard some static from the phone. "Hello?"

"Yeah, I'm here," he responded. "Just surprised."

I understood why. He was upset with me for not answering him when he tried to apologize. Normally I just forgave him right away whenever he apologized so he would stop whining about it.

"I'm sorry," I mumbled. There was silence. I shifted my eyes across the room, unsure if the power went out or something.

Then, I could almost hear him grinning. "What was that?"

I groaned. "I'm sorry."

"Yeah, Kyle, I don't know. Maybe there's something wrong with the phone—"

"I'm not saying it again!" I complained. Luke started giggling, which made me laugh. I think he could tell how serious I was because I never apologized.

"Thanks, Kyle." His tone shifted from giggly to serious. I heard him grunt before continuing. "I was upset because this is not the time for us to be fighting. We need to be there for each other. And I know you would never do that to Nick. I was just angry and mad, mostly at myself and—"

"Okay, Luke." I stopped him, not wanting to get into an hour's discussion about his feelings. "I get it. Don't worry about it."

A doctor burst into the office and looked around before his eyes landed on me. He scoffed, standing up straight. I tilted my head at him.

"You're not supposed to be in here," he announced. "What's your name?"

I smirked at him, holding the phone away from my ear. "Kyle Davis, sir."

He narrowed his eyes on me before realizing that I was the chief's son that was sent to the hospital then the psych ward. He quickly apologized before slamming the door and running away.

Coward.

What was he even doing in here?

"Wow, that's a new record. That was the longest you let me talk about my feelings. You must really be sorry." Luke chuckled. I rolled my eyes again before telling him I had to go. He said goodbye before hanging up.

~

The night sky was dark and mysterious. Not a single star. The moon was dull, barely lighting up anything, not helping me find my way home. I realized there wasn't any noise, so I looked around. No cars were on the road, not even miles up ahead. It began to get warmer under my coat. I took it off and held it in my arms; the breeze cooled me down until there was no more wind.

It's always windy here.

My feet trudged down the sidewalk. I looked ahead and saw a shadow figure a couple of stores down. The lights were flashing assorted colors, so it was hard to see. The red light flashed, and I saw a boy, about my age, grinning. My stomach churned at his face, making me feel uneasy. The light flashed blue and uncovered marks on his face. I couldn't tell what it was, but his face had them all over, and they were dripping. My legs started to wobble, and I almost lost my balance. The light flashed green, and the kid now had a creepy smile on his face, showcasing his teeth. I felt very light-headed and closed my eyes to ease the dizziness. When I opened my eyes, the light was white, and the boy stood there with blood dripping from his head and down his face. His smile and eyes stared into my soul, and my head started to throb. My legs gave out, and I fell.

The pain struck me, running down to my toes. My head stung with pain, and I winced. I looked in front of me and saw a pool of blood, and a metallic taste filled my mouth. Darkness started to take over me, and I looked up at the boy one last time.

Nick?

10

Day Fourteen

Why does this keep happening?
Why do I keep fainting?

I refused to open my eyes so I could recall everything that happened, peacefully. I was on the sidewalk, and there was this boy who looked a lot like Nick. And he was bleeding and smiling at me. I couldn't remember what happened after I fell, though. I blinked, my eyes opened, a dim light staring down at me. I could feel the heat hitting my face, and I wasn't sure if it was from the light or the lack of air in the room. I felt like I was choking on my spit. I didn't get a chance to stand up and look around before a door clicked open and I heard someone shuffling around. I shut my eyes again, my body shaking with fear. I had no idea where I was or who I was with. It wasn't until I heard that sweet voice that I knew I was safe.

"Kyle?"

Noelle?

I opened my eyes and sat up to see Noelle staring at me. She had a soft smile on her face, and her eyes were dark. Not mad or anything, just emotionless. Her hair was in braids, and she was just wearing a sweatshirt with very short shorts. I refused to look past her chin, though. She walked closer to me, her braids bouncing with each step she took.

"Noelle? What happened?"

She put down a tray of food that I didn't realize she was holding until then. She sat down on the bed, a few inches away from my feet. The covers were a dark purple with a thick, black outline at the head and foot of the bed, with the pillows matching them. The frame was dark oak, with a small headboard. The rest of the room matched with purple curtains over the windows and a wooden dresser. The room was barely lit, with one lamp on the other side of the room standing on the dresser.

After admiring the very vampire-like room, I turned back to Noelle, who was just staring at me. Her eyes were soft, but something was hiding behind them. She wasn't smiling because she was happy.

She's smiling because she feels like she must.

For me.

"Noelle." I spoke again, lowering my voice. I pushed the food out of the way. The buttered croissant with a fruit salad didn't seem that appetizing to me. I knew something happened to me last night. After I saw Nick. I could still taste metallic in the back of my throat.

"I was walking home last night—"

"Why were you walking home alone last night?" I interrupted, standing up. I pushed the covers out of my way and stood on the carpet floors, which were dark colored, coordinating with the theme. "That's beyond dangerous, Noelle! Especially with the whole Nick thing going on!"

She stared at me, her little eyes beaming up at me. I watched as her face grew a tint of pink before she looked away. "I was with a friend; she and her brother were walking me home. Then I saw you fall, and her brother helped me carry you to my house. There was blood in front of you, but I couldn't figure out where you were bleeding." She stood up and walked to the other side of the bed, almost pacing back and forth. "I was going to bring you to your house, but when I called, no one answered, and I wasn't just going to leave you. I left a voicemail telling them that you are okay and that you were staying at my house."

I started to feel dizzy again, thinking it was just because I got up too fast. "Did they call back?" She shook her head. "Well, thank you." I looked around and noticed my coat sitting on a chair. The chair had a violet-and-pink pattern to it, traced with dark oak.

This is like a witch's room.

"And, um…" I started, coming up with a lie for the blood. "There was an animal that was hit by a car. A bunny. I guess it was fine and jumped away."

I reached for my coat and started to shrug it on. A groan came from Noelle as she sat on the bed, facing the wall with her back to me. I waited for her to say something for a few seconds, and when she didn't, I knew something was up.

"What's wrong?" I asked, sitting on the bed beside her.

"Nothing's wrong, Kyle!" She scoffed at me. "You just don't care about anything!"

She stood up and stomped across the room, sitting in that ugly chair where my coat had been I stood up, my eyes following her. I glared at her from the other side of the room, taken aback by what she said. She crossed her leg and folded her arms.

Dramatic.

"What?" I barked. She jumped at my tone, I'm assuming. Her eyes flickered with bitterness, and her face turned paler. I thought she was about to vomit. I so badly just wanted her to be quiet. I wanted to cover her mouth with my hand until she stopped breathing.

Wait.

The thought entered my mind before I had a chance to even think about it. I'd never wanted to hurt Noelle before. I pushed it away, stomping around the room. I tried to forget about it. Which I did. I was really good at lying, even if it was to myself.

"Nothing, Kyle, I—"

"Noelle!" I yelled. "Just tell me what the hell is wrong!"

I had never used a loud tone with her, and I felt bad that I did. But I had so many things running through my head, making me irritable. I just wanted to leave, and Noelle was making it impossible. She snapped up at me, her nose twitching like a dog.

"I asked if you could hang out with me yesterday, and you blew me off. I practically saved you last night, and you barely thanked me. You were getting ready to just leave! Why are you ignoring me?" With each word, she stepped closer and closer to me. I didn't move from my position. I stood there at the foot of the bed with her only two feet away from me.

"I am not ignoring you, Noelle." I stepped forward cautiously. I knew Noelle was fragile, and I didn't want to set her off.

She stepped forward. "Then why? Why are you about to

leave?"

Her eyes brimmed with tears for a quick second. She brought her sleeve up to her face and wiped them away. I didn't realize that she was so hurt by me going to see Marie.

"I don't know." I breathed. She moved a couple of steps toward me. Her face was right by my chest. I was always taller than her. She was looking up at me, though. Her eyes gazing into mine. I gulped, pushing my gut, telling me to back away, down into the depths of my soul. I had a feeling she did the same. From her eyes shifting to mine, then to my lips, and back up.

I felt the heat of her breath on my face. She twitched her hand, and it grazed mine. Our fingers interlocked, connecting our bodies. I looked back at her perfect skin. Faint scars sat on the edges of her forehead, but I didn't care. This was the only time I had ever been close enough to her to see them. My attention shifted back to look into her eyes. She never seemed to have left my gaze.

"Noelle?" I asked, holding tightly to whatever was between us. She hummed as a response. "What's happening?"

She stepped closer to me. Her eyes had specks of gold in them as her nose nudged mine. Inches apart.

No.

She felt me back away. She knew I disconnected from her as her eyes shifted to a different emotion. Her eyes looked like they were going to fill with tears again, and I knew I had to leave. I turned when her hand caught my wrist. It was weak, but I didn't want to push her away too forcefully.

"No," I whispered. She let go of me, her hands reaching for her face so I wouldn't see the tears streaming down her red cheeks. I grabbed my coat and thanked her again. My feet traveled around the room as quickly as I could. I opened the door, the handle hitting the wall. I stood in the doorway, replaying what happened in my mind. I turned back to see her standing in the same spot. Covering her face with the sleeves of her hoodie.

"Noelle," I said. She looked at me. Her face was red and her eyes watery. I wished I could take it all back. The yelling, the arguing, and even whatever moment just happened.

"It's not good timing."

She nodded, trying to smile. "I know."

~

When I left Noelle's house, it was still pretty early in the morning. The sun was rising, but it was safe enough for me to go home. The sound of birds chirping made me feel like I was in a cartoon. No one was on the roads. There were no cars or any pedestrians. I thought about what happened at Noelle's house. I was wondering why she didn't push any questions. Maybe she was planning to but got distracted with our fight. I was glad Noelle didn't ask why I fainted or who the boy was in front of me.

Did she even see the boy?

Was he real?

Flashes of what he looked like came to mind. He seemed familiar to me, but I couldn't put a name to the face.

Was it Nick?

My memory had decreased since I started taking the medication. I thought that since I stopped taking it, I would be better.

I unlocked the doors to my house, and everything was dull. I didn't hear any music from the basement, and I noticed that Mom's and Dad's work bags were still home. I looked into the kitchen to see Mom, covering her head with her arms and Dad rubbing her back.

What happened?

Dad's head snapped up at me, without another second more, he started glaring. Mom must've felt his movements because she looked at me. Once she realized he was looking at me, she turned her head. She gasped, sliding the chair that she was sitting in back and running toward me. As she got closer, I could see the streaks of tears down her face and the dark circles under her eyes. She ran up to me and wrapped her arms around my back.

"Kyle!" she bellowed, moving back to see my face. "Where were you?" Dad stood up, coming over to me. I couldn't tell whether he was going to kill me or hug me. He did neither and just stood there with his arms crossed.

"I was with Noelle. I thought she called." Mom shook her head and then burrowed her head into my neck. I could hear her faint sobs. She muffled them with her wrist, trying to hide the fact that she was scared she lost me. I hugged her a little harder.

The familiar feeling of guilt entered my stomach. After losing Max and what happened with Nick not that long ago, I should've known better. I kept forgetting that people didn't know the same things as me. People didn't know what I saw.

"You should be ashamed of yourself, Kyle," Dad scolded. "Your mother and I were worried sick. With all the Nick stuff, we thought you would be more careful. We don't know what happened to that kid, and we don't want the same fate for you."

Dad tried to seem threatening, but his voice had the same fear about it as Mom's. I hadn't heard it in his voice in a long time, but it was very present. It almost scared me for how noticeable it was. Dad was never the type to show emotion. He was incredibly good at hiding his feelings.

It's almost as if he wants me to know he was scared.

"I'm sorry," I replied. "I was feeling dizzy, and I thought if I stopped at Noelle's and just stayed there for a bit before heading home, I would feel better. Noelle said she called you and left a voicemail, and I didn't think I would end up falling asleep."

Mom stayed where she was, crying into my shoulder. Dad nodded and patted me on the back. He never cries, except for when someone dies. I could tell I had him shaken up, though, because I saw him sigh before he turned around and headed back into the kitchen. Mom let out a shaky breath, heat rising in the spot she breathed on.

"Kyle, if you ever pull something like that again," Mom warned, stepping back from the hug.

"I won't!" I promised her. She wiped her face and told me to go change and get ready for the day. She gave me one last hug before going to Dad in the kitchen.

Climbing the stairs felt like a workout. Each step made something more present to me. Each thought became louder to me. Practically yelling in my ear. Making my head spin. When I reached the top of the stairs, my stomach seemed to have thrown itself against my body. It felt like a wave of stabbing pains just hit me at once. Bile rose in my throat, bringing the taste of metal with it.

What the hell?

I couldn't figure out what was scarier. The pain that made me feel like I was dying, the taste of vomit and blood sitting in the back of my throat, or the fact that it all seemed so familiar.

My feet pounded against the floor as I raced to my bathroom. The door slammed open when I pushed it, and I was worried my parents might have heard it. I stared into the mirror. My face looked like a ghost's. Dark circles under my eyes were the first thing to notice. Then it would've been my pale skin. The scar across my cheek was faint but still there. I gently brushed over it, the rough edges scratching my fingers. My clothes were dirty. Dried blood was sitting on them in a stripe as if I threw up onto them.

Is this real?

Or the mirror?

I felt something push its way into my mouth. I toppled over the toilet seat and started heaving into the bowl. Sitting on my knees, letting it all out. Once the feeling subsided, I leaned back and cleaned my face. I checked the toilet bowl to see what I puked. It was a thick red liquid. Dark red, though, really dark. Almost purple. I peeked closer inside to see clots of it bunched up throughout the toilet bowl. Then, I realized what it was.

It was blood.

I threw up blood.

11

Day Seventeen

Three days since I threw up blood. Seventeen days since I spilled it. Five days since I found out Nick is still alive.

Could be alive.

He could be alive.

There hadn't been any word on him since the forest. Everyone was still looking. Luke and I haven't because we were told we need to go through a full psychological evaluation before going out again. Since I was in a mental ward, they wouldn't even let me get the evaluation until my therapist gave the okay. Considering I didn't have a therapist, that was never going to happen. Luke promised me he wouldn't do it without me, though. I think that's more for his sake.

Not much had happened at school. No one talked about anything. Some of the teachers had come up to Luke and me to apologize, and it made me want to punch them across the face. Noelle and I have been ignoring each other. She will wave, but that's it. Yesterday was the first time she said anything to me since Tuesday. I was with Luke by my locker. He was talking about another dumb protest.

"Kyle, can we talk?" She cut Luke off, but I don't think she cared all that much. I nodded and told Luke I would let him finish his rant about global warming later. She led me to a hallway with fewer people and looked at me.

"I want to apologize about the other day," she announced. I went to speak, but she waved me off. "Wait, let me finish. It was out of line, and I'm still dating Nick, so it was really wrong of me to do that. It shouldn't have gotten that far. I don't have any rights to you or your friendship, so I apologize."

Her eyes batted up to mine, waiting for a response. A couple of kids that passed us stared and started snickering. I let out a huff.

"Noelle, it's fine. I'm in the wrong too," I admitted, looking around the hallway, getting an uneasy feeling. "But nothing happened. We were just yelling, and things got heated." Her eyes widened at that word. "Not heated!" I stuttered. "But you know what I mean."

A smile grew on her face. "Yes, I do. Friends?" She held her hand out for me to shake.

"Friends." I grabbed it.

Nick's missing but alive. I could feel it. There was no way that he died. He must be confused or lost. He's not gone.

Not yet.

Walking around the house alone was the worst. Shadows followed me wherever I went. It wasn't a shadow you could literally see, but more of a feeling. All my emotions were in this tiny bottle, waiting for the perfect moment to explode. Which didn't happen.

On Friday after school, I got a voicemail from Marie. My thoughts ran around, trying to figure out why she called me. Or more, how she called me.

"Come get me, loser!" she demanded when I listened to it. "I'm getting out of this hell hole!"

I was walking down the street on my way home when I got the message. Mom told me to come straight home to talk about her new work schedule; otherwise, I would've gone to Luke's house. He invited me over three times that week, and I never had the energy to go. I started to feel bad every time I blew him off because he would do those stupid puppy eyes at me, making my guilt pile up.

Idiot.

I called Marie back, and she answered immediately.

"Holy crap!" I responded. "Are you serious?" I switched my phone to my other ear; cars were passing through on my right, so I couldn't listen as well.

"Um, yes! Now, are you going to come and get me or not?" she asked. I heard some shuffling around, and I assumed she was rushing to pack her bags. She wanted to leave that place and never look back.

I groaned. "I can't. My mom wants me to stop at home to

talk about her work schedule. I think she is going to be home more often."

Marie understood after calling me a few names. Then she suggested that we met up at a cafe in two hours. I told her that was girly. She replied by telling me to suck it up and to become more secure with my masculinity.

When I got home, Mom just told me about how she was going to be at the hospital more that week, but it would go back to normal soon. It was the opposite of what I said, but it didn't bother me that much. Dad would still be home or Henry. Even though Henry stayed in his basement, it would make me feel better knowing he was there. After Mom and I talked, I told her about Marie wanting to meet up, and she told me I could. After waiting around the house, boring conversations with Mom about surgery, and trying not to think about anything, it was time to go to the cafe.

The walk wasn't so bad, only ten minutes from my house. Marie was waiting for me when I walked through the cafe doors. The smell of burnt sugar in my nose. I heard a chair scraping as someone stood up. I turned to see Marie jumping up.

"I'm finally out of the psych ward!" she bellowed. Heads turned in her direction, but she kept her smile on. It spread across her face, reaching both of her ears. She clasped her hands together and pushed a chair back with her foot for me to sit in. My eyes rolled to the back of my head as I sat down.

"It's kind of weird seeing you out of the hospital," I admitted, placing my phone down on the table. She sat down and agreed with me.

"Right? It's kind of weird for me too. But it's not that different. They still have me seeing the same doctors, like a lot."

"How long were you in for?" I asked.

She paused for a moment to think. While she was thinking, I paid attention to her face. I didn't realize it before, but she had freckles running along the top of her cheeks and across her nose. Her black curly hair was a mess, kind of all over the place.

If I saw her down the street, I'd probably think she was pretty.

"Five months," she stated, sipping her drink. Her top lip

perched over the mug, and her eyes stared at me.

"Oh."

"Yeah, but…" she started, placing her mug down. The sound of it clanging to the table echoed through the cafe. The cafe was small but decorated very nicely. There were bookcases throughout the place, a lot of oak wood signs, and the tables were covered with different pattern tablecloths. The chairs were wood as well, and there were about two per table. Only two other people were in the cafe, and one was about to leave. The other one was typing fiercely on her laptop. "It felt longer until you came. While you were there with me, it was the only time I felt safe and happy inside that place. There was a reason for me waking up."

Tears threatened to fall from her eyes; I watched them become watery. She smiled and refused to let them go. I knew she was trying hard not to cry.

It was not the same case for me.

It was as if all the emotions I was saving came hurling at me like a fastball. It hit me right in the head and burned through my skull. Tears fled from my eyes and ran down my face. She was taken aback, looking at me. I started sniffing and wiping my face, groaning. She erupted into laughter.

"It's not funny!" I growled. She held her stomach and almost fell out of her chair. People were looking at her again. Or the teenage boy crying beside her.

Oh god.

"No, it's just cute. Didn't think it would affect you that much." She snickered. The door slammed open. I had my back to the door, so I didn't see who it was.

"It doesn't." I rebutted harshly. She just rolled her eyes and smirked. I felt a hand on my shoulder. I hesitantly turned to see Noelle appear next to me, still with her hand on me.

"Hi." Noelle didn't seem to be talking to me. Her eyes were concentrated on Marie. It was like a glare, but it was as effective as a puppy glaring.

Marie looked up from me and to Noelle. "Hello?" Noelle brought a chair over and sat in the middle of us, but still facing just Marie.

"I'm Noelle." She put her hand out. "One of Kyle's closest friends." Marie barely grabbed her hand and then retracted it.

She looked at me, then back to Noelle, then to me again.

"Yeah," I added, failing at trying to break the tension. "Marie, Noelle. Noelle, this is Marie. I met her when I was in the hospital." Noelle didn't even look at me. Her face turned red as she stared at Marie. Marie was just drinking her coffee, batting her eyes between me and Noelle.

"How long have you guys known each other for?" Noelle asked, placing her elbows on the table with a loud bang. Once again, I felt eyes staring at us. We have a crazy girl, an emotional boy, and now a raging girl who's as threatening as a bunny.

"Okay, Noelle," I responded wearily. "What's up? Why are you asking these questions, and why are you so mad?"

Her cheeks cooled down to pink, and she stared at the floor. After a few moments of silence, she looked up at me. "Are you guys dating?"

The cafe boomed with laughter from both me and Marie. Even the store owners glared at us this time. I quickly apologized to them and hit Marie to get her to stop laughing. Noelle's face went pale as she looked at both of us.

"Oh, sweetie," Marie said, wiping a fake tear from her eye. "I'm gay." Noelle's eyes widened as she turned to me, her mouth open. I nodded my head and grinned, watching her squirm in her seat. Redness appeared on her cheeks again, and she suddenly seemed nervous.

"Oh, don't worry," Marie continued, "you're not my type." Noelle laughed and nodded. She relaxed in her chair, letting her back hunch over a bit. Her hand covered her mouth, muffling her giggles. Marie joined her, but all of a sudden stopped and announced, "But she is. Give me one second." I turned around to see a teenage girl walking into the cafe. She wasn't looking at us until Marie scraped her chair against the floor and walked over to her. This girl had blonde hair that was in a ponytail, and she was wearing a baseball cap. Her shirt was a jersey from a basketball team.

Oh, so that's her type.

Noelle smiled, watching them talk, her eyes glistening. I was confused as to how she could come in here all angry at Marie, then suddenly be fine with her and silently cheer her on from the sidelines.

"Were you jealous?" I blurted out. I didn't even realize I said anything out loud until her head turned to me. The tip of her ears turned slightly pink.

No.

You don't get it, Kyle.

You don't understand how this works.

They all came hurling at me. My thoughts. It was as if I was not in control of my mind. I wasn't even thinking of them myself. It was as if someone was whispering these things into my ear. I never felt like this before.

I've never hated myself like this.

"No, of course not," Noelle answered. Her face was still bright with a pink tint. My mind quieted down with her response. I could still hear them, but they weren't overpowering me any more. I looked at Noelle to finish. "I didn't want to lose you, as a friend, I mean."

I nodded, turning to the menu. I glanced across the wooden boards, trying to find something that piqued my interest. "You mean like how I lost you when you started dating Nick?"

We didn't talk much after that. She was silent for a while, then Marie came back over. Her grin said everything about what happened between her and Blondie, but she still decided to tell us. We left the cafe, with Marie rambling on about Andrea.

"She was so cute! Wasn't she?" Marie squealed. It's at these moments I wonder why we became friends. Noelle and I were walking a bit ahead of Marie. I had to turn around and give her a sarcastic smile. She either didn't notice or didn't care because she kept talking. "I know! She invited me to see her basketball game next week!"

I leaned over and whispered in Noelle's ear. "If she keeps talking, my ears are going to bleed." Noelle let out a giggle but covered it with her hand. She glared at me and pushed me away. Her hand put pressure against my chest, and when she took it away, it was still there.

What the—

"Kyle!" Marie yelled behind me. "What did you say?" I stopped in my tracks, causing Noelle to pause as well. Marie huffed at me; her eyes narrowed down on mine. I realized what was happening.

Oh god, not this again.

Please, not now.

Marie stared at me, waiting for an answer. My stomach felt like it was boiling. The heat rose, burning my lungs. I pursed my lips together, grunting quietly at the pain. I looked around and spotted an alley a couple of stores down. I booked it past Noelle to reach the alley before it was too late.

"Kyle!" Marie and Noelle called out. I heard their footsteps chasing me as I turned into the alley. Once I reached the end, they stopped. I could feel their eyes boring into my head. I hurled over and let the blood rush out of my mouth.

"Oh my god!" Noelle screeched, backing away. Marie stepped closer to me and started rubbing my back. When Noelle saw her doing this, she ran over to me as well. "What the hell, Kyle?"

I groaned, feeling another one building up in my throat before releasing it onto the ground. It burned all the way up my throat and through my mouth; I could taste the metallic-ness of it on my tongue. Dizziness took over, and I had to lean on the wall. Noelle helped me sit down against a dumpster. The smell reeked, making me gag again.

"What do we do?" Noelle shrieked, shaking as she held me. Her hands were on my biceps. My eyelids started to close, and my mind began to shut down.

"No!" I heard Marie demand. She held my head up, and I opened my eyes to see her glaring at me. "Don't faint!" I shook my head and tried to push her away with all the energy I had. However, it wasn't much. I could hear Noelle freaking out beside me, but I had no idea what she was saying. Ringing started to appear in my ears. I knew it was too late to try and stay awake. Blood dripped from my mouth and onto my clothes.

Blood, dripping.

I started remembering something that I didn't realize happened. There was blood, but I wasn't in the forest with Nick. I was in my bathroom. Alone, but there was blood. I think three nights after Nick and I fought.

The clattering of the knife falling to the floor boomed in my ears.

Blood dripping from my chest and traveling down my stomach. I looked at the mirror and realized what I did. The cuts were all over my pecs, short but deep. Blood was dripping onto the floor.

Dripping.

I felt the pain, the burning from the cuts being exposed to air. I could feel, that's what I was looking for that night. To feel again.

Murmurs were being exchanged between Marie and Noelle. They were standing in front of me now. The blood on the ground taunted me, bragging that it knew what I did to myself. I reached for the bottom hem of my shirt, which caught the girls' attention. Marie came rushing over to pull it back down.

"Easy there, cowboy." She grabbed it out of my clasp. "What are you doing?"

"I need to see."

Footsteps came toward me slowly. "Need to see what, Kyle?"

"If I hurt myself." Silence.

Noelle bent down next to me, placing her hand on my shoulder. "You would know that."

"No, he wouldn't," Marie stated plainly. "That's why he was in the psych ward. Subconscious self-harming."

I didn't have the energy to fight back and say that it wasn't a real thing. My eyes closed, and the last thing I heard before it went dark was from Noelle.

"Check. I want to see if he really did hurt himself."

"You don't know that! He threw up blood!" a voice seethed. I heard a scoff from another voice.

"Going to the hospital will make it worse, Noelle," Marie argued back.

I opened my eyes to find myself on a beige couch in Noelle's living room. I'd been in her living room before, but things had changed since then. Her rug now matched the light blue walls, and her coffee table was glass instead of dark oak.

"Stop yelling." I groaned, my head piercing with pain. I sat up, placing my back against the couch. Noelle sat next to me, her hand on mine. I didn't even realize the flutters in my stomach until she spoke.

"Are you okay? I wanted to take you to the hospital, but

Marie wouldn't let me." Marie stood in front of the table with her arms crossed. Her eyebrows were furrowed together, and her hair was up in a bun. I could tell it must've been a lot of trouble to get me here.

"It would've been worse; do you know how much longer they would've kept him there?" she asked, moving beside me. "He wouldn't get out for at least another month."

I nodded in agreement with Marie. "She's right. Bringing me here was a better plan. Thank you, guys. I hope I wasn't too much trouble." Noelle handed me a glass of water that was sitting on a coaster.

Of course, she is the type to actually use a coaster.

I accepted it, thankfully. My throat felt like sandpaper. It was like something scratching against the walls of my esophagus. The water trickled down and helped a bit.

"Nah, it wasn't so bad," Marie assured me. "You kept going in and out of consciousness and helped us. You don't remember that?"

I shook my head. Marie sat next to me, investigating my face. She was looking at me, but not in my eyes. She was almost studying my facial features. Then her eyes landed on my cup, which shifted my attention to my hand. Water dripped down the cup and soaked my finger.

Drip.

Dripping.

Bile started to stir in my throat. I felt it building up, waiting to pounce out. I quickly drank the water out of desperation to keep it down. Marie stared at me the whole time.

"What's going on, Kyle?" she demanded. I placed the cup down before turning to Marie. The taste of metal subsided.

"Nothing," I lied. "This has happened before."

That was the truth. What part they believed, I'm not sure. Marie huffed, still staring at me. Noelle was looking at her feet, shaking.

I hate that I caused this.

"Why?" Noelle squeaked, keeping her eyes on the ground. "Why is this happening to you?"

"Side effect of one of my medications." I lied without hesitating. I was starting to get good at that. "It's not dangerous until it happens four days in a row."

Another lie.

"I don't believe you," Noelle admitted.

She was now looking me in the eye. Her eyes dark, almost filled with anger.

"It's true. I just forget which one." Lies.

She stood up, not backing down from her intense stare. "When was the last time it happened?"

"Five days ago." Only three days, really.

Marie looked between the two of us, leaning back and smirking at me very obviously losing whatever this was. She crossed her leg and arms, laughing. Noelle glared at her, quickly shutting her up.

"And the time before that?"

"Didn't happen before that," I answered truthfully. It hadn't happened before, and I wasn't sure why. I was sure it wasn't going to happen again, so I didn't say anything to anyone. Otherwise, I would've been all of Mom's focus, and probably everyone else's too, instead of trying to find Nick. Nick, who was out there alone and scared.

I did that to him.

I could feel Noelle's glare when I announced I had to go. Marie said that she was going to walk me home to make sure I didn't faint again. Before I could protest, she yelled at me.

"Don't even, Kyle. I will slap you all the way to Mars if I hear a single peep about you being a man or whatever and that you don't need a babysitter. I'm coming, and if you try to stop me, I'll make you bleed myself."

Without another word, she stomped out the door. I grabbed my coat that was hanging on a rack in the corner of Noelle's living room. I looked back at Noelle to see her staring, still puffing hot breath out to signify her anger.

What did I do?

12

Day Eighteen

I didn't hear from either one of them since I left. Marie kept quiet the whole way to my house and left without another word. She didn't even say goodbye to me. I woke up the next morning to a text from her, though.

From: Psycho!
Hey! Things got a little heated yesterday and I just wanted to make sure you're ok.
Are you?

I quickly responded, saying I was fine and was going to spend the day at my house. She didn't answer, so I just put my phone down on my nightstand and got out of bed. I figured I needed a shower, so I turned on the water. Once I got in, the sound of the water rushing filled my eardrums. It ran down my face and cooled my body. I turned around to have the water splash me in the face.

The door suddenly closing made me jump. It wasn't loud or anything, just unexpected. I waited for someone to say something to me, like Mom telling me she was leaving. Or Dad scolding me about using too much of the hot water. I was even waiting for Henry to start yelling at me. I quickly peeked out of the curtains to be faced with nothing. No one was standing there. There was just a mirror with my reflection facing me and an empty sink. I faced the water again and continued my shower. Desperately trying to wash the dirt off me. It wasn't visible, but I felt it trying to crawl its way into my skin, peeling off the layers to get into my blood. I rubbed a washcloth against my forearm until it turned bright red and started to burn.

I shut the water off and stepped out of the tub. I was looking at my feet, watching the water fall from my body to the floor.

Splashing and making little pools. I wrapped my lower body in a towel, letting it claim most of the water. When I looked up, my mirror was different. Splotches of blood were smeared all over it. As if someone dragged their bloody hands along the glass. *Murderer* was spelled out in blood, dripping from some of the letters. Pain stung my chest as I clasped over it with my hand.

What the hell is this?

Who would do this?

I tore off my towel and started collecting the blood from the mirror. Dark red overtook the white towel as I wiped it across. The blood started to smear even more. I was erasing the words but not the fear. I couldn't read it any more, but it haunted me as I rubbed my blood-stained towel across the glass. It was a whisper that turned into a scream. As if someone was right next to me, accusing me of murder.

Murderer.

My breath stopped short. It felt like my lungs almost gave out on me. I had to pause to catch my breath which seemed to keep slipping from me. I waited three minutes to feel normal again, but my breath was still gone. I started to feel my body shake as the terror built up inside of me. I slid down my bathroom wall, holding the red towel in my hand. Blood splattered all over my body when I held it close, but I didn't care.

Am I dying?

Is this what it feels like to die?

I closed my eyes, trying to hide from the bloody mirror. I was choking on my fear, feeling it climb up my throat. I swallowed, pushing it back down. I could feel it bubbling up. Horror shook my whole body violently.

What do I do?

I then remembered what Marie taught me. She told me whenever I felt like I wasn't in control of my body and mind, to go through photos to remind my brain of a better time. I told her that it was stupid and to shut up.

It's worth a try.

I kept my eyes closed as I reached up around the counter that the sink was in until I found my new phone. Dad backed up my old one, so all the pictures were the same. I held it in front of me and opened my eyes so I could only see the screen. I clicked onto the photo gallery and started scrolling. I noticed a picture of me and Noelle.

This was before she and Nick got together.

She was my best friend.

I believe the photo was taken the morning after one of our sleepovers. Noelle's hair was out and wasn't brushed. Her pajama pants had cupcakes on, and she had on a white tank top. She was smiling from ear to ear, her white teeth brightening the photo. I sat next to her, my arm around her shoulder. I wasn't looking at the camera. My eyes were set on her.

My eyes were only ever set on her.

And she chose Nick.

I scrolled again and landed on a picture of Nick, Mark, and me. Mark was smiling with his eyes closed because the sun was gleaming down on him. It made him look washed out. Nick and I were grinning at each other. Our hands were behind Mark's back. I remembered that we were holding water balloons, about to throw them on his head. The next picture was evidence of that with Mark's hair soaked, and he was laughing. Nick ran out of the picture so you could only see his foot in the frame, but I stood there. Staring at the water dripping off his head. This was before Nick and I even thought of kicking Mark out of our friend group.

"I feel bad, Nick," I admitted. Nick was leaning against the school wall on his phone. He was texting Mark to come and meet us. A couple of days before, Nick told me what Mark had done and that he was fed up. He didn't want to be friends with Mark any more. I agreed.

"This is the best thing for the both of us," he explained. "Mark has done nothing but bring us trouble. And because his daddy is this big-shot lawyer, he gets away with it while we get crap!"

He put his phone back into his pocket and huffed. It was true, though. Mark was always getting us in trouble, and he barely suffered consequences. His dad was always there at the school and used the fact that he helped fund the school against them. But that's only when his dad was around. His parents were never there. Always on "vacation." Dad complained about it a lot because he had to take his cases when he wasn't there.

"My dad works with his," I muttered. Not quietly enough, though, because Nick snapped his head and looked at me.

"Yeah, but you get in trouble. Your dad doesn't bail you out like his dad does."

I nodded, knowing he was right. Dad always made sure I got consequences. He would make me leave the principal's office while they discussed what was best for me. I am almost positive Dad vowed to get me more detentions.

"Hey, guys!" Mark bellowed a couple of feet away from us. We both turned to look at him, and he looked awful. The dark circles under his eyes were obvious, even from where we were standing. The smell emanating off his body reached our nostrils in no time, causing us both to cringe. I noticed the redness in his eyes.

"Mark," I scolded. "Are you on drugs?"

"Hey!" He chuckled. "Get off my back, Dad." He grunted on the word Dad which caused him to cough. Nick's jaw was clenching. His arms were crossed, and I remember thinking if anyone looks like a dad, it was Nick.

"We need to talk," Nick warned. He took a couple of steps toward Mark.

Mark slurred, "What? Are you guys breaking up with me?" He started to laugh afterward, tripping over himself and landing on his face. "Ouch."

I rolled my eyes and walked over to him. I grabbed him by the back of his collar and stood him up. He lost a lot of weight; I felt it in my arms.

"Look at yourself, Mark," I criticized. "You're skinny. You must've lost a lot of weight. Your eyes are red, and I bet you haven't slept in days."

He cocked his head to the side. He suddenly winced in pain and grabbed the back of his neck. I let go of him and watched as he slumped to the ground again. He was on his knees, grunting. I heard footsteps behind me, and Nick appeared by my side. That was when I knew Mark was at his lowest. I bet Mark realized it too.

"Clean up your act, Mark," Nick demanded. "Do it for yourself because Kyle and I are done."

Mark looked up at us, his eyes screaming anger. "What?"

"You have caused nothing but trouble for us, Mark." I repeated Nick's earlier words. Nick didn't even flinch. He kept his stare on

Mark, who was now standing up. His limbs were shaking, but he managed to get on his feet.

"Trouble like what?"

"Like Noelle!" Nick exploded. He stomped to Mark and was inches away from his face. "Like what you did to Noelle."

"I thought she wanted me," he explained, pushing Nick away. "We only kissed, and I thought it was because she wanted me."

Rage was boiling inside of me. The sound of her name coming out of his mouth pushed it over. I felt the heat attack me like being submerged under lava. I didn't even realize I moved until I saw Mark bleeding from his mouth. He held his hand up to his lip and made the blood spread even more. Nick wasn't concerned. He never was when I reacted poorly when someone hurt Noelle. You should've seen Mark when I caught him with her. He couldn't go to school for a week. I didn't even remember it until Noelle hugged me the next day.

"She would never want you," I spat at him. Nick and I left after that. Mark was standing there, blood pouring out of his mouth and dripping onto the ground. His fists were clenched, and his eyes were burning into our backs. I then suddenly realized who I saw Mark as.

He was a monster.

I didn't go through any photos after that. I sat on my bathroom floor for what seemed like hours, naked. I didn't have enough strength to even try and wrap myself in a new towel. My brain was being tortured with a million questions.

Where did the blood come from?

How am I going to hide the towel?

Who would do this?

Why is this happening?

I felt like an old guy that you see at the beginning of an awful movie. Where he is all depressed, then turns his life around by falling in love or something stupid like that. My bare butt on the cold tiles made me realize how pathetic I must've looked.

Once I was able to distract my mind, I started to clean up. I grabbed the blood-stained towel and cleaned up the rest of the mirror. Wiping it away, smearing it even more. I had to get the towel wet again to get all the blood off the glass. The water stained red as it fell through the drain. Once the mirror was clean again, I washed the inside of my sink that had tints of pink all around it. I even poured bleach down to get rid of the stench. Mostly so I didn't have to smell it again. I put on clean clothes before heading downstairs to put the laundry in. I washed the red towel with a bunch of my red clothing so it wouldn't look different. Once I clicked Start on the washing machine, my phone started vibrating in the pocket of my jeans. Noelle's name appeared, and I immediately answered it.

"Hello?" I stuttered out. I wanted to slap myself for sounding like that.

"Kyle?" Noelle asked. I grunted in response. I knew we were in a small fight, but hearing her voice say my name made me want to run over to her and just hug her. To let the smell of vanilla sugar fill my nostrils. I knew it was her favorite perfume; I bought it for her a lot.

Noelle was the only person I could never really get mad at. My anger is the worst part of me, and sometimes I can't control it. But with Noelle, it wasn't like that. I had never actually gotten so mad with her that I even threatened to hit her.

"What?" I barked. She jumped at my tone. Her eyes flickered with bitterness, and her face turned paler. I thought she was about to vomit. I just so badly wanted her to be quiet. I wanted to cover her mouth with my hand until she stopped breathing.
Wait.

Noelle's voice pulled me away from the scary memory. I had completely forgotten about it until that moment. I did want to hurt Noelle.

"Kyle, I am so sorry about what happened at my house. I understand that I am not in charge, and you are allowed to do what you want to do." She started sniffing through the phone. I could tell she was upset, but I didn't say anything about it.

"I'm sorry too. You were just looking out for me."

Noelle was always looking out for me. She was my savior. Got me out of a lot of bad situations. For a while, I didn't want to be friends with her in case she got hurt, but she stuck around and refused to let me be stupid. I used to not care that much about my life until she came along.

"Anyways," she continued, "Wednesday is a teacher prep day, so we don't have school. Do you want to come over and hang out like we used to?"

"You mean before Nick?" my voice mumbled. I guess she didn't hear me clearly because she asked me what I said.

"Sure, but I have to hang up right now. I'll see you Wednesday." I placed the phone back down, not letting her respond. I could feel my veins popping out of my wrists.

Is she just trying to replace Nick with me?

Why is she doing this now?

What a little…

I paced around the room. I thought about what would happen Wednesday. I thought about what if I had killed her the day before. Would her family have known it was me? Would anyone?

Can I get away with murder?

Pushing away my thoughts, I went for a run. The heat was building up in my body and making me sweat. I needed to push the anger and hatred out on something else before I did something I would regret.

Should I kill her?

I didn't even bother to change except for my shoes. I grabbed my keys and phone and left the house. I let my feet take control, running around. I couldn't fight it; they wanted to go where they wanted to. I let my mind wander, trying to relieve myself from any more haunting thoughts.

Where am I?

I looked around, and the neighborhood was nicer than where I lived. Tall houses with balconies. Don't get me wrong, we could've afforded to live there. But Dad was a minimalist. We had more than enough. I walked past a familiar house, and I realized where I was.

Kill her.

Noelle's house beckoned me. It called me to go inside. I closed my eyes and imagined myself breaking in. No one was home except her, so no one would have known. I would use my keys. I gripped them in my hand, holding one in between my pointer and middle finger. A jab at the eye would cause her enough pain for her to know she shouldn't have tried to replace me. Then slicing her throat open, watching the blood pour from her perfect neck would have been more than satisfying to see. To lie next to her lifeless body.

What is happening to me?

I ran. I sprinted farther from the house before I could do anything. I was terrified of my mind. And my strength. I didn't know how far I would go. How far I could go to kill a person. To kill Noelle. I came across an empty road. I paced myself, still fighting the murderous thoughts in my head.

It felt like someone was squeezing my skull and a couple of times I lost my balance. My feet slowed the pace when I noticed a figure standing ahead. He was hunched over, leaning against a store window. I figured he was looking at something, but as I got closer, the blood dripping from his body made itself visible to me.

"Sir!" I called out, running to him. "Are you okay?"

He turned to me, his eyes bloodshot red. Scratches and wounds gushing with blood were all over his face, and I almost didn't recognize him.

"Mark?" I asked. I was only a few inches away from him now. Cuts were ripped into his shirt, and the cloth around them was stained with blood. He pushed himself away from the wall and started leaning toward me. I caught him before he hit the ground, and he grabbed my shoulders, trying to steady himself.

"Kyle, I didn't do this to myself. I…" He struggled, trying to explain what happened. I told him to shush as I pulled out my phone and dialed 911 for help. Mark was falling to the ground as I tried to hold him up with one hand; the feeling of blood dripping onto my arm shook me.

"It was Nick." My head snapped to look at Mark, to see if he was saying that or if it was a figment of my hallucinations. His eyes were peacefully shut, and his breathing started to slow.

"Nine-one-one, what's your emergency?"

13

Day Nineteen

"Kyle!" a voice rang out, distracting me from my thoughts. Noelle came running over to me and engulfed me in a hug. Her arms traced my spine as she placed her head onto my shoulder. I listened as her breathing evened out and steadied.

I was in the waiting room when Marie, Luke, and Noelle walked in. It was hours after I had arrived, but I didn't tell them where I was for a while. Mark was in surgery, and no doctor had talked to me for a long time. I remember watching the sun beam through the windows when the doctor came out and told me that they were doing everything they could.

It was dark when they found me.

"Hey, guys." I sniffed, rubbing my eyes. "How did you find me?"

Luke walked over to the seat beside me and sat down. He handed me a cup of coffee. Marie sat next to him while Noelle remained in my arms. She shifted so now she was sitting in my lap.

"Your mom told us what happened," Luke explained.

Marie nodded. "What she couldn't tell us is why you are torturing yourself by staying here for hours for some old friend of yours who I believe made your life a living hell."

Noelle peeked her head up and stared at me. My eyelids threatened to close and taunted me with the relief of sleep. Her hands ran up to my hair, and she started twisting it in her fingers.

I can't handle this right now.

I pushed her away slightly. Shifting my legs to the other side, forcing her off. She was taken aback, but she didn't say anything. She just sat down next to me and placed her hands in her lap. Luke gave me a look, but I didn't care enough to comment on it. Marie just stared intently at me, waiting for a response. I sighed and grabbed at my head, holding it in my hands. I let my eyes close for a second.

"Where are his parents?" Luke asked. He squirmed in his seat, trying to find a more comfortable position. Luke is six foot one, so small hospital chairs don't fit him. I watched the ground, looking at his feet move around. Soon, Luke placed them on his chair, so his head was now in between his knees. I chuckled at his little kid's stance.

"Out of town. I tried calling them myself, but they didn't answer." I huffed. He just nodded, then looked down. Marie was staring at him, bug-eyed at what she just witnessed him doing.

"You comfortable, Dopey?"

Luke slowly turned his head to face her. His smirk widened on Marie when she looked him in the eyes. His arms fell to the side, and he leaned forward.

"I can't fit into the chairs, and this is the only comfortable position. I'm sorry I'm so tall." Luke paused for a moment. He turned his head back to face forward, then he muttered, "Shortcake."

Marie's smirk dropped, and her eyes turned red. You could see the steam coming out of her head. Veins were popping out of her neck.

"Guys, not now," I begged. They both turned to me and apologized. I always thought that Luke and Marie would get along, but I guess not. Noelle told me that she introduced them in the parking lot because that's where they all met up. She said that they were not too happy with each other. I couldn't understand why, but it was the last thing on my mind.

"Kyle, why don't you go home, and then when the doctors know something they can call?" Noelle offered. I looked at her, and her eyes twinkled with hope. The way she was looking at me, she seemed to have been asking a lot more than me just going home.

What is she asking me?

"I can't." I fought. "I can't leave him."

"He was awful to you, Kyle," Luke argued. "He was always making you do things you didn't want to do and got you in trouble. I feel bad for him, I really do. But you brought him to the hospital, and you've stayed here for hours. You've done enough."

Marie nodded. "I agree with Giant John; you know that if that was you, he wouldn't be here. Hell, he wouldn't have even brought you here. He would've left you on the sidewalk, bleeding to death."

"You're right," I answered. They all looked at each other before getting up, except Noelle. She remained in her seat; she knew me too well to know that it would be the end of it. She folded her hands in her lap and waited for me to continue.

"I owe him."

"He's really gone, Mark." We were sitting on my bed because Mark wanted to check on me. His mom told him about Max, and he said that he needed to see me. My head was under my pillow, trying to mute my sobs. Mark was sitting upright next to me with his hand on my shoulder. We were so young, and he knew exactly how to act.

"I know, Kyle." He started patting my back. "Max was my little brother too, and I miss him. But it wasn't your fault!"

I sat up, pushing my pillow away from me. "Henry said—"

"I don't care what Henry said," Mark yelled. "He's an idiot. It was not your fault."

I looked down at my Spiderman bedsheets and felt upset again. I didn't know what bothered me more, Max dying, my family hating me, or the fact that Nick wasn't there. It wasn't Nick's fault he wasn't there. His mom wouldn't let him. She said that Nick doesn't handle death well, and after his dad's passing, he had to see a therapist. This would only set him back. I would only set him back.

"It is my fault, though, Mark." I sniffed. "I was the one who let him in the water. I didn't know."

"Exactly, you didn't know because no one told you. So, it wasn't your fault," Mark explained. He stood up and started pacing my room.

"How are you so good at this?" I asked, wiping the tears from my face. "How do you know what to say?"

He stopped walking around and looked at me. "I deal with death in my family a lot. So, I know what to say because I say it a lot."

"That's sad."

I don't remember if I said that out loud or if I was just thinking it. But Mark continued talking about it.

"I also know that they are in a better place now. Just like Max. I

bet he has a treehouse and is playing with a lot of toys in Heaven. Maybe reading that book he likes so much. The one he made everyone read to him when they came over. I've read it like a hundred times!"

I smiled for the first time in eight days.

"Who's Max?" Marie asked. It was a simple question, but I couldn't answer it. Hearing his name set off a rollercoaster of emotions. I just hid my head in my hands and tried to calm my breathing. Marie noticed she made me upset and kneeled beside me. "Oh, I'm sorry, Kyle. I didn't mean—"

"Max was his little brother. He died when Kyle was eight. Max was only five." Luke answered for me. He walked behind me and placed a hand on my shoulder. "I never met him, but I heard stories. He was a sweet boy."

It was silent for a while. No one said anything else. Marie remained at my side, Luke sat down in the seats behind us, and Noelle was sitting next to me. After a few minutes, her phone started ringing. She picked it up and answered, trying to whisper. Her eyes grew wide, and she started to grab her stuff. She hung up and explained that her mom needed her home. Something happened that her mom refused to tell her on the phone. She apologized and gave me a quick hug before going home.

"Kyle?" a deep voice rang out. I looked to see a doctor that wasn't in scrubs. I got up and raised my hand. He came over to me, checking over a clipboard.

"Hello, I'm Dr. Davern. I was scrubbing in on your friend's surgery. The good news is that it was successful, and he is in recovery."

Relief hit me like a tow truck. Luke stood behind me, and Marie grabbed my arm.

"However," Dr. Davern started, "we had to perform brain surgery because there was fluid in his brain by his frontal lobe, caused by his accident. His Broca area was damaged, and he has dysarthria." He noticed the confused looks on our faces.

"He lost his ability to speak."

"He can't talk?" Luke asked. The doctor nodded. He told us that one person could go see him, but he was still in recovery, so he was unconscious.

"I need to see him. Do you guys mind waiting?" I asked

Luke and Marie. I figured it would give them a chance to talk things out, not hate each other so much.

"Of course," Luke said.

Marie smiled at me. "Take as much time as you need."

They both turned around and sat down in chairs. The doctor led me down a hallway. The hospital was a lot smaller than the one Mom works at. There were a few staff members and not as much hustling going around. Nurses were showing each other videos online and laughing. It didn't even seem like people were dying. Or if the workers cared.

I should've insisted that they take him to Mom's hospital.

Maybe then he would've been able to talk.

This was just the closest one.

"It's a good thing you found him when you did, you know." Dr. Davern spoke, ending the silence between us. "Another minute and he most likely wouldn't have made it."

I bet they say that to everyone when giving bad news.

To make them feel like heroes.

I just grunted and kept my head forward. Passing by the rooms, I took note of the condition most people were in. I couldn't even see what was wrong with some people. No one had significant injuries, from what I could tell. Just people in beds with flowers and balloons surrounding them.

"We did have to place him in the children's unit because he is underage, and his parents aren't here," he explained while opening the doors. Inside was wallpaper with various kinds of animals in the forest. The lights were a lot brighter, and the nurses were walking around, doing things. One was pushing a wheelchair with a little girl sitting in it who had no hair. She also had a tube coming out of her nose and a huge smile on her face.

"Daddy!" she squeaked. An older man came running to her and hugged her.

"I'm so sorry I was late today, sweetie. I had to work another shift."

We continued walking down the hall, and the further down we got, the less kid-friendly it was. The wallpaper was ripping in some spots with stains on it. The lights were dimmed, and some were even flickering. We took a turn, and I already knew which room was Mark's.

The last room.

I could see him from the other end of the hallway. His head was wrapped in thick white bandages. Machines were surrounding him instead of flowers and balloons. A nurse stood by him, checking the machines and writing things down. She noticed me and left the room. I walked in, and the doctor said he would leave me for a few minutes. Mark was incredibly still; I didn't think he had it in him. The cuts on his face were cleaned up but still visible. I could see how deep most of them were by the edges. His eyes were shut, and his lips were cracking from dryness. I'd only been in this situation once, and it was when I was young. I didn't know what to do.

Mom held Max's hand; should I hold his?

No, that's stupid.

"You can come back in the morning if you'd like," the nurse said, coming back into the room. "Sorry, I need to check his vitals."

"It's okay." I blanked. "He is going to wake up, right?"

She paused. "He was awake earlier. That's when we knew he couldn't talk. We sent doctors to get you, but I believe they went to the children's waiting room. Interns." She rolled her eyes at the end and giggled. I felt the need to laugh with her, so I let out a small chuckle.

"Then I'll come back in the morning. Thank you."

She nodded and continued her job. I left the room without another word. I waved to Dr. Davern that I was leaving because he was with another person. He smiled and nodded before continuing to talk to the other man.

This place is unprofessional.

Mark would love it.

~

Marie and Luke were waiting for me when I came back. Marie was poking at his cheek, and Luke looked like he was about to slap her. He saw me and pushed her away, which made her stumble in her seat. Luke stood up and came over to me. "How is he?"

"He looks awful," I admitted. "And this place is awful. He was awake earlier, and they didn't even tell me. That's how they knew he couldn't talk."

Marie stood behind Luke, bouncing on the balls of her feet. "Wow, what a bunch of—"

"Unprofessional doctors." Luke finished for her. "I don't swear."

"No one asked you to, Frankenstein." She pushed him with her elbow to stand in front of me. "Can we go now?"

I nodded, and we headed for the exit. The chilly night air blew against my face, brushing the hair out of my eyes. Lights from the hospital shined on the ground as we left. Luke started to talk about his plans for the upcoming week. He said how school might be canceled for a snow day, which Marie disagreed with, saying how there's only a sixty-five percent chance of snow.

"Why do you have to fight me on everything?" Luke groaned.

"Because you are wrong about everything," she snapped back. We walked past Marie's neighborhood, which was filled with nice houses. Most three stories tall, with huge balconies. I watched as Luke's face dropped at the sight of them.

"I'll see you later, Marie," I said, giving her a quick hug. "Thank you again for coming."

"Sure thing." She smiled. She turned to Luke and pushed his shoulder. "Later, loser."

She ran off into the dead-end street, climbing the stairs of a huge house that was painted white. Her bright red door opened, then she disappeared inside.

"So, she's rich?" Luke asked when we started walking away.

"Grandparents are," I answered. "What's your problem with her, anyways? Marie is awesome."

Luke kicked a rock on the sidewalk, and we watched it roll into the grass. "When I met her, she had this weird vibe. I don't know; I just didn't think we would be friends. I bet she wouldn't even go to a protest with me."

"I don't go to protests with you," I pointed out. "In fact, I mostly make fun of you for them."

The street was empty, not a car or person in sight. Honks could be heard in the distance, and the wind was howling. The darkness felt calming to me, mostly because I had Luke with me this time.

"Yeah, but that's different," he explained. "You still support the causes. I don't think she would."

I decided to mess with him a little bit. "Causes like what? LGBTQ?" Luke nodded, and I laughed.

"What's so funny?" His ears turned red. I could tell he was getting embarrassed by me laughing at his ignorance. Which just made it even funnier to me. "What's so funny about being homophobic?"

"Luke," I said calmly, "why would she be against herself?"

Luke stopped in his tracks and faced me with his eyebrows furrowed together. His mouth was inching over to one side as he thought about what I said. I turned and continued walking. After a few seconds, I heard him yell, "She's gay!?"

"Yes, Luke," I replied, letting him catch up with me. "She's gay."

"That makes so much sense! It wasn't a weird vibe I got; it was my gaydar going off!"

I looked over at him, shoving my hands into my pocket. My fingers were starting to get cold. "Gaydar?"

"Yeah, you know. Like a vibe." I just nodded. He clicked his tongue before speaking again. "Ah, it makes so much sense! That's why she has these walls built up and fought me on everything. Out of fear that I wouldn't accept her because, in reality, she wanted me to be her friend." I gave him another look so he would elaborate. "I have like ten million psychology books. I study them for fun."

I had to ask. "For fun?"

He nodded. "I met someone that I wanted to diagnose. He always seemed off."

He'd better not be talking about me.

Luke and I made it to my house, and before we said goodbye, Luke gave me some news.

"I didn't want to say it earlier, but they figured out that the blood we found in the forest did belong to Nick. I guess they tested it or something." I nodded and thanked him for telling me, even though I already knew. Luke smiled and started walking home. I felt weird being dropped off at my house, but Luke insisted on walking home with me.

When I walked through the doors, I realized it was time to take my medication. No one else was home even though it was late. I thought at least Henry would be home, but the house was empty. I checked the counter for my pill bottles, and they weren't there.

Who moved them?

I sent Mom a quick text asking her if she put them someplace else. I was just going to wait for a response. After a few minutes, I concluded that she was busy at work. I started checking in places that I thought Mom would put them. I looked in drawers, cabinets, and even in the living room. All I found were utensils, cereal boxes, and quarters on the couch. I thought that she put them in her office.

I opened her door, and the chilly air hit me. I was only in a short-sleeved shirt. Goosebumps appeared on my arms and legs. I looked to the window and realized it was open.

Mom never leaves her windows open.

Maybe she was in a rush.

I quickly closed it before looking for my medication. I started pushing papers out of the way and checking under the desk. I bent down and went on all fours. I was too big, though, and my head hit the bottom of the desk. I felt something sharp jab me in the head.

What the hell?

I sat back down on the floor and reached my hand under the desk. I pulled on it and saw that it was a key. I felt the back of my head for the bump, but instead, I found a cut. When I took my hand away, it had blood.

Ow.

There was a locked drawer where the key fit. I unlocked it and slowly opened it. There was something in there being covered by a piece of cloth. I took the cloth away, and a small pistol was sitting in the drawer.

What?

I slammed the drawer back and locked it quickly. I put the key back where I found it and raced out of the room.

Growing up, my parents had always been against guns. Dad used to say that a man could defend his family without a gun, and Mom never liked guns. She said that they were too violent and that they didn't need them. She went to the shooting range once and left two minutes after being there.

"The noise they made was too loud," she told me, "and they

are dangerous."

Why would she have a gun if she hated them so much?

I sat down on the couch, waiting for her to come home. I couldn't move. I kept thinking about why she would have a gun. Nothing made sense to me. She didn't like guns. Every scenario I came up with didn't match up.

Maybe she found an interest in them?

No, she just talked about it last week.

She could have found it and didn't know what to do with it?

She would've turned it in.

"Kyle," Mom said, walking through the door. I didn't even hear her car pull up. "Honey, I just got your text. I moved them to the bathroom. I'm sorry I forgot to tell you."

I stood up and faced her. Her hair was pulled back into a ponytail, and she was still in scrubs. Her eyes had bags under them that I could see from five feet away. She placed her bag down and walked toward me with her arms held out. I returned the gesture.

Mom hugged me and started talking about her day. "I had to work late, a surgery came in, and I really wanted to do it. You won't believe what—"

"Why do you have a gun?"

She stopped talking. Her arms remained around me, but her mouth was closed. I wanted to apologize for going into her office, but I couldn't form words.

"Did you touch it?" she asked.

"No."

"Good," she replied. She pulled away from the hug and sat on the couch. After a few minutes of her messing with her outfit, she patted down for me to sit. I obeyed, wanting her to tell me. She coughed before answering my question.

"When you were really young, there was an accident here," she explained. "You weren't even three months old, probably. Henry was only two, so he doesn't know about this either." She took her hair out of her ponytail and ran her fingers through her hair. "Your dad had this big murder case. The man was accused of killing a family. Your father was his attorney."

I knew Dad took complicated cases. Ones where there doesn't seem to be any hope, but he always wins. I've never seen him lose a case. He always came home with a happy look on his face.

"Your father proved the man innocent. He opened a new case about the father of the family, Larry Johnson. He was the only one that survived." She sighed, shaking her head. "The poor family was murdered in their sleep. And yet not a single scratch on this guy. When the new case opened about Larry killing his own family, he got so upset and mad that he broke into our house and tried to kill your father in his sleep."

I was silent. I didn't know what to say. I have never thought of Dad in such a vulnerable state. He was always "the man" of the house. The one that would do anything to protect his family, but this one lunatic was able to break in.

"I was actually in the nursery with you when it happened. I heard him yelling from the other room, and I knew something was wrong. I grabbed you and your brother, then I ran downstairs and grabbed the phone. Dialing nine-one-one was the hardest thing to do because my hands were shaking. I ran to the neighbors to drop you guys off, then I came back for your father."

I looked at her and couldn't read her expression. It was as if she told this story hundreds of times.

"What happened next?" I asked.

"When I came back, your father was standing over Larry's body."

Dad killed someone.

"When the police arrived, they questioned us and such. One policewoman told me that I should think about getting protection for the family. She said that this time the guy was small, but with jobs like ours, many people would be getting mad and upset at us," she explained.

"Why would someone get mad at you, Mom?" I questioned. "You save people."

She grinned and placed her hand in my hair. "I can't save everyone. People die, and families can get upset about it. There was an incident with the chief of surgery years ago. A guy's daughter was pronounced dead, and the chief was the one who performed the surgery. It was a spinal osteomyelitis surgery, common but has a remarkably high death rate. Anyways, she ended up getting a secondary infection from the surgery and died from it. Her father came back to the hospital a few weeks later, walked right into the chief's office, and killed him. That's why we have so much security now. So, I am safe there; I just wanted to be safe here."

I understood why she had a gun, but one thing was left unclear.

"Then why did you act like you didn't like guns?"

She moved her head to the side. "Oh, I don't like guns. But I acted so harshly against them because I didn't want you boys to find it. Boys can be stupid and play and get injured. Or if one of you were suicidal…" She trailed off, tears forming in her eyes. "I just didn't want you guys getting hurt. Especially after Max, I thought of getting rid of it entirely. Everyone was just so depressed I didn't know what to do."

I nodded and hugged her. She sniffed and wrapped her arms around my neck, placing a hand on the back of my head.

"Promise me you won't ever look in that drawer again. Don't ever touch the gun," she pleaded with me.

"I promise."

I promise.

14

Day Twenty-Two

I went to see Mark in the morning, just like I told the nurse. Mom dropped me off on her way to work. She kept talking about how she hated the place I brought Mark to. At first, I thought she was angry at me for taking him there. But when I asked her, she denied it.

"Of course not, sweetie. I think you were smart about it. Considering it was the closest place, but I just hate that he can't speak any more. Poor boy."

We arrived at the hospital, and it didn't seem busy at all. At Mom's hospital, there are people all over the place. Even in the morning, doctors running, nurses searching for things, patients groaning. At least in the emergency room. This place seemed as if they had no patients. I walked inside, and everything was a lot different in the morning than at night. Nurses weren't sharing videos, they were drinking coffee and typing on their computers.

"Excuse me," I said to the lady behind the counter.

She looked up at me and said, "Mmm." But her fingers were still typing

"Um…" I struggled. "Where is the children's unit?"

She pointed in the direction of two big doors. "Down that hallway, then take a right and through another set of doors."

Anyone can just walk in here and go where the sick children are? That's not safe.

I followed the lady's directions and found the animal wallpaper. I was walking past the counter when someone stopped me.

"Sir, who are you here to see?"

I turned to face a guy who was holding a clipboard. Either he thought I was lost, or I looked suspicious.

"Mark Evans," I informed him. "He was brought here last

night."

His eyes lit up, and he grinned at me. "Are you the kid that found him?"

What the hell?

Am I some heroic news story here?

"Dude, you are amazing!" he sang. "I'll bring you right to him."

I thanked him in the nicest way I could and followed him down the hallways. I couldn't believe what he said. Did everyone here know what happened to Mark? And what I did? I didn't even do anything.

While we were walking, the guy told me about Mark's recovery. "He has made amazing progress this morning. He woke up, and he can make grunts and noises, he just can't form words. But he is fully able to comprehend what you are saying, and it seems like he has movement in his body. Lucky kid."

Lucky?

Mark's lucky?

He was beaten and can't speak.

We turned the corner, and Mark was sitting up in his bed. His head was still wrapped in a bandage. A nurse was speaking to him. She pointed down the hallway at me, which made Mark turn and look. I waved, hoping he won't be mad.

Please don't hate me for coming here.

Then Mark did something I haven't seen him do in a long time. Unless it caused trouble.

He smiled.

He actually smiled at me.

I walked into the room, and his smile was still very present. The nurse told me that she explained to him what happened, so he was fully aware of his condition. She also said that he healed quickly from the accident and that some policemen were going to coming later to question me.

Question me?

"Do they think I did it?" I asked, my palms suddenly dripping with sweat. You could sense the anxiety radiating off me. She gave me a concerned look.

"No, of course not, sweetie. They just want to see if you saw anything that could help them find the guy. Mr. Evans gave his statement. Well, as best as he could. They asked him if it was you, and he shook his head."

I looked over to Mark, and he grinned at me. This was the Mark that I knew. Before he started making trouble and getting involved with drugs. This was the Mark I was friends with.

The nurse left after checking his vitals. I apologized to Mark for what happened to him. He didn't seem that upset about it. As if talking was a burden to him. I asked if his parents had called, and he shook his head. When we were younger, Mark's parents would "leave on vacation" all the time, and Mark would have to stay at our place until they came back. The longest time was four months.

I sat down in a chair beside his bed, and I felt something poke my stomach.

"Oh right." I spoke softly, pulling out the pictures in my pocket. "I brought pictures so we could look at them. I thought maybe it would help." Mark smiled and nodded. I showed him the first picture. It was just the two of us. We were in a classroom, probably first grade, and we were grinning at the camera. We both had lost our two front teeth and wanted to show that we were twins.

"Mom wanted a picture so bad," I laughed. Mark did too, but it was a weak one. "I remember after this photo, we went out and got ice cream which hurt our mouths because our teeth were missing."

I showed him a few more photos of us and some with Nick. I watched his face become sadder.

"They are gonna find him, you know," I told Mark. "Nick will come back."

I couldn't figure out who I was trying to convince more, Mark or myself.

I flipped to the next photo and realized Mark wasn't in it.

"Oh, sorry, it must've gotten stuck with the rest. We'll just move on—"

Mark started grunting at me. His eyes widened, and fear was written on his face. He was staring at the photo, practically screaming. I looked at the picture and saw me, Nick, Henry, and Luke. Luke, Nick, and I were in front of the picture, posing with our arms around each other. Henry was in the back, throwing a ball at my head.

"Luke?" I asked. "What's wrong with Luke?"

Mark looked at me, his eyes red and bulging out of his head. They looked like they were about to pop. He started shaking, moving the bed around. His grunts were so loud the whole hospital probably heard them.

"Mark! Calm down!" I begged. Doctors came rushing in and instructed me to leave. I walked out the door and watched in before they shut it closed. People were trying to hold him down; one was injecting him with medicine, and others were frantically trying to find some way to help. Mark stared at me through the tiny window in the door, still fighting the doctors.

What did Luke do?

I was soon told to come back later when Mark was feeling better. When I asked if he was going to be okay, the nurse just said, "Probably," before stomping away.

I walked down the hallway that I was too familiar with at this point to be met by police officers.

"Hello, son," one of them said in a deep voice—raspy— sounded like he smoked a lot. The other police officer was wearing blue socks with pizza on them. I could see it because he pulled them over the bottom of his pants. As if he was proud to show them off.

They looked like the same person, just at different stages of life.

"Hey," I said back, "if you are looking for Mark's room, it's not a good time."

"Rough day?" Officer Socks asked. I nodded my head. "Too bad. Are you Kyle?"

What's with all the questions?

"Yes, sir," I informed him. I figured this was the questioning phase. They asked me to answer a few questions about the night I saw Mark. We went to the cafeteria, and they bought me a soda. I offered to pay, but they wouldn't let me. After I got my drink, we sat down at a table in the far corner where very few people were.

"Now, we want you to remember every detail of that night. Anything you can tell us, even the smallest thing, could help," Officer Smoker pleaded with me.

My feet slowed the pace when I noticed a figure standing ahead. He was hunched over, leaning against a store window. I figured he was looking at something, but as I got closer, the blood dripping from his body made itself visible to me.

"Sir!" I called out, running to him. "Are you okay?"

He turned to me, his eyes bloodshot red. Scratches and wounds gushing with blood were all over his face, and I almost didn't recognize him.

"Mark?" I asked. I was only a few inches away from him now. Cuts were ripped into his shirt, and the cloth around them was stained with blood. He pushed himself away from the wall and started leaning toward me. I caught him before he hit the ground, and he grabbed my shoulders, trying to steady himself.

"Then he fell to the ground," I explained, trying to recall that night. "I tried to keep him upright, but he was so heavy, and I was trying to dial nine-one-one as well."

"Did he say anything to you?" Socks asked, leaning forward on the table. Officer Smoker was writing things down on a notepad. I didn't know they actually did those things; I thought it was just a Hollywood myth.

"He said he didn't do it to himself," I answered. Their heads both shot up and stared at me. I thought I said something wrong, and I could feel my heart try to jump out of my chest. Warmth grew in my hands and down my back. I started to say the ABCs backward to calm myself down. Marie taught me that.

"Why would he say that?" Smoker questioned.

I took a breath in and drank my soda to wet my throat that turned to sand. "We were friends since we were like five. He got involved with a bad crowd and started doing bad things to himself. Drugs and such. He always looked horrible, so I guess he just thought I would think he did that to himself."

Socks nodded while Smoker wrote it down. They started whispering to each other. I ignored it the best I could. I figured I was in the clear.

"And you two were also friends with Nick Walter, right?"

I stared at them. I couldn't tell which one asked the question. I wasn't paying attention. I was thrown off by the question.

Nick?

Why would they ask about Nick?

"Yes. We were until Mark started getting us in trouble," I

confessed.

"But you and Nick were still friends?" Smoker asked. I nodded.

Do they think I'm the cause of this?

Of Nick?

Of what happened to Mark?

I was partly to blame for Nick, but I did nothing to Mark.

"Do you think I did this to them?" I asked. Socks moved his head to the side and started shaking it.

"No, of course not. Just one more question for you, Kyle," he said, smiling at me. He was trying to reassure me.

"Okay," I answered.

I couldn't believe these officers. They were just as stupid as this hospital. It seemed like no one knew how to do their jobs around here. Nick and Mark were two separate cases, with two separate stories. They had no relation to each other.

Smoker turned to me and asked, "Was it Nick's idea to cut Mark off from your friend group?"

What does that have to do with—

Oh.

They think Nick…

My jaw clenched subconsciously, making my teeth ache. I could feel my fists tighten, my nails digging into my skin, drawing blood. It dripped from my palm and onto my pants. Anger boiled inside of me.

"You think Nick did this to Mark?" I challenged.

Socks could tell I was upset. When he was about to speak, Smoker cut him off.

"We have a hunch. Nick left his family, his girlfriend, and friends. Signs of drug abuse. Now this happens? It's obvious what happened to the kid. Nick probably went to him for drugs, and when the kid wouldn't give him any, Nick got mad."

I should change his name to Stupid.

Because he is a stupid idiot.

"Are you dumb?" I questioned. His head snapped toward me.

"Excuse me?"

"Are you dumb?" I barked back. I stood up in my chair; a loud noise pierced through the room because of me scraping it against the floor. Stupid Smoker stood up with me. "You must be some officer to think a missing kid would do this to somebody! Nick wouldn't hurt anyone!"

"Kid, you need to calm down," Socks said, standing up.

"No!" I shouted, gaining the attention of everyone in the cafeteria. "This is ridiculous. Clearly, you guys don't know how to do your jobs!"

I stomped out of the cafeteria with all eyes on me. The officers remained in their position, whispering to each other like middle school girls. I wanted to punch them in the face. I wanted to scream and throw things at their heads. I made eyes with a little girl sitting at the table with her father. She was in a wheelchair wearing a beanie with a tube out of her nose. I recognized her from the first time I walked through the doors. The only thing I didn't see last time was written all over her face. It was fear. She was scared of me.

"I'm sorry," I whispered under my breath, continuing out the doors. As I made my way out of the hospital, memories came flooding back of the night I found Mark.

"Mark?" I asked. I was only a few inches away from him now. Cuts were ripped into his shirt, and the cloth around them was stained with blood. He pushed himself away from the wall and started leaning toward me. I caught him before he hit the ground, and he grabbed my shoulders, trying to steady himself.

"Kyle, I didn't do this to myself. I—" He struggled, trying to explain to me what happened. I told him to shush as I pulled out my phone and dialed 911 for help. Mark was falling to the ground as I tried to hold him up with one hand; the feeling of blood dripping onto my arm shook me.

"It was Nick." My head snapped to look at Mark, to see if he was really saying that or if it was a figment of my hallucinations. His eyes were peacefully shut, and his breathing started to slow.

~

After walking around the streets of Concord, I finally concluded I was delusional. There was no way Mark said Nick did that to him.

Maybe Mark was freaking out about Nick in the photo.
Trying to tell me it was him.

I thought back to the photos. Some before the last one had Nick in it. If it was Nick, then why would he freak out at that one? Unless it wasn't about Nick.

Luke?

Why would he freak out about Luke?

I let my thoughts run wild as I paced the corner. I couldn't figure this out; it was like a mystery without any hints or any clues that I must find out on my own. And it was all real, and it was all happening to me.

My phone vibrating in my pocket distracted me.

From: Noelle
Hey! you're still coming over, right?

I had completely forgotten about our plans until she texted me. I was never like this; I always remembered if I had plans with Noelle before. I guess it was because I had nothing else to do. Now it's like my head can't take any more memory.

To: Noelle
Yeah, I'll head on over now.

She sent a smiley face in response, so I made my way over to her house. She lives by Marie, so I knew the way. The next neighborhood, actually. It wasn't as rich as Marie's place, but it was still nice. Noelle's house was always clean, not a dirty spot in sight.

I knocked on the door before it even opened; I sensed something was off. On the other side, Noelle stood in yoga pants and a tank top. Her hair was frizzy and all over the place. It looked like she had just woken up. She rubbed her eyes and smiled at me.

"Hey," I said, stepping into her house. She trailed off into the kitchen, me following her.

"Hi," she replied, grabbing a box of cereal. "Do you want any?"

"No thanks," I responded. "What's with the pajama look today?"

I knew I shouldn't have said that. I knew it before it came out of my mouth, but I said it. It was out in the air, hanging there, waiting for her response.

She looked up at me and giggled. "Trying something new. I don't have anyone to impress right now, so thought I would dress down. You like?"

Okay, that was so not Noelle.

"Uhh…" I started, making my way toward her. The tank top had a yellow stain on it across the stomach area. The yoga pants had about three holes in the front. Something was wrong.

"I love it."

Her face dropped. Her eyes that were previously lit with freedom, turned to a darker tone. Her grin fell into a frown, and she threw her cereal box to the side.

"Don't be nice to me, not today," she muttered, stomping away from me. I heard her slippers slide into the living room. I trailed after, confused as hell as to what just happened. I found Noelle sitting on her couch, her knees in her face. I went to sit down next to her but noticed a bunch of crumbs on the cushion. I started to pick them off and placed them in my palm to throw out.

"No!" she yelled, pushing her knees away from her face and grabbing my wrist. "Don't start helping me clean!"

"I just wanted to sit there," I muttered. I placed the last bit of crumbs in my hands and threw them out in the bathroom. I heard her groan and stuff her face into a pillow. "What is going on with you?"

I sat next to her and waited for her response. She slowly sat up, holding the pillow in her arms. "I wanted to see if you would tell me the truth about how I look."

What?

"Nick always told me the truth."

I nodded. "Well, he was your boyfriend."

"But that's the thing!" she exclaimed, throwing her hands up in the air. She turned and stared into my eyes. "I didn't want a boyfriend that told me the truth."

She must've seen the confused look on my face because she kept talking.

"I want a boyfriend who tells me the truth, but not in certain situations. Like my appearance, I want a boyfriend that will always tell me I look good. Even when I don't. Or won't judge me when I get into a slump. I want a boyfriend like y—"

She suddenly stopped talking and covered her face with the pillow. I took the pillow away and threw it on the ottoman. She stared at the ground, and her face turned red, along with the tips of her ears. I watched as her nose twitched like a rabbit.

"Like what, Noelle?" I asked.

Please.

After a few minutes of silence, I sighed and stared at the floor with her. Dark oak covered with a lavender rug. I tried to remember if it was the same as last time. Mrs. Seong-Hun liked to redecorate often. She doesn't have a job or many things to do, so she takes on new projects all the time. She even built me a skateboard once. It broke after one trip to the skate park, but I didn't need to tell her that.

My thoughts halted when I heard sobs next to me. I looked at Noelle, and tears were streaming down her face. Even when she was crying, she still looked perfect. Like a porcelain doll. I leaned in closer to comfort her, which made her cry even more. I moved back out of fear that I was the one doing this to her.

"No—" She spoke softly. "—it's not you." She grabbed a tissue from the coffee table and wiped her face. "I just feel so guilty."

"About what?" I asked, leaning back in. Watching her cry was the hardest thing I had to do. I hate seeing girls cry, especially Noelle.

"Nick," she admitted. "I don't love him. I never did. He was my first boyfriend, and he always talked about how we would end up together." She blew her nose into the tissue. "But I didn't love him, and I didn't know how to tell him. I liked him. A lot. I really did."

A noise grew from inside her; I couldn't tell if it was a scream or a sob. I just sat there, letting her talk it out. I didn't know what to do, though; she was so upset. I didn't know if what I wanted to do would make her feel better or worse.

"And that's not even it, Kyle." She cried. "I'm such a bad person because he is missing and—" She let out another cry again, blowing her nose. She looked like a mess. A sobbing, snotty mess.

"That's not even the worst part because I'm in love with someone else."

My ears tuned everything else out. I watched her mouth move; it could've been another sentence or a scream, but I couldn't hear it.

Who is she in love with?

Do I have to compete with another guy?

When will she realize that I want her?

I deserve her.

I was lost in my thoughts, anger filling me. When I looked back at Noelle, she was silent. Her mouth was closed, and her eyes stopped watering. She was just looking at me. Staring at me. Before I knew what was happening, her lips were on mine.

She kissed me. The moment I had waited years for finally happened. Noelle Seong-Hun was kissing me. She chose me. Not Nick. She was kissing me.

And I felt nothing.

~

I left her house soon after that. We didn't talk about it; we didn't do it again. Her mom pulled into the driveway and invited me for dinner. I was going to stay until I saw the hundreds of text messages from Mom asking me to come home. I told Mrs. Seong-Hun that I had to leave.

I practically ran home. Mom was supposed to work tonight, so something must've happened. My head raced with a million reasons as to why Mom wanted me home. I thought that Henry or Dad were hurt. But when I got to the driveway, only two cars were there. Mom's and Dad's.

Henry?

I knew he was supposed to be at work, but maybe something had happened. A nail went through his foot? Chopped his hand off on a saw?

I opened the door to find Mom and Dad sitting at the table. Mom had tears in her eyes while my dad comforted her. It reminded me of the time this happened with Max.

"Our baby is gone," Mom cried. She turned and placed her head into my dad's arms. He wrapped them around her, holding her tightly. "He's gone."

"I know, honey," he whispered. "I know."

I was sitting on the stairs, crying about Max. It was all my fault.

I killed their baby. I didn't mean to, but it was my fault. They didn't know I was awake and was listening to them.

"What are we going to do?" Mom asked, sniffing. She pulled away from Dad and rubbed her eyes. They were bright red, like a fire truck. Her hair was all messy and was very obviously not brushed. She was holding a bunch of papers.

"Sh, let's not decide that right now," he said, pulling her up from the dining table. "Let's go to bed."

They were trying to figure out what to do with the body of my little brother.

They ended up burning him.

"Kyle," Mom whispered, waving me over to the table. I walked slowly toward her. I noticed another person sitting at the table that I didn't see before. Ms. Walter was sitting there, with her head in her hands, sobbing.

No.

"Kyle, sweetie, I'm so sorry."

I won't believe it.

"Come here, son," Dad ordered me.

I backed away.

No, he can't be gone.

Because then it's my fault.

Ms. Walter stood up and walked over to me. Her arms wrapped around my shoulder, but I couldn't move. I stood there, numb.

No.

Ms. Walter sat back down, still crying. "I'm so sorry, Kyle."

This is all my fault.

I did this to him.

"Kyle," Mom said to me. "They found his body a few miles into Warner. He was beaten but alive and made it all the way there until…he died."

15

Day Twenty-Three

I couldn't sleep. I couldn't bring myself to even close my eyes. Fear was sitting in my stomach, making every move ten times harder. If I went to turn on my side, the unknown of what was lurking in my room made me sick. I would roll back over to be faced with darkness. After three hours of that, I decided to turn on the light. I watched my windows to make sure no one was watching me. Every time I looked away, my gut screamed at me to look back. To make sure I wasn't being watched. And every time I did, I was only met with the tree outside my window. The entire night, my thoughts were consistent with the same idea.

It's your fault.
You killed him.
He's dead because of you.
You did this.
They will know soon.
They are going to kill you next.

It was as if someone was hunched over my shoulder whispering these things into my ear. It sounded like someone else was in my room, reading my death note to me as a bedtime story. Whenever I imagined the face that was speaking to me, I saw Nick. Nick's bloody, disfigured face with a dent the size of a rock in his skull. I imagined him opening his mouth, taunting me.

"You murdered me." He hissed. "You're a murderer."

I murdered him.
I'm a murderer.

Before I knew it, the sun shined through the windows. It proved that no one was watching me, and I had enough energy to get out of bed. When I stood up, I could still hear the voice telling me things I already knew. Making the pain of knowing the information worse.

Stop…

I slammed my head with my fists to quieten the attacks that were screaming at me. I pulled my trembling hands from my hair and focused on them. They looked like they were vibrating; I couldn't stop them. The thoughts only grew louder as I gave up the urge to fight back. There was nothing I could do. The accusations were right.

I am a murderer.

I walked past my bathroom, peeking inside. The room was lit by the sun coming in through the window. My sink was gross and dirty with toothpaste I forgot to clean out. I pushed on the door slightly to see the mirror. I stared at my reflection, trying to remember how much progress I made. I was doing good. I was happy.

That was before you knew.

Before you knew you were a murderer.

I closed my eyes for a moment, reliving what had happened to me these past few weeks. Nick being dead, then missing. And I was doing better. Now he's dead again. I was stuck in a train that was just traveling in circles, and there was no way out.

Well, there is one way out.

When I opened my eyes again, a boy was standing right beside me. I could've touched him. He had no expression on his face. He was just staring at me through the mirror. I was too tired to fight back. I didn't close my eyes; I didn't break the mirror. I looked back at the boy.

"Nick?" I asked him. He did a slight nod. I watched as he turned and faced the window. I followed him there. He reached his hands up to unlock it. His hands were covered in dirt and blood. I then noticed how much blood was on him. His shirt was covered, and it was dripping onto his pants. Dirt was all over his body, and there was a gash along his cheek.

He looks like me the night he went missing.

Nick unlocked the window and slid it open with ease. He pushed the screen door out and let the fresh air in. It hit both of us at the same time. Nick closed his eyes and started humming. He did that all the time when we were younger.

My hands started to sweat. I could feel my heart jumping

out of my rib cage and slamming into my chest. For once, my head was empty. It was like my brain left my body here to fend for its own. Nick opened his eyes and pointed out the window.

"Your turn."

When I turned to see him, he was gone. Not a trace of him even being there. No blood or dirt left behind. The wind stopped blowing in my face, and I realized the window never actually opened.

Murderer.

I didn't change my clothes. I didn't even put on deodorant. I threw on a black hoodie and made my way to the stairs. Before I took one step, I could hear faint voices below me.

"I'll drive him, Henry." Mom bickered. "You don't do anything to help out your brother. His best friend just died, and you can't even give him a ride to school!"

I heard chairs scraping against the floor and metal clanging together. Footsteps stomped around in the kitchen.

"He shouldn't even be going to school," Henry argued. Which was a good point. "And besides, I'm the last person he wants to be trapped in a car with."

"He needs to go to school because he can't be alone right now. I tried to call off work, but we have about twenty burn victims from a barbecue that went wrong, alright? And about fifteen interns who don't know what they are doing," she explained, marching around. I could hear her heels click against the tiles each time she made a step.

She thinks I'm going to kill myself.

Maybe you should.

I took a step on the stairs, making sure it creaked by adding pressure. Shushing echoed up the stairs, but the walking around continued. I dragged my feet into the kitchen and stood in the doorway. My father was sitting at the end of the table on his phone. He had burnt pancakes in front of him, untouched. Henry was next to him, in his uniform, poking at his plate of pancake batter. Mom was standing by the oven wearing an apron. Her hair was tied back into a messy bun. When she turned around to face me, she was covered in flour and batter.

"Hi, Kyle," she greeted, huffing. "How are you doing, sweetie?"

I am a murderer.

How do you think I'm doing?

"Fine." I sighed. I tried to walk toward the door, only to be stopped by my worrying mother.

"Where are you going?"

The door was painted black a few months ago. It was starting to chip on the edge. The blue paint underneath it was revealing. I told Dad to chip off the paint, then paint it, but he said no. A few days later when it started to chip on its own, he agreed that it was a clever idea.

"School," I barked. She either didn't notice my snappiness or chose to ignore it because she kept a smile on her face.

"But I made pancakes." She held up a plate of burnt pieces of pancakes mixed with uncooked batter.

She's trying to kill me, isn't she?

If she knew the truth.

"I'm good."

Dad stood up and started stretching his arms. A loud yawn escaped his mouth. He turned to me with his hands on his hips and offered me a ride.

"I'll take you to school. It's only a little out of my way."

Mom said goodbye to me and told me to be safe. While she hugged me, Henry flipped me off. I normally would return the favor, but my arms were too weak to even lift. Henry noticed this too and just smirked at me.

If I get caught.

He's the next to go.

Dad and I made our way to his Ford Escape. I climbed into the front seat while he started the car. For most of the ride, we were silent. The radio wasn't even turned on. Which meant that I had nothing to focus on besides my thoughts.

Murderer.

You should just die.

No one wants you here anyway.

It felt like the voice was whispering to me from the back seat. I kept shifting my eyes to the mirror to see if anyone was sitting there, but there was no one.

I can't punch out my thoughts.

"How are you doing, Kyle?" Dad asked, his eyes pacing from the road and to me. I shrugged when he was looking my way. He nodded, facing back toward the road.

"Nick was a good kid."

He's dead.

"He was a part of our family as well."

He's gone.

"We knew him since he was a kid."

I killed him.

"We just can't mope around about it."

What?

Dad cleared his throat and took a sharp left turn. We were only a few minutes away from my school at this point. I could even see it down the street. I prayed that a car would come crashing into us and kill me. Just me.

"Nick's passing is sad. I was even angry about it, but he wouldn't want us to be depressed about it, so we have to move on."

We pulled into the school, and he parked a bit away from the building. We were in the last line of the parking spaces. No one was around us; everyone was closer to the school. Nothing had changed. People were still outside, laughing and chatting with their friends. As if a kid that they had been going to school with forever didn't die.

"You don't know anything about Nick, so don't act like you do." I spat at him. His eyes widened, and he opened his mouth to yell, but I slammed the door and jumped out.

"Kyle!" he barked. I shut the door with a loud bang and stomped away. Luke wasn't waiting for me by the stairs, and Noelle wasn't hanging out with her friends. They both skipped school. Rightfully so, he was close with them. I just couldn't be alone.

I got to the stairs where Luke and I would meet. Instead, I was greeted by another bloody Nick. He was sitting on the steps, hunched over. He was wearing a backpack that was stained with a dark liquid. I stared at him for a few moments before giving in and sitting down next to him.

"You aren't real," I muttered. He nodded but kept his head facing the concrete. I wanted to push him, knock him over, and run away. My muscles refused to give into that. I had enough energy to hit him, but there was no running.

Nick looked up at me, bruises all around his face. The blood from earlier was gone, but the dent remained. It looked like it had gotten deeper, reached more inside of his skull. He smiled, showing his cracked teeth off. Some were missing, making him appear younger.

"We should do it, you know," he whispered in my ear. It didn't even register with me that he spoke until a few minutes after.

"What?" I asked. Not sure what I was asking, though.

"I have pills. We could both end it in the bathroom. They are just sitting on your counter," he responded, shoving his head into his hands.

"Pills?"

He looked back at me and smirked. Blood from his backpack started pouring out and reaching the steps of the school. He turned his head to the side, his throat showing that now was sliced open. It didn't even look cut because of the dark blood pouring from his neck.

"To die," he replied.

"Kyle?" a voice behind me asked. I turned to see an older lady standing. She smiled at me and asked me to follow her to the principal's office. I agreed reluctantly and left the perfectly clean spot at which I was sitting.

No blood.

No Nick.

The lady led me into the principal's office. Mr. Finn sat at his desk, typing loudly on his laptop. He didn't even notice I was there until the lady cleared her throat.

"Ah, Kyle." Mr. Finn spoke, giving me a warm smile. "Sit."

He motioned to the chair in front of his desk. It was a wooden chair with a black cushion on it. There were three of them lined up there. I looked at the chairs and sat in the middle. The lady left the room and shut the door behind her. Hearing the door close made me feel trapped. My body immediately came up with an escape plan.

Windows.

Grab the chair and throw it out the window.

The glass will shatter, and you can use one of the pieces to defend yourself.

I pictured myself grabbing the glass. I could see the moment

I took the sharp weapon and plunged it into Mr. Finn's neck. His cry for help I would hear, with the blood trickling down. I would be pushing it in so hard I would start to bleed. Our blood combining on the floor, making a little pool.

"How are you, Kyle?" he asked, folding his arms. He held a pen in his hand, clicking it. The noise echoed in my skull until another voice appeared.

"He wants to kill you with that pen."

I didn't need to look to know who was talking. I could feel Nick beside me, hear his breathing. I knew he was sitting in the chair next to me, feeding me these lies.

But I didn't care that they were lies.

I believed him, anyways, because I wanted to.

He wants to kill me.

Nick leaned in closer and whispered in my ear, "Because he knows."

He knows.

Mr. Finn tilted his head to the side, waiting for a response. I just nodded, which made him smile.

Is he making fun of me?

"Of us," Nick replied.

I turned to look at Nick. He wasn't bloody or bruised. He didn't have teeth missing. He wasn't mad at me. He wasn't trying to get me to kill myself. He didn't have a dent in his head. He wasn't yelling at me. He was smiling.

He is trying to help me.

Save me even.

"Nick was a friend to many people. Touched the hearts of so many. Even mine," Mr. Finn rambled. "Such a good kid didn't deserve such fate."

"He wanted me dead," Nick informed me. "He wants you dead."

Wants me dead.

"However," Mr. Finn continued. He took off his glasses and started rubbing his eyes. "Life doesn't stop."

Nick snorted next to me. Which made me snort. Mr. Finn shot a look at me, which made me want to scream that Nick did it first. I realized that if I had said that, it wouldn't have been long until I was back in that psych ward.

"I wanted to see if you would help me plan an assembly for

Nick. Students could talk about him, and we could all get to know him a little better. It would give everyone closure." Mr. Finn smiled, looking all proud. As if he single-handedly just saved every depressed kid in America.

"No," Nick snapped.

"No," I repeated.

Mr. Finn was taken aback. He shook his head and frowned, a line creasing in between his eyebrows. "I'm not sure you understand—"

"We understand perfectly!" Nick barked, standing up. I copied him, stating the same words besides for the "We" part.

"You don't care about me!" Nick screamed.

"You don't care about Nick!" I screamed.

He has control over me.

I believe Nick.

"You only want to feel good about yourself! I'm not playing your stupid games!" Nick bellowed. I followed suit, except angrier. I was fuming. My nose started bleeding from how tightly I was clenching my jaw. I felt it drip down my face and onto his floor. I didn't stop yelling, though. I'm not entirely sure what I said or what I did because I was just following Nick. Soon I was out of the office, slamming doors and frightening people. When I walked out of school, I was alone again. Nick was gone.

Stop leaving me.

Suddenly, there was this burst of energy. Like power surging through me that I needed to release.

I took off running.

I couldn't stop. I had to keep going. My lungs felt like they were going to give out any second, but I pushed myself. Cars honked as I crossed the road. Birds flew away at the sight of me. People on the street stopped and whispered to each other. I was sprinting at this point. My feet found grass but kept going. My heart was about to burst. Trees swayed past, and I crushed branches underneath me. I stopped and realized where I was.

"Hey, man, get away from me!" I screamed at Nick. His eyes followed me, red with anger. I could see the steam coming from his ears, and I knew I was in trouble.

"No! Why would you say that to her?" he barked at me, pushing my chest. I felt his fist and my temper run out of patience. I looked at his hand before looking him in the eye. His were focused on mine, and I knew we were in a fight.

"She deserved the truth," I said.

"BS!" he fumed. "You told her lies!"

I don't know what happened next. Calling me a liar triggered something within me. I used my hands and placed them on both of his pecs and pushed him as hard as I could. I watched as he lost his balance and fell backward. Before his head hit the ground, there was this loud noise. A gunshot. It blasted through my ears, and I had to cover them, or else I would've gone deaf. I looked around me and saw no one.

"Damn hunters," I muttered under my breath.

I looked at Nick and watched as the blood came pouring out of his skull.

But here he was, standing in front of me. Not lying on the ground, bleeding to death. He was five feet away, standing where I pushed him.

"Push me," he ordered.

"No." I fought back. He walked closer to me, his eyes rolling to the back of his head, then bouncing back. I watched as blood stained his clothing.

"Push me!" he yelled louder. I shook my head, and he grabbed me by the shoulders, forcing me to stand still. He opened his mouth to speak, but no words came out. He just screamed in my face, his breath forcing itself onto me. I could feel his spit fall onto my eyelids. When I opened my eyes, he was nowhere around me. I was alone again in the forest.

I ran over to him and watched as his eyes followed me. He knew he was dying. I saw that his head landed on a rock. The top part of the stone couldn't be seen, so it must be lodged in his head. I watched the thick blood come rushing out, and I tried to cover it with my hands, but there was nothing I could do.

His eyes stared into mine before the blood from his head came pouring down his forehead and covered his eyes. I tried to wipe it away, but it was no use. It was all coming down, and it was coming fast. I watched as his lifeless body lay there; no Nick left any more. I knew what I had to do.

I ran.

"Why did you leave me, Kyle?" he begged behind me. I turned, expecting to see Nick. But when I looked, it was a little boy. His features were the same as Nick's, and I realized this was Nick when he was younger. The little boy's eyes stared into mine, pleading for his life with them.

"It was an accident." I cried. I fell to my knees. "I'm sorry."

"No!" Nick screamed. "Please don't kill me!" I reached down to him and grabbed his shoulders to calm him.

"I didn't!" I sobbed back. "I won't hurt you!"

Nick ran from me, pulling away from my grasp. He started screeching at the top of his lungs, calling me a murderer. Screaming for his mom. Calling for his dad to save him.

I fell on my knees, weakened by the boy. He pained me in a way I didn't know existed.

"Please!" I begged. "Come back! I won't hurt you."

I started sobbing. I couldn't help it. The tears came out uncontrollably, and I started to choke on them. I started wheezing; my lungs couldn't keep up.

"Yes, you will," a voice harshly whispered in my ear. "You killed that boy."

I turned around and grabbed whatever was speaking to me. I felt something, someone. But they pulled away. My eyes were filled with tears; my vision was impaired. I couldn't see who it was. I couldn't tell whether it was my head messing with me or if it was real.

Was it real?

"Please." I sobbed. "Kill me."

I started begging for the thing or human to kill me. I begged Nick to kill me. I begged the little boy too. I begged anyone that was listening to kill me.

"I deserve it!" I pleaded. "Please!"

I lay on the forest ground, sticks and rocks shoving themselves into my back. I lay there until the sun went away and the night fell. The trees became more lifelike, and nearby noises filled me with fear. I lay there until I knew that nothing was going to kill me that night.

Except me.

There was one person I needed to talk to. One person who would understand. I walked the whole way to their house with my head low. I felt ashamed, and I didn't want anyone to see me. I walked up the stairs and knocked on the door. It swung open with ease, and a voice called out to me.

"God, you look awful."

I looked up to be met by Marie. I didn't know who else I was expecting, considering I walked to her house. Her black curly hair was out and all over the place. She was wearing pajama shorts and a T-shirt that said multiple swear words on it.

"Don't just stand there like a weirdo; come in," she said, pulling me inside the house. Her house wasn't at all what I expected it to be. Everything was white and gold; crystals lined the chandelier. There was a bar with barstools in the hallway.

Her room, however, was exactly how I pictured it. Black walls with posters everywhere. Clothes flung around the room, empty containers, and wrappers on the floor. The radio and speaker set sat on her desk with a bunch of albums. She even had a guitar.

"Why do you look so gross?" she asked after pulling me inside her bedroom. "Seriously, did you roll around on a farm?"

I looked down in response. I felt the mood shift and her worry appeared. I sat down on a chair that was stained with some sort of liquid.

"Are you okay?" she asked, the concern in her voice rising.

"I need a favor," I whispered. She walked closer to me, placing a hand on my shoulder. "I need you to tell my mom and dad that I love them."

"What?" she asked, raising her eyebrows.

"And tell Noelle that I love her too."

Realization hit her, and she opened her mouth to speak. I hushed her before she got a chance to say anything, though.

"And Luke. Please tell him that he gets dibs on anything in my room. He'll probably donate it all to charity, but it's whatever—"

"Kyle, are you asking me to say your goodbyes for you?" Marie cut me off. "As in, you're killing yourself?"

I looked up at her with tears in my eyes. I expected a laugh or a mocking tease or some joke that I'm not doing it without her. But her face turned soft, and she sighed instead. She climbed onto my lap and held my head in her arms.

"You aren't doing anything, Kyle. I'm not going to let you," she promised. "What happened to Nick isn't your fault."

"I killed him, Marie," I confessed.

"No, you didn't." She fought back, stroking my hair. She sat up and started playing with it. "It was an accident. It's not your fault."

I closed my eyes to let myself breathe. Marie didn't see me as a monster that deserved to die. And she knew everything. She didn't want me dead.

I opened my eyes to see Nick standing in the corner. He was smiling at me, blood dripping from his mouth. The dent was back, and it looked like he was smashed by a semi-truck. His clothes were ripped and bleeding from the holes. His legs were covered in dark bruises. There was one gash across his whole face. It lined from the top left of his forehead to the bottom right side of his jaw. Just barely missing his eye. He started to move his hand across his neck and pointed at me. He opened his mouth to speak, and when he did, I heard him right beside my head.

"You're next."

Marie must've noticed me shifting in my seat because she stood up and faced the corner I was looking at.

"Is he over there?" she asked. I nodded, gulping a lump in my throat down. The taste of bile appeared.

Marie walked over to the corner and stood there. Nick moved to the side to let her pass through. She looked at me and asked, "Where is he?"

"Next to you."

"She can't see me," Nick said, staring at me as if he was reaching right into my soul.

"You don't scare me," Marie barked. I turned to look at her, expecting her to be facing me. But she was staring right at Nick. He looked at her and tilted his head to the side, confused as to why she was talking to him.

"Is he listening?" she asked. I nodded. "Good. Listen here, Nick, go away because you are making my friend here uncomfortable. And me as well."

What is she doing?

She's talking to air.

Nick looked taken aback. The bruises from his legs disappeared, along with the cuts in his shirt.

"You aren't real!" Marie screamed.

He's not real.

He isn't real.

Nick's blood seemed to have dissolved from his body. His mouth had closed, and blood wasn't pouring from it.

"Now go away," Marie finished, staring at the wall.

It's just a wall.

"Go away!" I demanded at the boy. Tears burned through my eyes. I looked at the spot where Nick had been, and there was only a wall. Just a plain wall.

Marie looked back at me and whispered, "Is he gone?"

I nodded, sitting on the floor. Exhaustion pounced on me like a tiger. My eyes were so heavy; I just wanted to lie down on the floor and sleep. Marie sat next to me and smiled.

"You better now?"

I shook my head. "I still killed him."

"Then you need to tell the police," she stated. I would've sat straight up at that, but I was so tired I couldn't move. "Explain to them what happened, and maybe they will take it easy on you."

"Easy on me?" I scoffed.

"They probably won't even believe you," she offered. "But it will help you if you confess. You won't be like this all the time."

It made sense, what she said. That's what scared me. If that was my only way out of being stuck with a bloody Nick for the rest of my life, then I had to take it.

I was going to confess.

16

Day Twenty-Four

"How dare you say that to her?" I barked. I felt my hands reach up and push the person in front of me. I watched as Nick's eyes ran out of patience. They glowed red. I narrowed down on him, anyways.

I was fighting with Nick as Nick.

He's gonna kill me.

"She deserved the truth, alright?" Nick said.

"That's a load of crap!" I fumed. "You told her lies!"

I could tell that I triggered him. He placed his hand on my chest and used so much force to push me backward. He watched as I lost balance and fumbled with my feet. I fell back, about to land on a rock, when a noise went off. A gunshot. My head hit the top of the rock, and I could feel it crack my skull. Nick looked around us, tracing the woods.

"Damn hunters," he muttered.

I watched the blood pour out of my head and reach the leaves on the ground. I watched as Nick ran over to me, fear growing within his eyes. He placed his hands on my skull to stop the bleeding, but it was too late. There was too much. He stared into my eyes until blood covered them. He wiped away what he could, but he realized that he had just killed me. He took one last look at me before taking off running.

"It should've been me."

I sat up in bed, tormented by what I just saw. I couldn't help but break down crying. Was Nick still alive when he hit his head? Did he watch me run away? Could he tell how sorry I was?

My breathing became heavier and harder to catch. Tears streamed down my face. I could feel butterflies flapping their wings inside my stomach, but worse. Their wings were made of razors and poison. That's what it felt like.

I turned to my side and turned my light on. I looked around my room, practically saying goodbye to it. I didn't know if I was ever going to see it again. I only had one part of my day planned; the rest of it was up to the cops. They could arrest me on sight.

Can they do that?

I checked the time, and it was only four in the morning. The panic of not knowing ate me alive. The sting of bile burned the back of my throat. I couldn't handle it any more. The fear and anxiety of not knowing what was going to happen to me was killing me. I pulled my phone out and I sent a quick text to Marie.

To: Marie
I can't wait any longer. I have to go tell them now.

I knew it was too early, and I knew she wouldn't respond, but I thought I would let her know. So when she woke up and thought about going to see me, she'd know it was too late. I got out of bed and noticed Nick standing there. His body was sitting straight up, his head almost cone-shaped because of the dent in his head. His clothes were torn, and the blood was back. He was holding an old action figure of mine. One that I let him borrow, and he never returned.

"You won't be here for much longer," I told him. "I promise you that."

He pouted his lips before laughing.

"Yeah, we'll see about that."

Not real.

I walked away from him and trailed downstairs. I grabbed a jacket and left Mom and Dad a note. I told them that I was sorry, but I had to leave to do something. I told them that I was okay and I would see them soon. I walked past the basement to see if Henry was up. His light was off, so he was either out or sleeping. I left the door, closing it as quietly as I could.

I can't take this any more.

I have to confess.

Each step made my stomach churn even more. Made my thoughts louder than they were before. I knew I was doing the right thing, but was it the wrong time? Did I wait too long? My phone vibrated in my pocket, but I ignored it.

I made my way to the police station, heading up the stairs. I didn't want to stop and think because stopping and thinking would lead to me leaving, and it would only make it worse in the end. I pushed away my gut telling me to run and turn back. I went against every instinct telling me to stop.

There were only three officers on the floor. They didn't even look my way when I walked in. A lady at the front desk was signing some papers when she glanced up and finally saw me.

"How can I help you, sweetie?" she asked, putting her papers to the side.

"Uh…" I blanked. I thought about it one more time. Leaving and never coming back. But I knew if I did, the guilt would claw at me until I gave in.

"I wanted to talk about Nick Walter, the missing—" I corrected myself. "The boy that died."

Two of the officers were looking at me now. One of them stood up and waved me over. She looked nice, and she had a smile on when I walked over. Made it easier to confess.

"Hey, kid," she greeted me, telling me to sit down. I sat in a black fold-up chair that was placed in front of her desk. "What's going on?"

This is it, Kyle.

Just tell her, and you'll be free.

"Nick Walter was my best friend," I started explaining.

She gave me a look and patted my shoulder. "I'm so sorry, kid."

I nodded and went to continue my confession when the doors slammed open. Both doors hit both sides of the walls and got everyone's attention.

I guess I could've done that.

Marie stomped into the station. The lady behind the desk was about to scold her when Marie's eyes settled on me. She shushed the lady and came running over to me. The officer I was with stood up and placed her hands on her hips.

"What is the meaning of this?" she demanded.

Marie grabbed my arm with one swift motion and smiled at the officer. "I'm so sorry about this. He's my brother, and he hasn't been taking his crazy pills like he's supposed to."

"What?" the officer and I said at the same time.

I pleaded with her. "Marie, stop I—"

"So, whatever he told you, please disregard. I just found out he hasn't been taking them for a while now, and he gets loopy and says things he doesn't mean and that aren't true." She rambled, holding me up. "We have to get going now; Mom's waiting."

Marie pulled me out of the station, saying goodbyes to everyone and apologizing that her crazy brother disrupted their morning. When we were finally out by the street, away from the building, she let go of me.

"What the hell, Marie?" I asked, pulling away from her.

"I just saved you, that's what," she remarked. "Nick died from a gunshot."

What?

"No, he died from a head collision because I pushed him!" I argued back.

"Sh!" she yelled, pulling me further from the street. We were in an alley. "I went to your house when I got your text to see if you were okay, but your mom said you left to do something. She said she woke up from the sound of your door closing."

Damn.

"Anyways, when I got there, your mom said she had the autopsy report about Nick. He died from a gunshot wound to the head. They believe that he was beaten, made it out of town before getting shot in the head," she concluded.

I was quiet for a few minutes before asking, "What does this mean?"

She smiled and hugged me.

"It means you're free."

~

With everything going on, I completely forgot to check on Noelle. I was worried about what I was going to do; I didn't even think to call her. After I dropped Marie back to her home, I sprinted to Noelle's house. I ran through someone's backyard and hopped two fences, but I made it there. There were no cars in the driveway, so her parents weren't home. I knocked on the door, and a few seconds later, Noelle opened it.

She looked a mess. Tears were streaming down her face; her eyes were red and puffy, and her hair was pulled back into a ponytail with strands of hair out of place. When she saw me, she broke down, crying even harder.

"Noelle," I cooed, trying to get her to relax. She turned around and walked inside, leaving the door open for me. I closed the door gently behind me and sat with Noelle on the couch.

"I just feel so guilty," she cried, wrapping her arms around me. My first instinct was to push her off and run. Instead, I sat there and let her cry in the crook of my neck.

"I mean, first Nick goes missing, then I figure out my feelings and kiss his best friend, and then he dies!" she wailed. "Why did he have to die?"

My heart ached for her, but not in the way it normally did. I didn't want her. I pitied her. I had empathy, but love wasn't attached to it. I wasn't in love with her.

I'm not in love with Noelle?

"This must be someone punishing me, right?" Noelle asked, pulling away from my neck. I felt the tears drip down my shoulder and onto my back. "I'm going to Hell because I kissed my boyfriend's best friend when he was missing."

I didn't know what to say. I looked down at the ground and thought about it. She sobbed silently, covering her face with a tissue. I had the sudden urge to yell at her.

"Noelle, listen," I said as calmly as I could. "This isn't about you."

She snapped her head up at me. The tissue fell from her hand and landed on the floor. Her eyes crinkled. "What?"

"This is about Nick. He just died. He's gone, and you are worried about you going to Hell? He might already be in Hell!"

"That's not funny," she muttered.

"But you get my point," I grumbled, standing up. "He's dead, and you are sitting here saying, 'O why me?'" She nodded, staring at the ground. She slowly bent down to pick up her tissue and held it in her hands.

"You say you don't want a boyfriend who would tell you the truth, but you need one, Noelle," I told her. "That's why you stayed with Nick. Because you guys worked well together, and you knew that deep down."

She refused to look at me.

"I'm going to figure out who took him from you," I

promised her. "Why don't you go clean up." I walked a few steps before pausing. "And try not to cry any more today."

Her eyes glistened, shimmering with hope. She slightly nodded, walking upstairs. I left the house and started walking to my own. I was alone, fully alone. There was no dead Nick talking to me any more. I didn't picture him bloody, dead, or hurt. I remembered him as the boy he was.

"Kyle!" Nick called out to me from his car. "Jump in; we are going to be late!" This was at the beginning of the school year; Nick had just gotten his license, and he wanted to drive me to school. Sure, it was illegal. But only if we got caught. I jumped into the front seat and grinned at Nick.

"Ready?" he asked. I nodded. "Okay, go!"

At the same time, we both threw our middle fingers out the window and at Henry, who was waiting in his car to leave our driveway. Henry yelled slurs at us, but Nick drove away before he could do anything. I started laughing in my seat, buckling up.

"I needed that," I admitted. "He was such a psycho yesterday."

"Ugh," Nick replied. "That's annoying." I nodded, agreeing with him.

The night before, Henry decided it was a clever idea to rip up all my homework into shreds and use it to make a fire in the fireplace. We never used that fireplace, but Henry wanted to, so he did. What was I supposed to do the next day at school? Tell my teacher my brother took my homework and burned it? I had Mom write me a note asking for another day to do it. Nick wanted to ask me what happened, but he knew better than to push it. He continued driving, his eyes on the road.

After a few moments, I realized we weren't going the right way.

"Geez, Nick, you are so stupid." He raised his eyebrow at me. "You are going the wrong way!"

"Nope," he argued back. "I'm going the right way."

I groaned. "No, the school is back that way."

I watched his grin grow from ear to ear. "We aren't going to school."

I sat up in my seat like a child, suddenly very interested in what he had to say.

"There's a carnival in town, and they are closing today so," Nick informed me, "we aren't going to school today."

That Wednesday, we spent the entire day eating a bunch of greasy, sugary carnival food, then riding unsafe rides till we were going to puke. On our drive home, we got phone calls from our moms telling us how mad they were and how badly we were going to get punished. We had to keep muting the phones so they wouldn't hear our laughter. We didn't care what our punishment was. We wouldn't have traded that day for anything else. He dropped me off at home and asked me, "Did you have a good time?"

"Yeah," I said suspiciously. "Why?"

Nick shrugged his shoulders and took off. The next day I found out why Nick took me to the carnival.

He didn't want Noelle to confront him about cheating on her.

17

Day Twenty-Eight

It had been a few days since they figured out what happened to Nick. After my almost confession to the police, Mr. Finn called to tell my parents that I could take as much time off as I needed. As long as I got my work done, I didn't need to go back to school until April. He also, very subtly, told my parents I needed therapy. And by subtle, I mean he said, "I believe Kyle needs therapy."

Noelle, Luke, and obviously Mark also got excused from school. Mark didn't have to do any work, though, because of his condition. I had been trying to stop by and see him, but the hospital only let me talk to him for five minutes at a time. Then they claimed he needed rest and escorted me out.

His parents never called back. I doubt they even knew what was going on with Mark. They had no idea that their son couldn't speak any more. I thought about it, and I don't think they would've cared. His parents had never cared about him. He had no one.

It was Tuesday, which meant that I was home alone for the first time since Nick died. Mom took off work the day before to stay home with me, but she said that there was a big surgery at work. Henry was working, and Dad offered to stay home, but I told him to go to work. I could tell he didn't want to stay; his eyes averted mine when he told Mom he would call out.

"No. Go," I said, breaking the few seconds of silence after Dad's generous offer. "I was going to go to Luke's, anyways."

It wasn't a lie; Luke did ask me to go over to his house. He just said that he and his mom were at a protest for whales or some other ocean animal, and he didn't know when he would be back. He said he was going to text me when they were home.

Dad grinned and nodded, sitting back in his chair. I could

tell Mom disapproved of this, but she didn't say anything. She continued combing her hair in the bathroom. After a few minutes, my phone rang.

"Hello?"

"Kyle." A soft voice greeted me on the other line. "It's Ms. Walter."

Oh.

I cleared my throat, trying my best to sound contented for her. "Hey, Ms. Walter."

Dad gave me a weary look from the couch, and I ignored him. That also got Mom's attention, and she paused while putting her earrings in.

I heard her hum through the phone. "I was wondering if you and Luke would want to come over later tonight to talk about Nick and perhaps go through his room to see if he has anything of yours. You can invite your mother too."

Mom stepped closer to me with her hands at her hips. Dad lost interest and was watching the news on our TV. Henry stomped up the stairs when Mom shushed him. He rolled his eyes and walked past me into the kitchen.

"Sure, I'll call Luke and let him know," I answered. I could feel her smile on the other line; she had a very distinctive smile. Her one dimple would appear on her left cheek, and her smile lines would crease. Sometimes she'd close her eyes impulsively. Wasn't ever sure why, but I didn't bother to ask.

"Thank you." She sniffed. "I'll see you later, then."

I hung up the phone and placed it in my pocket. Mom was staring at me, waiting for me to tell her what that was about.

"Ms. Walter wants me and Luke to go over and go through Nick's room to see if he has anything of ours. She wants you to come too."

Mom nodded, grabbing her bag. "I'll have to see if I can make it, depending on how long this surgery goes and if anything else comes in that I'm needed for." She kissed me on my forehead and headed out the door, saying goodbye. Dad left soon after, and I didn't even notice Henry leaving. I was sitting on the couch, watching TV, when Luke told me he was home.

From: Luke

Hey, just got back. Want to come over?

I shut the TV off and quickly responded.

To: Luke
Sure. How was the protest thing?

I opened the fridge to be reminded that we never have any food. I peeked into the cabinets to find an open sleeve of crackers. I figured it was better than nothing, so I started munching on them.

From: Luke
Do you actually want to know, or do you just want me to say good?

He's right; I'm never actually interested in his protests. I asked him a few times and let him ramble on about how they spread awareness about trees dying in some country, but then they got too long. He realized I was never listening, so he just said good, and we talked about anything other than his charity events.

Sure, it makes me a bad friend, but do I care? Besides, he never listens when I want to talk about a video game or something that involves harming anything. Like paintball.

To: Luke
I'll be over soon.

I headed out of my house after I sent that text. The streets were busier than they normally were. A lot more people on the sidewalks, and there were a lot of cars on the road. The constant noise in my ears felt calming to me because, for once, it wasn't my mind playing tricks on me. The noise was real. It wasn't a figment of my imagination.

When I made it to Luke's street, my phone started vibrating. I thought it was Luke calling to see where I was, but it was the hospital Mark was staying at. At first, I got worried, thinking something happened to him. But then I remembered the last time they called me was because they wanted me to go see

Mark that day. I ignored the call, thinking that I would go see Mark the next day.

I made it to Luke's house and knocked on the door, immediately being greeted by his mom. Don't get me wrong, I love Ms. Cloud. But she can be a lot sometimes. She opened the door, and her outfit screamed unusual colors to me. She was wearing a blue shirt that had the Earth on it. Her long purple skirt flowed down to her ankles with patterns of flowers. Her hair was dyed green on the sides and up in a bun. Her earrings looked like they were made of plastic forks.

"Hi, Ms. Cloud!" I greeted her, stepping inside. She grinned at me and gave me a quick hug.

"Kyle!" she exclaimed. "It's been so long!"

I nodded, taking my shoes off at her doormat. She had awfully specific rules about wearing shoes in the house. While I placed them in the corner, I noticed a pair of shoes that I didn't recognize. Ms. Cloud saw me looking, and she laughed.

"Oh, those are Caroline's shoes," she explained, pointing to the dining table. There sat a woman with short black hair. She was dressed in a button-up and jeans. Her earrings were two giant hoops intertwined with each other. She smiled and waved at me. "She's my girlfriend."

That was the third girlfriend I met of Ms. Cloud's. The first one turned out not to be gay and went running back to her husband. The second one moved to another country. And then this one. I waved back at her and told Ms. Cloud I was going to Luke's room. She nodded and went back to the dining table with Caroline.

Luke was sitting on his bean bag chair, reading when I walked in. His room was painted bright blue, and his walls were bare. No posters or anything. His desk was meticulously organized with a cup for pens. His bed was made, and there wasn't a dirty spot in his room. He looked up at me and smiled.

"Hey!" He put his book away. He had two bookshelves by his chair so he could read comfortably. He let me sit there once to read, but when he left the room, I just fell asleep.

"Hey," I responded, plopping onto his bed. "Ms. Walter wants us to go over to her house later."

He stood up, stretching his arms out. "For what?"

"I think to talk about Nick and go through his room for our

stuff."

Luke nodded, walking over to me. He lay down on his bed and huffed. "It seems like Nick has been gone forever." I stayed silent.

Should I tell him?

"I just wish I could've seen him before it all happened," Luke continued.

I did.

It sucked.

"Who would shoot a teenager?" Luke questioned. "This is why guns are bad."

I just nodded, letting him ramble on about gun control. I never argue with Luke when he goes on his rants; I just don't listen. For a moment, I let myself think about what Luke would do if I told him. That I saw Nick before he died. I pushed him, and I ran. Would Luke be mad? Would he tell on me? Would he have done the same?

"I'm going to go in the bathroom," Luke announced. "I'll be right back."

He left the room, shutting the door behind him. I sat there, trying to convince myself to tell him.

He deserves the truth.

Maybe leave out the part about running?

And pushing him.

Maybe just say you got into a fight.

I stood up, running my fingers through my hair. I couldn't figure out what to do. I paced the room, weighing my options. He didn't need to know, but I felt like I owed it to him.

As I walked around the room, I noticed a drawer on Luke's desk that was slightly open. I went over to it and looked inside. It was empty, except for a phone sitting there. The phone had no case, revealing the silver on the backside. I turned it over, and the screen was blank until I turned it on. A picture of Noelle kissing Nick on the cheek appeared.

What?

The phone slipped from my hands, clattering noisily when it fell. I cursed myself, grabbing the phone. I held it inches away from me.

Why would Luke have a picture of Noelle and Nick?

Unless it's not Luke's phone.

I stared at the picture again before typing in the passcode.

If this is Nick's phone, then his password should work.

The phone opened automatically, and the apps appeared. Surprised, I lost my grip on the phone, and it fell again, sliding to the wall. My mind shut down, leaving me helpless at that moment. I could feel the sweat drip off my face.

Why does Luke have Nick's phone?

Footsteps going up the stairs startled me. I ran to the phone, made sure it wasn't broken, and closed it. I threw it back into the drawer and shut it. The second I closed the drawer, I realized I should have taken the phone.

Wait.

I turned to open it back up, but the door opened, and Luke appeared. I turned back toward him and smiled, leaning against his desk.

"What are you doing?" Luke eyed me, slowly stepping into his room.

I chuckled, swallowing a lump in my throat. "Just looking at your messy desk. Seriously, Luke, clean up your crap."

Luke threw his head back, laughing, before he sat back down on his bed. I took the chair out from under his desk and sat there. Luke gave me a look, wondering why I wasn't sitting next to him, but I ignored it.

I felt uneasy knowing Luke had Nick's phone. A million questions ran through my head, most of them concerning me. Luke just smiled awkwardly at me every few seconds while I was lost in my thoughts. After an awkward moment of silence, I figured there was only one way I could break it.

"How was your protest?"

~

Luke and I didn't talk much more after that. He went back to his book, and I was lost in my never-ending worrying thoughts about how Luke got Nick's phone. I stared at the drawer, and it taunted me with my stupidity because I didn't take it.

Should've taken it.

I could have just slid it into my pocket.

He wouldn't have known.

Luke glanced up at me occasionally, and I just pretended to be watching a video on my phone. It was like that until it was time to go to Nick's house.

I guess Ms. Walter's house now.

We said goodbye to Ms. Cloud and Caroline and left. On the walk over, I stayed quiet while Luke had occasional opinions about things we were passing.

"Look at that tree; it's dying."

"Oh, why can't people just walk; they are polluting the air."

"That reminds me of a protest I went to…"

I nodded and grunted along for most of what he was saying, still stuck on how he got Nick's phone. I tried to push the thoughts away, but the more I tried, the more questions I had.

Maybe they hung out before and left his phone?

But then wouldn't Luke have told the police or me?

Luke and I made it to the house, and I noticed Mom's car sitting in the driveway. I looked up to see the bright red door that I've walked through so many times.

I was wandering outside of the house. I was probably five or six, maybe younger. Mom was busy finding Henry an outfit to wear. We were going to go to my grandparents' house, but I didn't want to go. So, while Mom was distracted with Henry and Dad was watching a game, I snuck out the door. I walked a few streets down; cars passed me by without another thought. I noticed this kid sitting on his lawn with a red door behind him. He was holding a yellow truck and was moving it through the grass. I ran up to him and watched him play.

I realized that he looked a lot like the kids I stole toys from at school. I thought I could steal his, and he would cry. I wanted to make him cry. I snatched the truck from his hands, and that's when he looked up at me.

I was expecting tears, screaming, and even him fighting back. But he just smiled and let me take it.

"That's okay," he said. "I can share."

I was taken aback. I wanted to see him cry. I wanted to make him cry and beg for his toy back. But he didn't. I grinned and sat down. I started playing with it, and he watched me, still smiling. After a few minutes, he jumped up, gasping.

"I got this new toy, and I think you would like it a lot. Come on!" He raced toward his door, and I followed suit. The first time I walked through that door.

I opened the door, seeing that it was unlocked. Luke and I walked in; Mom and Ms. Walter were at the table drinking out of their mugs.

"Hey, hun," Mom said, placing her mug down and hugging me. She gave Luke one too before going back to her seat. Ms. Walter waved at us before speaking.

"Forgive me; my feet are so sore. I'll give you a hug later, boys."

I nodded, knowing that she's a waitress and is on her feet all day. Nick used to massage her feet to help ease the pain.

I wonder what she does now.

She told us that we can go through Nick's room for anything that is ours or if we wanted anything.

"Wait." I hesitated. "Are you getting rid of his stuff?"

She gave me a faint smile, nodding. "I can't keep it all. I'll get some things, but that's still his room. I don't need all of the gadgets he had."

I could tell she was having a difficult time talking about him, so I just nodded. Luke and I walked down the hall, passing the game room they had.

Game room is a bit too much of a stretch. They had no pool table or arcade games. It was a room filled with board games and cards and a table in the center to play on. There was a couch behind it with stains from soda and pizza.

"You cheated!" Nick laughed. We were about nine at the time, and I was invited over for a game night. Nick pointed a finger in my face, accusing me of taking Monopoly money. I did cheat, but I wasn't going to let him call me a liar.

"I did not!" I defended myself, sticking my nose up in the air. Ms. Walter was giggling from the couch, drinking her soda to hide her laughter. Nick crossed his arms and started screeching again.

"Then how did you have all that money?"

"You landed on my property like five times!"

Nick shook his head. "It wasn't worth that much!"

Ms. Walter grabbed another slice of pizza from the box, still laughing at the fact that we were arguing. "I don't know, Nick; you did land on it a few times."

I beamed at Ms. Walter, who winked at me. Nick gaped at his mother for betraying him. He took his hands and acted as if a sword went through his body, and he fell to the floor, throwing his hands into the air. Ms. Walter snorted at the sight of her son playing dead. I giggled, standing over his body.

I growled, lunging after him. He rolled to his side, missing my pretend punch. Ms. Walter stood up, clapping her hands together.

"Boys, boys. No need to fight. Let's go get ice cream."

Nick and I were tangled together, rolling on the floor. We both stopped and grinned before racing out of the room and into the kitchen.

Luke was ahead of me, standing by the picture frame on the wall. It was a picture of Ms. Walter and Nick at some fair. Nick was grinning from ear to ear, and Ms. Walter had that smile on her face. They had their arms around each other, holding on tightly.

"It's just not fair." Luke choked. I could see tears welling in his eyes, but he pushed them away. One slipped and slid down his face. He quickly wiped it away, and I placed my hand on his shoulder to let him know it was okay.

The phone.

Why would Luke have his phone?

I retracted my touch as if I burned it on the stove. Luke didn't notice my reaction and continued walking down the hall. My stomach was flipping around as I followed him. Every thought in my head screamed to confront him, but I ignored them as best as I could.

What if I hallucinated it?

What if I'm not better and Luke sees me as a crazy person?

I pushed all feelings and thoughts deep down to my core and tried to keep them there as long as I could. I passed by the bathroom, where Nick and I got ready for our first high school dance.

"Dude, I'm not getting ready with you in the bathroom," I complained to Nick. "That's what chicks do."

At this time, I thought saying chicks was so cool. Which made everyone's eyes roll to the back of their head when I opened my mouth.

"Come on, it will be fun," Nick rebutted. "Besides, no one is going to see."

I groaned and stepped inside the tiny bathroom. The walls and tiles matched, which made me feel uneasy. The sink was small, with an even smaller mirror hanging over it. The two of us could barely fit in the bathroom. We had to take turns sitting on the toilet while the other got the mirror.

Nick sat down on the toilet and tried his best to do his hair. He would comb through it, then peek in the mirror, then sit back down to fix it. I told him to go first, so then I was sitting on the toilet while he did his hair.

"What do you think about me asking Noelle to dance with me tonight?" he asked out of nowhere. I scoffed at him, putting on the shoes that Dad got me. He raised his eyebrow, waiting for an answer.

"I don't care," I replied, truthfully. I really didn't care. She was just a friend of mine. It didn't bother me.

Nick nodded, returning to his mess of hair. He grabbed gel from the counter to make his hair spike up. When he did, he frowned, then just flattened it out. I peeked into the mirror just to straighten my tie. The door slammed open, and our moms were standing there with their phones, blinding us with the flash.

"Smile!" Mom yelled, snapping pictures of us.

"You boys look so cute!" Ms. Walter exclaimed, shining the light in our faces.

Nick and I both yelled, telling them to get out. I closed the door, locking it. Nick laughed and looked back into the mirror.

"They just love us."

"A little too much," I muttered.

Luke and I ended up in Nick's room after what seemed like an hour of us roaming around. His room was thrown around. Clothes everywhere, books on the floor, posters that fell halfway down. No trash from what I could see other than some plastic bottles. I started going through his clothes, seeing if he had any shirts of mine, while Luke went to his bookshelf. I picked up one shirt that belonged to me. It was something that had a band logo on the front. I hadn't listened to the band in a long time. I held it in my hands, something telling me to put it back down. I sighed and placed it back on the floor.

"I can't do it either," Luke admitted, holding two books. "They're still his." He placed them back on the shelf and walked toward me.

"What should we do?" I asked, kicking some jeans out of the

way. It revealed another shirt he borrowed from me. This one was stained badly with what looked like pizza sauce.

"Why don't we just clean it," Luke offered, picking up a magazine. I turned to him, and he continued. "Like make it neater so Ms. Walter doesn't feel like she has to get rid of anything. That way if we ever did want our things back, we could just grab them."

What he said made sense, but the idea of cleaning my dead best friend's room made me feel sad. I thought of Ms. Walter and how hard she worked and how alone she must have felt in this house without Nick, so I agreed.

We spent the next two hours cleaning Nick's room. I started in his closet, hanging up things that fell off hangers and placing things in his drawers. Luke cleaned up his desk and bed, making them look neat. One side of his pillow had a large purple stain, so Luke just flipped it over. We both cleaned up the floor together, throwing things out in his trash can. When we finished, we heard a knock at the door.

Mom stood there in the doorway and smiled. She walked in, giving both of us a hug. "You guys are so sweet." After a few moments, we heard a gasp from the hallway.

We all turned to see Ms. Walter with her hand over her chest. Tears swelled in her eyes, and she looked at us. "You boys did this?"

We nodded. Luke said, "We didn't want you to give his things away, so we just tidied it up."

Ms. Walter beamed at us, pulling us in for a hug. Luke and I were at her sides, facing each other, while she lay her head on top of ours. Luke stared into my eyes, and for a split second, they changed. Then he smiled.

What I saw behind his eyes was something I have never seen before. It was quick but not unnoticeable. Fear built inside me as I realized what it was.

Anger.

18

Day Thirty

I ignored Luke as best as I could. It felt like he did the same because he never reached out to me either. It was as if we both had an unspoken agreement about not talking to each other. I wasn't sure why he wasn't trying to speak to me, but I thought it was for the best.

My days were spent being consumed by varied reasons as to why Luke had Nick's phone and why he looked angry at his house. Luke was never angry. He was the peaceful, happy kid that always had a smile on his face.

Was he faking?

This morning my parents announced that I was going to see a therapist. I tried to resist, but Mom said it was completely necessary.

"We were thinking about it before," she admitted, getting ready to take me. "Then Mr. Finn advised us to so that pretty much made us sure that you needed one."

"Remind me to thank him." I rolled my eyes. She huffed and gave me the stare. She eyed my pajamas and pointed to my room without saying a word. I groaned aloud and dragged my feet up the stairs. I quickly changed into sweatpants and a hoodie. My eyes caught my reflection in the bathroom mirror.

That damn mirror.

I stood in the doorway between my room and the bathroom. The sun was burning through the windows, shining onto my white tiles. I walked inside and placed my hands on my counter. I looked into the mirror to find my reflection staring back at me. I observed him, making sure there weren't any tricks my mind was playing with me. After a few minutes, I realized that the only thing in the mirror was myself.

Take that, stupid mirror.

See? I don't need therapy.

I walked down the stairs to be met with my impatient mother, standing there rolling her eyes at my outfit. She was dressed in a purple blouse and a black skirt.

"No scrubs today?" I asked.

"No," she muttered, shoving her phone into her pocketbook. "I am taking you to therapy, and that is all I'm doing today."

She rushed me into the car, complaining that we were late. The office wasn't that far from our house, but it felt forever. It felt like bees were swarming in my stomach, making me feel queasy. Mom kept telling me I was going to be fine, but I didn't believe her.

We arrived after a few minutes and walked inside. The place was odd for a therapy office. I thought it was going to be dimmed lights and wood-themed, with dark cushioned seats. The couch was bright blue, and there was a magazine stand made of marble. The lighting was quite blinding and seemed brighter than the sunshine outside. I sat down on the couch while Mom met with my therapist. They were in there for about ten minutes, and I passed the time reading a cooking magazine.

"Kyle?" a deep voice asked. I looked up to be faced with the exact therapist I was expecting to meet. His oval-shaped glasses sat on the bridge of his nose. He was wearing a brown jacket over a beige shirt, paired with some brown trousers. His head was shaved to a buzz cut, and he was wearing suspenders.

"Yep," I announced, standing up. "That's me."

And I had such high hopes for this guy.

He walked me to his office, where I passed Mom, who was leaving. She gave me a quick hug and told me she would be waiting. I walked inside and noticed his office matched the lobby of this place. Everything matched except him. He sat down in his baby-blue-colored chair, and I sat down on the couch.

"Hello, Kyle," he stated. "My name is David Collins." He took out a folder and already started to write things down.

I didn't even do anything yet.

"Hello," I replied, cautious of what I was saying. I felt the bees sitting in my stomach stinging me with each second that passed by.

"So, have you done therapy before?" he asked, still writing things down. His pen moved in the same motion on different areas of the paper, which made me wonder what he was writing.

I shook my head. "No, sir."

"Alright, let me walk you through it," he offered, shutting his folder. This was the first time his eyes were looking at me since we walked through the room, and my gut screamed at me not to trust this guy. "Everything you say is confidential. I will not share it with anyone, not even your parents."

That's good.

"However," he stated, "if I feel like you are going to hurt someone or yourself, I have to report it."

I nodded, everything making sense. "Got it."

"Good." He smiled, opening his folder back up. "Now, with that being said, have you thought about hurting others or yourself?"

Is he serious?

I was waiting for him to laugh and ask me an actual question, but he was staring at me blankly. He was seriously asking me this. I just shook my head. I watched as he wrote it down, scanning the papers before continuing the questionnaire.

He went through this entire packet of questions that "got to know me better." After we finished the folder, he placed it to the side and grabbed a notebook. After writing a few things down, he looked up at me and smiled.

"Now, Kyle, let's talk about Nick."

Nick?

"How do you know about Nick?" I asked.

"Your mother informed me about Nick and Max in our brief meeting. She said that's what she is worried about the most."

"There's nothing to be worried about."

He nodded, almost mocking me. The bees had flown away and were replaced with boiling hot lava. I felt my tongue ignite with curse words I wanted to scream at this guy.

"When was the last time you saw Nick?" he asked.

I thought about it, and I realized I could tell him the truth; he wouldn't say anything to anyone. If I left out the actual hurting people part, I would be safe.

"We were in an argument," I admitted.

"About what?"

"A girl."

He wrote this down in his book before asking me to elaborate.

"He started dating this girl named Noelle," I explained. "She was my best friend, but I had feelings for her." His pen clicked. "And that day, she came to me upset about her relationship, saying that she thought Nick was cheating on her." Pen clicked again. He pushed his glasses up his face and started writing.

"Did he?" Dr. Collins asked.

I shrugged my shoulders. "I don't know. He claims he didn't, but I don't think Noelle would lie."

He nodded. "And you and Nick fought because he cheated on Noelle?"

I shook my head. "No, we fought because Nick thought I was the one to tell Noelle. When I saw him get so heated, I poked fun at him, which just got him even madder. And he pushed me, which got me mad."

His eyebrows furrowed together as he tried to keep up with my story, writing it down. My hands itched to snap that pen in half. After writing for a while, he looked up at me and asked me another question.

"So, you killed him?"

My heart jumped out of my chest. I could feel my bones shaking to my core. Shivers were sent down my spine.

"What?" I spat.

"I asked when was that—"

I stood up, not letting him finish. "Don't lie to me!"

His eyes widened as I jumped up. He put the notebook down before standing up with me. "Kyle—"

"No," I barked at him. "Shut up!"

It came in flashes. It was as if I blacked out. I only remember bits and pieces of the rest of that session. Glass breaking. Yelling that came from me. Someone was bleeding. The door opening. Bookshelf being knocked over. When it was over, I finally saw the room and the blood on my hands. I was the one doing everything. Dr. Collins stood there with his arms crossed next to my mother, who was wide-eyed at everything. Her eyes landed on mine before turning to Dr. Collins.

"I'm so sorry. We will pay for everything to be fixed." She apologized, taking out her checkbook. Dr. Collins nodded, taking the check without hesitation.

Don't give him money.

"I fear Kyle has some anger issues that I cannot resolve," he started, staring at me. "I believe anger management would be best suited for him. However, I would be fine to see him after he completes it."

Blood trickled down my hands, dropping onto the carpet. It was blue, so the red would stain. The pain wasn't bad; it just stung. I turned my hand to the side to let the blood fall onto the ground.

"Kyle!" Mom scolded, grabbing my wrists. "Stop that."

I held my hand up to stop the blood as she asked. Dr. Collins asked us to stay for a few more minutes so he could talk about my diagnosis.

I was here for five minutes; how does he know about my diagnosis?

"I know it may seem early, only one hour..." he started, sitting down on his chair. "But I have some thoughts besides anger management."

An hour?

I was breaking things for an hour?

Mom and I sat down on the couch across from him. I was holding my bloody hand in my lap, so I didn't get it on anything else. It created a pool of liquid in my palm, swirling around.

"I believe Kyle has PTSD from Max and Nick dying," Dr. Collins admitted.

I shook my head. "No, I don't."

Mom shushed me and told Dr. Collins to continue.

You're really believing some nerd with glasses over your son?

"While his 'fit' was going on, he claimed I was accusing him of murder," he explained.

"I thought this was confidential?" I challenged.

He looked at me, nodding his head. "It is, unless it could harm you or others. I think you blame yourself for Max and Nick dying. Some things that were stated were worrying me that you might hurt yourself."

I rolled my eyes and sat back, still being careful with the blood. Mom leaned forward, listening intensely. I wanted to tell her not to believe him, but she would've just shushed me.

She and Dr. Collins talked for a few minutes before we left. I was given a paper towel to clean up my hand. I dipped the edges into the pool of blood, watching the white cloth turn bright red, soaking up the blood. Dr. Collins gave me a weird stare, but I ignored him, dipping all the edges into the blood.

I had no idea what they talked about. My ears felt blocked; everything was faint for me.

I'm sure I was being yelled at by Mom when we left. She pushed me into the car, threw her bag into the back, and then reversed. I watched her mouth open and close a bunch of times. I couldn't tell if she was talking or breathing through her mouth. The entire car ride was silent for me. Not even the sound of passing cars filling my ears like they normally did.

We arrived at home, and Mom got a phone call. I stayed in the car with her, my hearing coming back. She grabbed her phone and answered it.

"Hello?" She looked at me. "Yes, I'll come in. Not a problem. Bye."

She hung up, grabbing her bag. She started shuffling things around, grunting.

"They need me to go into work. Henry will be home soon, so you won't be alone for long."

My parents were so afraid to leave me home alone since Nick died. Which meant that I didn't get the chance to start figuring out who would kill Nick.

"That's okay," I told her. "I'll be fine."

It would give me time to think about who would do this to Nick. I left the car and ran inside the house, but not before waving goodbye to Mom. I went to my room to find an empty journal. I started to write down everything I knew.

Nick and I were in a fight. I pushed him, and he fell. But I didn't kill him; there was a gunshot. I thought it was hunters, but someone was trying to kill him. Or me.

The realization hit me. That person could have been trying to kill me and missed. I took a shaky breath in, trying to calm myself. The lock on my door taunted me, telling me to lock it. I obeyed the orders out of fear. I sat back down to continue writing.

Someone knew about our argument and didn't say anything. They could've been a witness and blamed the whole thing on me, but they didn't.

Why?

If someone saw us in the woods and saw me push him, why wouldn't they just go to the police? I leaned back in my chair, knowing that nothing made sense. I had no idea why someone would've wanted me or Nick dead. Then I remembered Mark. If Mark was on drugs, maybe it was he who shot Nick. But he was beaten almost to death after Nick went missing.

Luke had Nick's phone after they announced he was dead.

How did he get the phone?

A door opening and closing downstairs startled me, making my chair fall backward. I could hear Henry walk through the house. I knew it was him because of his car outside. I went down the stairs to find Henry in the kitchen with a plastic bag. It looked like he had gloves and hydrogen peroxide.

"What are you doing with plastic gloves and hydrogen peroxide?" I asked, poking at his bags.

He turned around and rolled his eyes. "Not that it's any of your business, but a bird hit my car and splattered blood all over the side. I read online that that stuff gets it out."

I nodded, sitting down on the chair by the table. Henry turned back around and continued going through the cabinets. He finally gave up and just grabbed a water bottle from the fridge.

"How was therapy?" Henry asked, sitting down in front of me. I was shocked that he was even asking me questions.

"Um," I said. I didn't want to admit what happened at therapy.

"It was fine."

He nodded, taking a sip from his water bottle. He swallowed before speaking.

"Mom said you went crazy on the dude and tried to kill him."

My head snapped up to meet his taunting eyes. He smirked at me, knowing he got the reaction he wanted. I watched as he shrugged his shoulders and chuckled at me. I felt my nose twitch with anger.

"You don't know what you are talking about, Henry," I spat at him, pushing my chair back. "I got mad, that's all."

He pointed at my hands and grinned. "Is that why you're bleeding?"

I looked down to see blood pouring from my previous glass cuts. I hadn't realized I was clutching my fists until then. My nails must have reopened the wounds that crossed my palms. They trickled from the middle of my palm and to the bottom on both sides, almost reaching my wrists.

"Shut up, Henry," I warned him. I could feel heat radiating off my body. I wanted to hurt him. I wanted to grab him by the head and bounce it off the dining table.

"At least I don't need to see a therapist," he pointed out, walking away. His back was facing me now, so I couldn't see his face.

"That's because you have more problems than a therapist could solve." I snorted. "You're a psychopath."

As soon as the word left my mouth, I regretted it. I watched his head snap to the side. His face wasn't smirking any more. His eyes were dark. I watched as he threw the water bottle to the side, the plastic breaking open and spilling water everywhere. Before I knew what was happening, he was standing in front of me with his hand wrapped around my throat. I could feel his grip getting tighter as I lost the ability to breathe. I tried to yell, but his hands were holding my vocal cords. All that came out of me were grunts. I watched as his eyes turned darker and darker. I could feel the color draining from my face. My eyes wanted to pop out of their sockets because of the pressure. Henry just grinned and tightened his grip on me.

I pried at his hands, trying to get them off. But they wouldn't come loose. It felt like we were standing there like that for hours. I even tried kicking him, but I could only land them on his knees, which didn't affect him. He kept holding on to my throat, making my lungs beg for air.

I hope I pass out.

I could feel darkness swarming me. I was waiting to black out, so I didn't need to feel my lungs burning without oxygen. His eyes maintained on mine the entire time, like a lion killing its prey. Suddenly, it was gone. Like a switch, the anger left his eyes, and his face dropped. He let his hands loose, and I fell to the floor, gasping for air. Henry stared at me, watching as I grabbed at my neck, filling my lungs with air. I still felt the pain of his hands there; I still felt the scorching hot pain my lungs were going through. I looked back at Henry, who had a blank expression on his face.

"I'm going to my room," he stated, grabbing his bag then leaving. I watched as he walked down the stairs, slamming the door behind him.

I lay on the kitchen floor, begging to pass out. Begging that I would forget this happened. That this was a hallucination. That my brother didn't try to kill me.

Please.

19

Day Thirty-one

I tried my best to ignore Mom and Dad, so they never saw the marks around my neck. I wanted to tell them what happened, but I didn't think they would believe me. I had just gotten out of the mental hospital because of subconscious self-harming. They would send me right back.

Luckily, I didn't see them that morning. I heard Mom knocking on my door, and I pulled my blanket all the way so it was practically covering my entire neck and pretended to be asleep. She just opened the door, looked at me, then left. I crawled out of bed when I knew Dad and Mom were gone, and I went into the bathroom. The mirror showed me a swollen neck that was badly bruised. I didn't want to try to speak out of fear of worsening it. Redness circled my eyes that looked bloodshot. Anyone looking at me would think I was high.

I threw on a hoodie and hid it as best as I could. Walking downstairs, I knew Henry was still home, so I kept my head down. He was sitting at the dining table on his phone. He didn't even look at me when I left through the front door. I texted Marie and told her that I was going over to her house. She didn't reply, but that didn't stop me.

Parts of my bruised neck were showing from the front of the hoodie, causing stares. I tried my best to hide it, but you could see the marks of the hands that choked me. A mother took her children and crossed the road with them, just to avoid walking past me. I knew it was my fault because when I turned around to look at them, she was crossing back over.

I made it to Marie's and knocked on her door, eager to get inside. Marie opened the door, facing the ground. She was looking at something on her phone.

"Hey, Kyle," she said, moving out of the way. "I was just about to text you back, but I got distracted on—" She looked up to my face. "Holy hell! What happened to you?"

I pushed past her, walking straight up the stairs. I heard her mumbling about me being a rude guest, but I didn't want her grandparents to see me. I shuffled into her room, pulling my hoodie back. She stomped in, stopping when she saw my entire face.

"Kyle, are you high?" she asked, just staring into my bloody eyes. She focused on my neck. She gulped, taking a step closer to shut the door. "Did you do that?"

"No," I groaned, my voice hoarsely toying with me. It was a struggle to even get my throat damp enough to speak. Swallowing was even more painful this time than the last time this happened.

"Woah. Don't talk," Marie said. "You'll just make it worse." She placed a pillow at the edge of her bed for me to lay my head on. "You need to rest."

I nodded, putting my feet up on her bed. Her pillow was soft and covered with a band logo.

"Was this Henry's doing?" she asked, taking my shoes off.

Marie might not have realized it, but she had motherly instincts. She would've never admitted it either. In the hospital, she always made sure I was eating and checked up on me constantly. Any time another patient would give me trouble, she was right there, backing me up. Even now, she takes care of me in a way I never imagined someone would. Not even my parents.

She was my sister.

My family.

I didn't say anything, and that was more than enough of an answer for her. She placed my shoes down before pacing the room. I felt her anger bouncing off the walls. Her arms were crossed, and I could see her nostrils flaring.

"I'm going to kill him," she threatened. "Doesn't he care about you at all? He knows you've been through this before; this could cause serious, permanent damage to your throat."

I closed my eyes and let exhaustion take over. Marie was still fuming, with her veins popping out. I didn't fall asleep, but I was happy just lying there.

"I bet he's the one that killed Nick."

I sat up, pain shooting from my neck down my spine. I

gasped at the sudden discomfort and reached for my neck. Marie came stumbling over, helping me sit up straight.

"That was kind of stupid, Kyle," she fumed. I eyed her while moving my neck in a circular motion to relieve the pain. Marie sat there with her eyes furrowed together.

"I'm fine." I tried to convince her in a raspy voice. She shushed me again before standing up. She pulled out a notebook and a pen and handed them to me. I hesitated before grabbing them, realizing I had no other choice.

—Is this really necessary?—

Marie was standing over my shoulder, reading as I wrote.

"Yes," she replied. "Now, was this Henry's doing?"

I went to nod, but the pain from my neck stopped me. I groaned, writing down my answer. I watched as the second I wrote Y, she was steaming.

"Why?"

I shrugged my shoulders, then thought about it.

—He is psychotic.—

Ever since we were younger, Henry had a weird obsession with pain and items that caused pain. Mom would find him playing with knives or scissors. He had a fish when he was five but took it out of the water to watch it suffer. Mom bought him a new one, which he strangled with his fingers. As he grew up, he stopped killing things. But his obsession with dangerous objects grew. He started playing with fire, burning anything flammable I had. Guns were something on his list, but Mom and Dad never allowed him to. If he knew about the pistol in Mom's drawer, someone would probably be dead.

"I can see that," Marie agreed. "Was he always like this?"

—Yes. Except he never got this physical before.—

Henry never hurt Max or me until Max died. Then Henry used me as his punching bag. Nothing too scary, but enough to make me cry and get him in trouble. Growing up, I feared Henry. Even with Max. Everyone did. I would overhear my parents wondering what to do with him. Max was the only one who wasn't afraid of Henry. He would play with him and not get mad when Henry broke a toy. And he was the first one to greet him when Henry came home from school.

Marie got quiet and sat down on the bed. "I was just rambling earlier, but..." She paused for a moment. "Do you think he was capable of killing Nick?"

Henry was scary, but there was no way he murdered Nick. I knew he wouldn't have done that.

—No, because Henry isn't capable of killing humans. There's no way. Besides, he has no reason to kill Nick.—

Marie nodded, leaning back on her bed. She stared at the ceiling for a while, keeping her thoughts to herself. I nudged her so she would talk to me. She looked at me from her position before groaning and sitting back up.

"It's just, it doesn't make sense to me as to why someone would kill Nick," she confessed. "I never knew the guy, but I did a lot of research on him, and no one hated him!"

I should tell her about the phone.

—Luke has Nick's phone.—

I handed her the notebook and watched her eyes widen. She snapped her head back to me and pushed it back into my hands. "Elaborate, please."

—I was at his house and found it in his drawer. It was Nick's phone. A picture of Noelle and Nick was in the background, and I unlocked it with his passcode.—

Her eyes scanned the paper, grinning with each second that passed. She stood up, running over to her desk. I went to follow her, but my muscles were sore. Marie came back to me, showing me a new notepad that flipped back like a policeman's one.

"I stole it," she admitted. Her pen traced the paper, eyes going back and forth. "This is an investigation. Everyone is a suspect unless proven otherwise."

I snatched the paper from her.

—This isn't some stupid game. My best friend is dead.—

She looked at me with empathetic eyes; she held the notebook down in her lap. "I didn't mean it that way, Kyle. But you know damn well that the police aren't going to do anything. It's in our hands now. We are going to find out what happened to Nick."

She was right. The biggest lead that the police had was that the blood from the forest was his, and he was killed with a gun. Anyone with a DNA tester and half a brain could've figured that out. Ms. Walter complained about how the police said they had nothing. That the guy in the forest was a pro. He knew what he was doing.

I nodded. Marie smiled, continuing to write down things in her little notepad. Her eyes lit up, and she turned to me.

"We should go back to his house and steal the phone!" She grabbed my arm, gasping. "There could be clues that could help us."

I shook my head. I wasn't going back into Luke's house until I knew it was safe. Deep down, I knew Luke couldn't hurt anyone. He goes to protests to give rights to trees—there was no way he could do this.

But what if it's all an act?

"I get it," Marie said. "We will just have to do our investigating from far away." She put her notebook in her back jean pocket. "Besides, Luke doesn't seem like the murdering type. Maybe he just found the phone and didn't know what to do with it."

I grunted in response, making my throat burn. I almost had to gasp for air. My phone started ringing in my pocket, and I pulled it out. The hospital where Mark was, was calling me. I pointed to it and showed it to Marie.

"What do they want?" she asked. I shrugged my shoulders. She snatched the phone from me and answered it. I tried to grab it from her, but she pushed me away.

"Hello?" she asked. I couldn't hear what the hospital was saying. "This is his sister."

I dropped my hands and almost laughed at her. She narrowed her eyes at me before putting her finger to her lips to shush me. I leaned back, knowing there was no way I was getting the phone from her.

"Okay, I understand."

I sat up, fear stunning my body. I wasn't sure what had happened, but my mind was tormenting me with what they could've said.

"I'll let him know. Yep, goodbye."

Marie hung up the phone, giving it back to me. She placed her hands in her lap and started eyeing the room. I sat there, patiently, waiting for her to tell me what they said. After a few seconds, I hit her shoulder. Not hard, but enough to get my point across.

"Ow!" she yelped. "What was that for?"

I gawked at her, holding up the phone. A smirk rested on her face as she leaned back.

"That was a private phone call."

My hand slapped her shoulder again.

"Okay! Ow!" She started giggling. "You hit like a child. Anyways, they said that they want you to go in and see Mark. He's been asking about you."

I grabbed the notebook and pen.

—He can't speak; how is he asking about me?—

"Perhaps the same way you are talking to me," she guessed. "Come on, let's go see Mark. I can be your voice."

She stood up, patting my legs. When I remained sitting still, she grabbed my arms and forced me up.

"Look, I can be you." She cleared her throat and started talking in a high-pitched voice.

"Hi, I'm Kyle. I don't like feelings." She made her voice crack a couple of times, which made her burst out laughing. After a few minutes of her giggling like a little girl, she sighed.

"Alright, I'm ready to go."

~

Marie and I got to the hospital, and it was the same as it always was. Not a lot of people doing their jobs. I shrugged my hoodie up and held it there so no one would notice the handprints on my neck. I knew exactly where to go, so I just passed the front desk.

Marie whispered behind me, "Don't we need to sign in?"

I shook my head, swallowing a little bit before whispering back. "They don't care."

Whispering was the only thing that didn't cause me pain. It stung a little, but it was worth it if I could talk now and then. Marie followed me down the halls and into the children's part. It was almost silent when we walked in. I noticed only one nurse was working, and not a lot of kids were around.

The nurse's name was Shelly. I had met her a few times before while visiting Mark. She was the only one that did some amount of work. Not enough for her to gain all my respect, but more than others there. I waved, and she smiled, asking me to come over.

Great.

I made my way over to her, leaving Marie behind. She hadn't noticed I left until a few moments later when she came running behind me.

"Next time, tell me when you are leaving to have a conversation with someone," she muttered in my ear, smiling at Shelly. I just grinned, wanting to laugh at her.

Shelly put her phone aside and leaned forward on the desk. "Kyle, is this your girlfriend?"

Marie gagged, tilting her head to the side. Shelly had a confused look on her face.

"No," Marie said, "he's my brother."

"I'm not your brother," I whispered harshly.

"He's sick," Marie explained. Shelly nodded, still looking at us wide-eyed. "And my brother."

I groaned. "She's my friend."

"Best friend."

I rolled my eyes, waving Shelly goodbye. I grabbed Marie and pulled her down the hallways.

"I don't want you to be my voice any more," I complained. She gasped, yanking her arm out of my grasp.

"Why?" she cried. "I did such an excellent job!"

I chuckled at her, turning into the hallway where Mark was staying. I could see him, and he looked a lot better. He wasn't as tired-looking, and his head wasn't wrapped in a very thick white bandage any more. Well, it looked thinner to me, but I don't know much about those things. He grinned when he saw me, waving Marie and me down. Marie waved back.

I realized that Marie had never met Mark. She only knew stories of what I told her, and up until a couple of days ago, she hated him. Now she was grinning at him, beaming.

When we walked in, I realized that Marie was right earlier. He was holding a whiteboard and an erasable marker. He held it up to show us what was written.

—Hello!—

We smiled, sitting down in the hospital chairs. I took the one closest to Mark while Marie sat down in the corner. Mark started to wipe his board before writing again.

—How are you?—

I opened my mouth to speak, but Marie did it for me.

"We're good," she answered, walking over. She stood over

me and placed a hand on my shoulder. "Our poor boy has a sore throat and can barely talk."

Mark's face fell, and he stared at me. He pointed to my eyes that were still red. Marie turned to see what he was pointing at and nodded.

"Yeah, he was crying and rubbing his eyes."

I poked her shoulder, shaking my head. She waved her hand in my face, telling me to shut up. Mark showed us his whiteboard.

—Why was he crying?—

I looked at Marie since she was apparently so good at winging it.

"He misses Nick."

Really?

Mark nodded, writing something down again. It took him a few minutes, so I gave Marie a look. She scrunched her face up as a response.

—It's okay. Me too, but they will find him.—

Find him?

He doesn't know.

I looked up at Mark, who had hope filling his eyes. He gave me a soft smile. Marie was staring at me. I could hear her swallow a lump in her throat. She cleared her throat, eyes trailing around the room. I couldn't believe that this hospital wouldn't tell him anything.

I thought about the last time I was here, when Mark was freaking out about the photo that I showed him.

Freaking out about Luke.

I held my hand out for his board, and Mark gave it to me; Marie peeked over my shoulder to look at what I was writing.

—Do you remember the last time I was here?—

Mark read it and started thinking about it. He shook his head at me.

—Do you know who did this to you?—

He read it; his eyes darkened. Marie took a step back, never seeing this side of Mark before. He shook his head and started writing something down.

—I can't remember.—

A doctor walked in, smiling at us. "Oh good, he has visitors."

"Yep, is there a chance we could talk to you in the hall?" Marie asked, pointing to me. The doctor nodded, stepping out of the door. Mark's face was confused, but Marie assured him everything was okay. That we just wanted to know the treatment plan.

Marie shut the door so Mark wouldn't see us yelling at a grown adult. The doctor was looking nervous the second he saw our pissed-off faces.

"Tell me, do you know about Nick Walter?" Marie asked.

The doctor nodded, looking toward the ground. I couldn't believe that this was the hospital I trusted with Mark's life. This man, who spent how long in med school, was being scolded by two teenagers.

"That's why we called Kyle," the doctor admitted. "We wanted him to break the news to Mark. Since they are so close."

Marie nodded. "I get that, but now there's a kid in there who thinks one of his best friends is still alive. Why couldn't you guys explain it to him and then let Kyle fill in the details at a later point, so Mark isn't left in the dark."

Damn, she's good at this.

I just had to keep a straight face on the whole time while Marie yelled at this man. She even started pointing her finger at him and saying how unprofessional the hospital was. The doctor tried to speak multiple times, but Marie cut him off. After a few minutes, the doctor said that there was some other news.

"Just hold on to your news and wait until after we tell Mark that one of his best friends is dead."

We walked back inside to a Mark who was smiling giddily. His eyes brightened when he saw us. I felt every bone in my body tell me not to tell him. To keep him sheltered. I could see that Marie was feeling it too. I didn't want to tell him.

"Mark," I whispered. I leaned closer to him so he would hear me. His eyes dropped, and his smile went away. He pushed his board aside and looked up at me.

"Nick's body was found a few days ago."

I watched his reaction. His face stayed the same. He was just looking at me. His eyes didn't get watery; he didn't grunt or make noises. He just sat there. After a few minutes, I saw a tear slip from his eye. Mark grabbed his board.

—Thank you for telling me. He will be missed.—

I nodded, not pushing it further. Marie was standing by the doorway when the doctor said something to her.

"What?" she screamed, startling everyone within a twelve-mile radius. She looked at Mark and apologized. I watched as she stomped into the hallway. I told Mark I would be right back and followed her out.

"What do you mean he's being transferred?" Marie asked.

"Who's being transferred?" I whispered, looking at the doctor.

"Mark," he explained. "His parents haven't returned any calls, so Mark is being transferred to another facility in New Jersey where they help kids like him, and they work with social services."

"That's a load of bull—"

I grabbed Marie's shoulder, shaking my head. She groaned, crossing her arms over.

"Does he need to move out of this hospital? Why can't social services come here?" I asked.

The doctor avoided my question. "They would be able to help him more there."

"Oh, come on," Marie complained, "you are going to move him to another state where he knows no one just because they couldn't help him find his mommy and daddy?"

I peeked into the window to see Mark speaking with a nurse. Well, writing to a nurse. He noticed me in the window and smiled. He wiped away his previous message and wrote a new one. He showed me his board through the window.

—Isn't the nurse hot?—

I started laughing at him while he grinned at me, erasing it.

I can't let him leave.

He's the last brother I have left.

I lost Nick and Max; Henry was never a real brother to me.

I can't lose him too.

"Why can't he really stay here?" I asked. The doctor looked sheepish, rubbing the back of his neck.

"Okay, we can't afford the things Mark needs to get better," he admitted. "We barely had enough materials to do his surgery the first time, and we fear that if he needs another one, we won't be able to provide it."

Marie stared at the ground. We both knew this hospital wasn't the first choice, but we had no idea the struggles they were going through.

"You could transfer him to Concord General Hospital," I told him.

The doctor shook his head. "There's no way this kid could afford it."

"He will be fine. His dad is a lawyer," I barked.

He argued back. "His dad hasn't reached out to us—"

"Then my parents will take the bill, don't worry about the money."

The doctor sighed, looking at Mark, who was sitting patiently on his bed. "I'll talk to him. This is a decision that he needs to make." He went inside Mark's room, shutting the door behind him.

Marie smirked. "Isn't that your mommy's hospital?"

20

Day Thirty-Three

Mark agreed to be transferred to Concord General Hospital. He had to sign a bunch of papers since he had no family left, which he completed the same day. The next day he was transferred. Mom welcomed him with open arms. She demanded that her staff gave him the best treatment.

Mom had always had a soft spot for Mark, even when he was not so great of a kid. She would stand up for him when his parents weren't around. Always making sure that he was well-fed and had a place to sleep. She saw him as the orphan boy that needed saving. Mom and Dad decided to become Mark's legal guardians. They hired a lawyer and applied for guardianship.

The lawyer came in the next day to give us some news.

"We have a court date!" he announced. "You guys will need to go to court to fill out some papers along with a filing fee, but we are almost there."

They were all sitting around the dining table, having drinks to celebrate. I never understood why Dad did that. He would come home from a court case then say that he needed to change for the celebration. I decided to exclude myself from the party and go see Marie. She had given me some makeup to put on my neck to hide the bruises. The swelling and red, bloodshot eyes were pretty much gone. It doesn't pain me any more to talk either. It just took a lot of ignoring my family to heal properly.

Marie and I met up at the cafe that we went to when she had just gotten out of the psych ward. I arrived a little late, which pissed Marie off.

"What's the point of setting a time if you aren't going to show up until later?" she asked, crossing her arms. I rolled my eyes at her and placed my book bag on the table.

She stared at it, raising her eyebrows at me.

"I thought about what you said," I admitted. "About going to take Nick's phone."

Her eyes glistened, and she slammed her police notebook onto the table. I was going to ask, but then I decided what was the point. She wasn't going to give me a normal answer.

"We could go in and take it, but only the phone," I told her. "I brought gloves, flashlights, and a key he gave me. Along with snacks."

"Why flashlights?" she asked, digging through the bag. "It's still daylight."

"Yeah, but they are home right now. I just happen to know that tonight they are leaving town for a bit. Some charity event in Connecticut."

Marie grinned, leaning back in her chair. "Alright, Mr. Investigator. Guess we have time to spare."

I nodded, looking around the cafe. Not very many people were here, one guy in the other corner typing on a laptop. I remembered the last time we were here; Marie met a girl.

"Marie," I said, grabbing her attention. "How did things go with that basketball girl?"

"Not well," she said, scooting closer to me. "She was so clingy, and I don't know. Her personality was not that great…" I eyed her. "Okay, she was boring."

I laughed at her bluntness. We sat in the cafe for a while, just talking. She was telling me about her therapist appointments and how well she was doing.

"Oh, I completely forgot," she said. "How was yours?"

"Fine." I lied. "He was boring."

She chuckled at me, shaking her head. "Most are."

I didn't want her to get worried about me blacking out and throwing things. I didn't want to scare her, either. Most people wouldn't have been friends with me if they knew that I had anger problems. Nick wasn't afraid.

God, I miss him.

I realized that I never got the chance to miss him. I went through guilt, anger, depression, and fear, but never sadness. When I thought I had killed him, I jumped right into the dark phase where I was terrified to even leave my house. I never even thought about him being gone.

"The sun's going down," Marie informed me. "You know what that means."

I pushed my thoughts away and smiled at her. "Yep, let's go break into someone's house."

Marie and I cleaned up our table and left the cafe. The sun was still setting, so there was some light guiding our way. The sound of honking in the distance was the only thing you could hear. Trees stood still, not a single leaf blowing around. There was no wind this night, which was strange for the middle of March.

By the time we got to Luke's house, it was dark. The only thing helping us see were the flashlights I had. Marie held one in her hand while I carried everything else. We walked to the door, and I opened it with my spare key. The door creaked open, inviting us in. I told Marie to leave her shoes outside, and she gave me a strange look.

"Ms. Cloud doesn't like shoes in her house," I explained, leaving my sneakers under their porch bench. She groaned, plopping her boots next to mine. She gave me a sarcastic smile before going inside. I checked our surroundings to make sure no one saw us. There was nothing around besides the other houses and an empty road. When I made it inside, Marie had her hands touching a small skull that was resting on a shelf. I ran over to her, prying the thing from her grasp.

"We cannot touch anything!" I exclaimed, placing it back where it was.

"Why not? We have gloves."

I rolled my eyes. "If it moves, she will notice."

"Whatever. What's she doing with a skull, anyways? I thought she was all peace for animals and such."

I nodded. "She is. That was their old hamster's head. She likes to keep something to remember them by."

Marie had a disturbed look on her face, looking back at the skull.

"Messed up, I know."

I had Marie follow me to Luke's bedroom, slapping her hands when they reached out to grab stuff. After walking down the hallway, we entered his room, closing the door behind us. I sighed, anxiety finally kicking in. I realized that if we got caught, I didn't know how we would explain this.

Someone could've seen us.

They could've called the police already.

I was so angry with myself for acting like this. I was never like this before. I was the one suggesting these crazy plans, not the one worrying about them. Marie saw the look on my face and asked me what was wrong.

"How do you do it?" I asked her. "How do you just do these things without being nervous?"

She smiled. "I always have a plan if things go wrong."

I raised my eyebrows at her, not believing it.

"Test me," she challenged.

"Police arrive?"

"Show them your spare key, tell them you are house sitting."

"They come back early?"

"You forgot something last time you were here, so you thought you'd just stop by and grab it."

"Alien encounter?"

"Let them take me."

I stared at her, impressed. I slow clapped to show her, which made her laugh. She pointed to her head and tapped on it a few times.

"I always have a plan ready."

Knowing that she was prepared for the worst made my fear ease up. I reached for the drawer, grabbing the phone from it. I unlocked it again to make sure it was Nick's, and sure enough, it slid open. I placed it in my backpack, zipping it back up.

"Alright, let's go," I told Marie. Suddenly, the sound of a door opening and closing rang through the house.

Crap.

Marie looked at me with wide eyes, holding on to my arm.

"I'll go see," I whispered, pulling her hands off my bicep. I went for the door but felt a pull on my back. I turned around to Marie, who was trying to zip my bag.

"What?" I asked her.

She sheepishly held up a flashlight, swinging it around.

I turned back around and walked out the door. I tip-toed down the hall as quietly as I could. The sound of television became louder with each step I took. I peeked into the living room to see a woman sitting on the couch. She had short black hair, and her feet were up on the table.

Caroline.

I felt a hand grab my shoulder, and I opened my mouth to yell but was soon muffled by another hand. I turned to see Marie standing behind me. I pushed her away from me, giving her a look.

"I got curious," she whispered. "Who's that?"

She nodded her head toward Caroline, who was chugging a beer.

"Caroline, Ms. Cloud's girlfriend."

"Does she have a daughter?"

I slowly turned to stare at Marie. "I don't know. Why don't you go ask her?"

She scrunched her face up, turning back to head to Luke's room. I followed suit, trying to come up with a plan. When we got back to the room, I closed the door gently.

"What now?" Marie asked, waving her flashlight.

I looked around his room and noticed a window. I pointed to the window, sliding it open. I looked out and realized it led to a rooftop.

Luke's house is strangely built. His first floor is up pretty high because he had about seven feet in between the ground and his porch. His basement is above ground. It was fun to hide under the porch when we were younger but a pain right now.

I scanned an escape plan from outside and realized what we had to do.

"Okay, so we will go out this window and onto the roof. Then we can jump to that tree over there, climb down it enough to safely land before running." Marie gawked at me, thinking about the plan. She nodded before stepping out of the window. I followed behind her, my feet touching the tiled roof. I watched her grab a thick branch and start monkey climbing her way to the trunk. I let her climb down and get off the tree safely before I went. I held my hands out, grabbing the same branch. My feet were still resting on the roof when I looked down. The fall was quite far. I felt a shift in the tree, and when I looked up, the branch was starting to snap. There was no backing out from the position I was in, so I had to look for a new way out.

Splinters were cutting into my skin while I was finding a new branch. I spotted one a little closer to the ground. I swung my legs a little before jumping. I heard Marie gasp as I flew. But I caught the branch and slowly started to make my way down. I reached the grass before realizing that we didn't have our shoes.

"We need to grab our shoes," I told her. I ran to the front of the house, Marie following me. I saw that the bench where our shoes were was right in front of the living room. One wrong move, and Caroline would catch us. I gulped as I climbed up the stairs, as quietly as I could. Creaking was heard all the way up, but I didn't think it reached her ears because of the TV. Once I got to the last step, I lay down on my stomach so she wouldn't see me from the windows. As I army crawled my way to our shoes, wood stabbed my abdomen. I finally reached the bench and grabbed our things. I repeated the same process back and handed Marie her shoes.

"Thank god, now let's get out of here," she exclaimed, grabbing my wrist.

"Marie," I said, looking at her hands. "Where's the flashlight?"

She stopped in her tracks before turning to me with a terrified look on her face. I groaned, running my fingers through my hair.

"I'll go grab it," she said, walking toward the side of the house. "I know where it is."

I watched as she scaled the tree perfectly. Then I realized something. I walked to the door and knocked on it. The TV noise shut off, and footsteps approached the door. Caroline appeared in front of me.

"Kyle, right?" she asked. "They aren't home right now."

"Yeah, I know," I said. "I left something here last time in Luke's room. I was wondering if I could grab it."

"Of course! Take off your shoes, though," she warned me. I slipped them off and placed them in the same place I did before and walked inside. I said thank you before running to Luke's room. I slammed the door open to see Marie's back. At the sound of the door opening, her body turned into a cat's one when they get scared.

"Who are you?" I gasped in a girly voice. Marie turned

around, fuming. She started hitting me with the flashlight.

"That's. Not. Funny!" After she was done, she asked me, "How did you get in here?"

"I asked Caroline."

She hit me a couple more times after that. I just laughed and took the hits.

"You're mad now, but…" I said, taking the flashlight from her. "She only knows about me, so back out the window you go."

Marie's mouth gaped open, and she narrowed her eyes at me. I left Luke's room, closing the door behind me. I said thank you to Caroline one more time before slipping out the door and grabbing my sneakers. I ran to the front of the house, just in time to see Marie jump to the tree again. Before she did, she gave me the finger.

She handled the jumps perfectly and found her way to the ground, running at me. She put her boots on while swearing. She grabbed the bag from me and started marching down the street and back to my house. I followed closely behind her, scared of what she was going to do next. The entire walk was silent.

When we got to my house, she just walked right in and up the stairs. I followed behind her, seeing Mom stare up the stairs. She turned to me and asked me who that was.

"Marie," I explained. "My new friend."

Mom huffed. "No girls in your room—"

"She's gay!"

I ran to my room where Marie was already waiting for me. She had the bag on the floor, and she was sitting on my bed.

"I'm sorry, but I didn't think about it until you were already on the roof!"

She huffed. "Whatever, let's just look through the phone."

She slid off the bed and onto the floor with her back against the bed frame. I sat across from her, reaching my hand into the bag. I felt around for the phone when I felt something else. It was a book. I took it out and showed it to Marie. It had a faux leather cover and a buckle that snapped open.

"What is this?" I asked her, throwing it in her lap.

"A journal I found in his room," she said, holding it in her hands. "I bet you if he did this or had any idea about it, it would be in here."

"I thought we were only taking the phone?"

"We were," she said, "until I saw this."

She unbuckled the book and started flipping through the pages. I went back into the bag for the phone until I felt it. I pulled it out and went to unlock it when Marie started talking.

"Kyle, you need to see this."

She shoved the book in my face to show me a very disturbing drawing. There was a boy with a knife through his chest. The blood was running down his shirt, and his face was drawn to look like he was screaming for help.

"What the hell is that?"

"This journal is filled with them." She began flipping to another page. This time it was a little boy drowning at the bottom of the pool while another boy stood above the water looking at him.

I snatched the book, staring at the picture.

Is that Max?

Is that me?

"I think it's Luke's drawing journal," Marie said. I stood up, dazed by what I was seeing.

"It can't be," I said. "There must've been a mistake. Luke wouldn't have drawn these pictures. He wouldn't do that."

"Did Luke even know Max?"

"No," I told her, "but kind of. He knows of him, and he knows what happened to him."

I threw the book onto my bed, hearing it hit the mattress. Marie stayed silent, sitting on the floor. She picked up the phone and handed it to me.

"There's only one way to really know if Luke would do this."

I grabbed the phone and sat back down. I turned it on and was greeted by Noelle and Nick. I unlocked it for the third time and was shown all his apps.

"Where to first?" I asked Marie.

"Texts."

I clicked the messenger app. The last one was from me telling him to meet me by the woods. After that, it was Noelle, saying she had a wonderful time. Then his mom asking what he needed from the store.

An uneasy feeling rose in me, guilting me into turning the phone off. I handed it to Marie, unable to go through it any more. He was dead. It felt like I was betraying him.

Again.

Marie opened it, asking for the passcode. I told her, letting her look through it.

"What are you going to look through?"

"Deleted messages," she told me without looking up. "I mean, if you had the phone of someone you just murdered, wouldn't you delete messages that would seem fishy?"

I waited a few seconds before thinking that the whole thing was ridiculous. I stood up and started pacing the room, unsure of what to do. After a few minutes, I was ready to give up.

"Luke is disturbed, but he's not a murderer."

"I wouldn't say that just yet, Kyle," Marie answered, throwing the phone in my direction. "Look at that."

I caught it, looking at the screen. At the top, it read, *Deleted Messages From: Luke.* I scanned the messages until one of them caught my eye. It was sent from Luke.

Dude, I'll kill you.

21

Day Thirty-Four

"Are you serious?" Noelle asked, putting the phone and journal down. "Luke had these things?"

Marie and I were in Noelle's living room, giving her all the evidence we found. We told her that morning that we were coming over because we had something to show her. When we got there, I had to explain that it was about Nick. I pulled everything out of the bag and gave it to her. She scanned the pages of the book, then looked at the text messages Luke sent to him the night that he died.

"We were in his room, and that's where everything was," I admitted, sitting down next to her.

She shook her head. "No, Luke wouldn't do that."

"Exactly what Kyle said," Marie said, pacing around the room. "But it was all there."

Marie said she had swiped the journal from under his mattress. It was sticking out, and she noticed the cover, so she grabbed it. She knew that I wouldn't have taken it if I had known, so she just put it in my bag.

"No," Noelle said in disbelief. She took a breath in, shakily letting it back out. "Luke, he wouldn't do that. Or draw those things. Especially the thing with you and Max."

The drowning picture wasn't the only thing that had Max and me in. There were multiple sketches where Max was dead at my hands. I tried to hide that it affected me so much; that one of my closest friends believed I murdered my little brother.

"I know," I agreed. "But they were all in his room."

Noelle nodded. "Yeah…" I watched as her eyes began to water a little bit. She sniffed, wiping her nose. "Nick was shot. Luke hates guns."

"So, we go back," Marie stated. "Look everywhere in his room. No gun? Then he's in the clear, and someone tried to frame him."

She watches too many crime shows.

She paced the room, thinking. "Or it means he has a partner that did it for him, and he just did the beating part."

Noelle let out a small sob, muffling it with her hand. I tried to comfort her, placing my arm around her shoulder, but she pushed me away. My hands fell to the couch cushion, and I just stared at her.

"Or," Marie said again, "he already got rid of the weapon." She looked at Noelle and realized she was crying. "Oh shoot, sorry."

Noelle faced the other direction, shielding us from her teary face. "No, it's fine. I just need a minute." She got up and went down the hall and into a room. After a few moments of silence between Marie and me, I decided to go see if Noelle was okay.

I walked down the hall and recognized the room she went into. It was the library. We used to spend so much time there together. I barely read, but Noelle always had her nose in a book. I knocked on the door and opened it to see Noelle facing the bookshelves. The entire room was lined with oak wood shelves. You couldn't even see the color of the walls. Bean bags sat around the room as reading spots. There was one big comfy chair in the middle of the room. It looked very odd, but with all the bookshelves, there was no other place to put it.

"What, Kyle?" she barked, not bothering to even turn around.

I walked further into the room. "I came to check on you."

"Since when do you care?"

What the hell?

"You know I care about you, Noelle. Why would you think—"

"Because of everything, Kyle!" She cut me off, throwing her hands in the air as if she had just given up on something. She whipped her head around to look at me. "Last time you were here, you said that I belonged with Nick. The time before that, we kissed. And then today, you tried to hold me."

I shook my head. "Noelle, I was trying to help you today. You were sad—"

"So, you decided to screw with my feelings?"

Her whole body was facing me now. She had her arms

across her chest, holding onto her shoulders. She was shaking, tears streaming down her face. She had to keep wiping them away. She stood on the other side of the huge chair as if it was a shield.

"No," I said cautiously. "Noelle, I never meant to hurt your feelings. I care about you because you're my family. When you cry, it makes me upset because I don't like seeing you hurt."

"That's not love?"

I shook my head. "It's a different type of love. You kissed me because you were lonely and thought I was your only option."

Her head snapped to mine. "That's not true."

"Even if it wasn't true," I continued, "I'm not okay with being second best."

"You're not second to me," she said.

She walked toward me, placing her hands into my hair. Her eyes stared into mine. For a split second, I let myself think of what life would be like if I did love her like I thought I did. I let myself wonder if I could have been happy with Noelle. If we would've lasted forever.

I pushed her hands away, facing the door. "Noelle, I don't want you like that."

I could tell it was harsh. I felt her move away from me, taking steps back. But I knew it was needed for her to understand. Anything that I thought was love wasn't with Noelle. She played me. Maybe not intentionally, but she did. She toyed with my feelings, and perhaps I did the same to her, which is why we wouldn't work.

"You said that you hated seeing me hurt." She sniffed. "Yet you cause me the most pain."

I thought I would've been more upset about what she said, but she was simply scared. She lost her boyfriend and didn't want to lose her best friend.

"Noelle," I called softly, "you don't understand. You don't love me. You love having someone. I was your next option." She paused for a moment, thinking about it. "But you don't need a boyfriend to survive."

I left the room, leaving her in the library. I felt like I was having the same conversation with her over and over again. She needed to get it into her head that her boyfriend was dead, and she didn't need to replace him.

I realized that I only wanted Noelle because I couldn't have her. When she wasn't dating Nick, I had no feelings for her whatsoever. I never even thought of her like that until Nick told me he did. Slowly it started, the obsession with needing her. Noelle wasn't trying to stop me either, though. She liked the attention. She liked having options.

I walked back into the living room, where Marie was sitting on the couch. She stood up when she heard me coming.

"You heard?" I asked.

"The walls aren't soundproof," she said. "I'm sure the neighbors heard."

I laughed, plopping down onto the sofa. Marie sat next to me, kicking her feet up on my lap. Noelle came out a few moments later, her face bright red.

"Okay, so what's the plan?" she asked, sitting on the ottoman. Marie gave me a side-eye, and I just shrugged.

"We haven't gotten that far yet," I admitted. "This was kind of the last thing we planned out."

Marie nodded, looking at Noelle. "We know that we should keep our distance from Luke. Unless there are other people around."

We all agreed, saying that it was safer that way. My phone went off, and the name Luke appeared on my screen. I stood up, fear running through my body. I felt my throat go numb, inhibiting my ability to swallow.

"What's wrong?" Marie asked. I showed her my phone, and her eyes went wide.

Noelle sat up. "What?"

"Text from Luke," Marie told her.

From: Luke
Hey, I just got home from the charity event in Connecticut. I was wondering if you wanted to hang out at my house later? My mom is going out with Caroline again.

"What does he want?" Noelle asked, trying to peek at my phone.

"He wants to hang out with me later when his mom won't be home," I explained. Marie snatched the phone from my hands. Noelle shuffled over to her to see the text as well. The air around me felt thick, making it harder to breathe. I didn't know what I was afraid of.

Noelle said, "Just tell him you can't. Say you need to see Mark or something."

I nodded, still focused on trying to catch my breath. Marie started typing something, her fingernails clicking against the screen. She turned it to Noelle for approval. Noelle grabbed the phone, read it over before pressing Send.

I sat down. "What did you say?"

"Just that you were going to the hospital because the lawyer that's dealing with the guardianship case needs you to," Marie explained, throwing my phone to me.

I gulped. "Do you think I'm next?"

Noelle looked at me with a strange expression on her face. "No. We don't even know if he's at fault for all of this."

What if he is, though?

And I'm next?

"Kyle, we don't know anything," Marie said. "Don't go crazy."

The feeling never went away. My gut screamed at me to do something.

"Maybe we should go to the police."

"Are you crazy?" Marie yelled. "Do you have any idea how much trouble we would get in? You knew information about the case and didn't say anything! We broke into a house and stole things! We'd get arrested before they even looked at the pretty boy with a protest sign!"

She was right. Marie and I would be far gone before they even thought of Luke as a suspect. Noelle was sitting with her hands folded in her lap. Her eyebrows were knitted together, and her lips were pinched.

"What does Kyle know about the case?"

Marie snapped toward me, swearing silently.

She's going to know.

Oh crap.

It felt like I completely lost the ability to even move my mouth. What was she going to say? Would she go to the police? Noelle was staring at me, with her head tilted to the side.

Marie turned to face her, smiling. "Luke. That he had the phone and Kyle didn't immediately turn him in."

Noelle's face dropped, and she gave a slight nod. I knew she didn't believe us, but for right now, it was okay. Bile bit the back of my throat as the fear of Luke with a gun came into my head.

"Do you guys think I need protection?"

I left Noelle's house about twenty minutes later. They both told me that I was fine and that I didn't need protection. But it didn't settle right with me. Something was jabbing at my bones, telling me I needed to protect myself. I tried my best to ignore it. Marie offered to walk me to my house so I wouldn't be so scared.

"Haha," I said sarcastically. "You're so funny."

Noelle was already in her room. She said she needed space and time to process everything. Marie was standing on the porch with me.

"I'm serious, Kyle," she said, running her fingers through her hair. It was so curly that her hand got stuck, and she had to yank it out. She sighed, clenching her fists. "If you are this scared, then I'll walk you home. I, personally, think you are fine."

Marie was just staring at me, waiting for a response. To be honest, I did want someone walking with me. I wanted to feel like even if someone attacked me, I had someone there to get help.

I mentally groaned. "No, it's fine. Then how would you get home?"

She looked at me, rolling her eyes. "I'll be fine."

My phone started ringing, and *Mom* flashed on the screen. Marie peeked over my shoulder to see who was calling me.

"Hello?" I asked when I answered.

"Hey, sweetie," Mom said. I heard rustling in the background. "How are you?"

"Fine," I muttered. Marie took my phone and put it on speaker. I shook my head at her, but she shushed me. She was always trying to get into my business. I snatched the phone back but left it on speaker so she could hear. I didn't see the point in trying to hide anything from her.

"Okay, so I thought I would let you know that Mark has a bowel obstruction, and we need to do surgery."

My heart dropped. I didn't know how severe that was. I barely knew what it was. Marie had a strange expression on her face. She looked at me and shrugged.

"Is he going to be okay?" Marie started walking around the deck, her boots clicking against the wood. My body was vibrating so much that the phone was shaking in my hand.

"Yes," Mom assured me. "It's a simple procedure. He will be fine."

I thanked her for telling me before hanging up. Marie had her nails in her mouth, still pacing the floor. She turned to look at me. "Are you going?"

I nodded, shoving my phone into my pocket. "I want to be there when he wakes up."

Marie agreed with me, saying that it was sweet. Which made me want to hit her, but I pushed my violent thoughts down and just started walking. I had to google directions because I had no idea how to get there from Noelle's house. Surprisingly, it wasn't far.

On my walk, my phone started to ring again. I thought it was Mom calling me about some changes, but the number was unknown. I answered it, anyways.

"Hello?"

Up ahead, an older man was walking his dog. The dog seemed to have been a mixed breed of German Shepherd and Husky. His tongue was hanging out, which looked adorable. The older man was on the phone too, but he gave me a slight wave, anyways. I returned it and continued to walk past him.

His face gave me déjà vu. As if I've seen him before.

"Kyle Davis?" a voice asked on the other side. "This is Officer Thomas with the New Hampshire Police Department."

My breath hitched unexpectedly, and I froze. "Yes, this is him," I managed to answer.

Shivers traveled down my body, and for some reason, I felt like I was back in the forest. With Nick running behind me, yelling. The wind brushing against the hairs on my arms and legs, making goosebumps appear.

But there was no wind, no Nick, and I was most definitely not in the forest.

"Good," the voice said. It was a female speaking, seemed young. "Are you available to come in on the twentieth for an interview? Nothing bad; we just need to ask you a few questions about Nick Walter."

I nodded, realizing my mistake soon after. "Sure."

They know.

They know, and they are going to arrest me.

"Perfect! I'll see you then."

The call disconnected, leaving me frozen in the middle of the sidewalk. I couldn't move. My limbs refused to work. I could feel sweat building up in my palms and under my arms. It wasn't until I was moved by another person walking by, bumping into me. They paid no attention to me and continued to move down the street. I needed that nudge to move forward. The rest of the walk was me having to deal with the many thoughts running through my head.

I finally made it to the hospital and signed in. I noticed Mom at the end of the hallway, talking to some other doctors, when she noticed me. She was in scrubs, so she had just gotten out of surgery. She held a finger up to the doctors and started walking in my direction.

"Hey, Kyle." She hugged me, holding on. "How are you doing?"

"I'm good, Mom," I responded, hugging her back. "Were you doing Mark's surgery?"

She shook her head, releasing me. "There are some rules regarding doing surgery on people you know. And with the whole guardianship thing going on, we decided it was better for me not to. I was doing a heart transplant with our cardio head."

I listened to her story of how the heart wouldn't beat at first, then they did something to get it going. I didn't understand what she was saying, but I was trying to. Sometimes, when Mom told me stories with a lot of medical terms, I would ask her what they meant. She would tell me but then forget where she was in the story, so eventually, I stopped asking and just pretended I knew what a scalpel was.

"Let's go wait in Mark's room. I told the surgeons that I would be in there when they were done."

I followed her down the hallway. We passed by the exit doors while there was a shift change. I noticed that the alarms weren't blaring. I pointed it out to Mom.

"Yes," she said, "we switched the cameras for motion detectors that we just shut down during the shift change so it wouldn't blare all the time. It was starting to make patients want to leave."

"Oh." That was all I said. We continued walking for a while until we finally got to the room. It was empty; no one else was in there. The sun was brightly shining through the window, casting a shadow on the bed. A TV hung in the corner, a chair sitting below it. I took a seat on it, waiting for some news about Mark.

A girl walked past our window, peeking inside. Her face was empty as she opened the door and walked in. She was in her scrubs, her red hair coming out a little bit. She asked to speak with Mom privately. They went into the hallway and stood in front of the glass. The girl started talking, and Mom's face dropped. I read her lips, asking what happened.

It might not be about Mark.

Mark will be fine.

Mom stomped away from the girl and passed the door. I ran outside and followed her.

"Mom, what's happening?"

She was practically running at this point. She stopped, turned, and held my shoulders.

"Everything will be alright, okay?" she told me, her eyes looking around. "Go back to Mark's room and wait for me in there."

She sprinted off, heading toward the surgery rooms. I stood in the hallway for a bit before the redhead rushed me back into the hospital room. I was convincing myself that it was about someone else. That Mark was okay, and he would be out soon.

I can't lose him too.

"Max!" I screamed. The dark water made it hard to see. It was nighttime, so that didn't help. In the ocean, I could make out a figure of a little boy. His face was staring at me. Looking peaceful, but I knew better.

Max was drowning. His pale body was just floating in the water. I reached to grab him, but every time I got close to him, he would be washed away by a wave. I kept screaming for him, yelling for him. But nothing worked. I couldn't save him.

When I woke up, the nightmare was replaying in my mind. It was mocking me, telling me it was my fault my little brother was dead. I started shaking, tears streaming down my face.

"Kyle?" a voice reached out to me. I turned to see Mark lying on the floor. His head was on a pillow while he was snuggled with a blanket. "Are you okay?"

I sniffed, wiping my face free of snot. "Yeah, just a bad dream."

Mark sat up, pushing his blanket off. He climbed up to the bed and lay down next to me. "About Max?"

I nodded, placing my head on the pillow. He sighed, closing his eyes. "I'll distract you. Try to go to sleep while I talk about different things."

I tilted my head to him, furrowing my eyebrows together. I was confused by what he meant. He opened one eye, glancing at my face.

"Just close your eyes and listen."

I followed his orders, shifting to my side and closing my eyes. Max came back into my head, his dead, drowned body screaming for help.

"There was a girl named Julie..." Mark started. Max disappeared from my head.

"She had long red hair and pretty blue eyes. She was a warrior..."

I didn't have another nightmare that night. I had a dream about a warrior named Julie. I woke up the next morning with Mark lying by my side.

I was okay.

I leaned down on the bed and did something I hadn't done since Max died.

I prayed.

I had no idea to whom or what. Maybe the universe. Whatever was listening, that's who I begged and pleaded to for Mark's life. I asked them to spare him. He was the only person I had left that genuinely loved me and cared for me. Sure, there was Noelle and Marie, but they didn't know me as well as Mark did. They weren't holding my hand as Henry screamed from his bedroom when Max died. They didn't see me cry for days on end and never left my side. They never rambled on about some fairytale to make sure I didn't have nightmares about my dead little brother. Mark was there for all of that. He knew me at my worst when I was only eight, and he stayed. He was one of the ones that stayed.

I knew nothing of God, but it seemed like it was the only thing I could've done to help at that moment. I folded my hands like I did when I was younger. Images flashed in my head. Mom sobbing. Dad consoling her. Henry yelling in my ear, blaming me for everything that happened to Max. Tears were running down my face as I prayed that Mark would be okay.

I'm useless.

My hands felt a hard plastic board in the sheets of the bed. I pulled it out to see it was Mark's writing board. The message wasn't erased.

—Thank you so much. I am so grateful for you, Mrs. Davis, and Kyle to be in my life. I'd probably be dead without him.—

Tears formed, and I didn't even try to hold them back. I had done awful things in my life, and Mark slipped up a couple of times, and I just abandoned him? I was disgusted with myself for leaving him on the ground, obviously in pain. Nick and I could've helped him. Instead, we dropped him like he was trash.

I waited for what seemed like hours. Not a single person passed in this hallway. I even stood outside the door to see if people were avoiding me, but there wasn't a doctor in sight. I almost fell asleep when I heard the door opening. Mom walked in with her head low and her surgical cap in her hands.

"Mom?" I begged.

"Kyle," she said, leaning down beside the chair I was sitting in. "He had a rupture from a direct artery during surgery. When I got to him, everyone told me it was too late." Tears brimmed in her eyes, and she wiped them away. "I tried, but they were right. It was too late. He's gone."

She held me in her arms; my face burrowed in her neck. I felt the sobs try to climb their way out of me, but I muffled my mouth with my fist.

Why does everyone keep leaving me?

22

Day Thirty-Seven

I ignored everyone for a while. Marie and Noelle found out the same day from Mom. She thought having friends by my side would help. I heard them down the stairs and locked the door. They sat by it for a while, talking through it. Marie told me about how her therapy appointments went, while Noelle just told me about school. She decided to go back because she couldn't stand being home alone for so long during the day.

Mr. Finn told me that I could take more time off because of Mark's passing. I emailed him back, thanking him for it. My parents didn't try to make me leave my room. I heard them talking about it in front of my door, then deciding against it.

I cried a lot. About Mark, Nick, and Max. I lost all of them. I didn't get to go through the sad stage with Nick and Max because of everything that was happening. Henry whispering into my ear, telling me it's my fault. Me watching Nick die in front of me and not doing anything. Now with Mark, they were all hitting me at once. When I would stop crying about one, the other would pop into my head, and so on.

I tried to watch shows to distract myself, but nothing was working. My days consisted of sitting on my bed crying to the sound of *The Simpsons* in the background.

One day, Mom appeared at my door. She told me Noelle was here to talk to me. I heard her footsteps walking away, then smaller ones coming toward my door.

"Hi, Kyle," she said. "It's Noelle. I wanted to talk to you."

I shut my TV off so I could listen.

"I thought a lot about what you said." My door pushed a little forward. It wasn't open, but I could tell she was leaning on it. "About me needing a boyfriend. I realized you were right. I was scared of being alone because I hadn't been in so long."

I crawled out of my bed and onto the floor. I leaned my back against the door and rested my head on it.

Go on.

"I don't love you. Not like that, anyways. But I care about you a lot. So, I'm not leaving because you need a friend." She slid something under the door. It was a piece of paper. When I opened it, she had written the word hug on it with a heart.

"You just lost someone close to you within an awfully close time frame of losing your best friend. You shouldn't be alone."

I wrote on the note, thank you, before sliding it back under. I could see her smile in my mind.

"You're welcome, Kyle."

She didn't lie either. She never left the door. She kept talking about random things, never leaving a space of silence between us.

"I never knew Mark like you did," she confessed. "I know you guys went through a lot. With him doing drugs."

I coughed. "I should've been there for him."

She paused for a moment. "You were there when it really mattered."

I stood up, holding onto the knob. I heard shuffling on the other side. The cool metal tormented me. I unlocked it; the clicking echoed in my ears. I slowly turned it to reveal Noelle grinning brightly on the other side. Her hair was down, and she was in pajamas. She held her arms out to hug me, which I gladly accepted. Her head was sitting on my shoulder. Mine was resting on top of hers. After a few seconds, she let go.

"Are you okay?" she asked. I just nodded.

Noelle stayed for a few more minutes before having to leave. Her dad wanted her home for dinner. She said that she could skip it and stay with me if I needed her.

"No, I'm okay," I assured her. "You don't want to get in trouble, do you?"

"Guess not." She laughed.

Mom had offered to drive her home, which Noelle gladly accepted. I didn't go for the ride, but Mom arrived back home after ten minutes. She asked me how I was holding up.

"It just sucks."

That was all I could bring myself to say.

Dad's car pulled up in the driveway, and Mom told me to

go upstairs because she had to talk to Dad about something. I figured it was about me, so I made my seat right at the top of the stairs. I heard Dad walk in the door and Mom greeting him. Everything got faint, so I crawled a few more steps down the stairs to hear better.

"He needs this," she said. "Anger management could help."

"No," Dad disagreed. "He doesn't need to go to some class that teaches him to be less of a man."

Dad is standing up for me?

"Being a man is breaking stuff in a therapy office? Really?"

I heard a loud noise, like someone slamming their hands onto the table. I almost jumped and ran up the stairs.

"Being a man is getting angry at people who deserve it!" Dad shouted. I could imagine the vein popping out of his neck. I've seen it a couple of times myself before when he would get mad at me. I've never seen it happen with Mom, though.

"Now is the best time for it," Mom argued back. Her voice slightly rising. "He just lost another one of his friends and spent the last three days locked up in his room!"

"He's trying to cope!" Dad yelled. "I get that. But about the anger management, I would be lying if I said I wasn't proud of him for doing what he did."

"Proud of him?" Mom snapped.

Proud of me?

"A fight?" Dad asked me three years ago. "With whom?"

Nick was messing with some guys at our school by hiding their clothes after gym class. I told him not to do it, but he was already dead set on doing it. He scattered them around the classrooms and left. The next day when they found out it was Nick, they met him after school to fight him.

Don't get me wrong; Nick could hold his own. But three on one wasn't fair. Nick asked me to just be near in case of something happening. I watched as the three guys almost beat Nick to a pulp before jumping in. At least, the last thing I remembered was seeing Nick on the ground, bleeding, before rage struck my body, and I blacked out. The next thing I know, three guys were on the ground, groaning in pain. Nick was in front of me grinning, and Mr. Finn had ahold of my wrist.

He called Dad to come get me for fighting. He wanted to talk about suspension, but Dad waved him off, saying he would shoot Mr. Finn an email. He was completely silent on the car ride home until we got to the driveway.

"Three guys. A year older. Why?" He turned the ignition off.

"It wasn't a fair fight," I complained. "They beat Nick until he was on the ground bleeding! I made things fairer."

Dad started to rub the bridge of his nose. "So, you mean to tell me, you took on three older guys and came out of the fight without a scratch on you?"

I nodded.

"I'm so proud of you."

I ran to my room once I heard footsteps coming in my direction. I jumped onto my bed just in time for Dad to walk in. He opened the door, throwing his hands into his pocket.

"Hey, kid," he announced, stepping further into my room. He was swaying back and forth. It had just occurred to me that he hadn't been in my room too many times. It was almost uncomfortable for him to be standing there.

"So, I was just talking to your mother about your anger problems," he told me, putting air quotations around "anger problems."

Dad had never been the talking type. He wouldn't scold you for a long time. Just a firm one-sentence yell, but that was it. Mom was the talker. She would go on and on about what you did was wrong, and you should apologize, and then when you think it's over, it wasn't. Five minutes later she would say something else that she probably mentioned earlier but reworded it.

Dad came over and sat on my bed, looking at his surroundings. It was like watching a puppy go to a new house for the first time. Seemed fine, but fear was written in their eyes.

"She seems to think it's a problem, but I think you're fine," he admitted. "I'm supposed to be convincing you to work on it because it's dangerous, but…" He paused, taking the time to show me his teeth in a slight smile.

"I know you know what you are doing."

I don't.

I don't even remember what happened.

I smiled back, nodding along. He patted my knee before standing up.

"Oh, and just for future reference, don't go all macho with your mother down the hall." He gave me a wink before heading out my door. I sat there, trying to figure out what the hell just happened.

I don't need to go to anger management.

I pulled my phone out and called Marie. It rang a few times before she picked up.

"Hey," she said. "How are you?"

"Fine," I answered her. "Guess what?"

It was late now; there was no light left outside other than the moon.

"Are you sure you're okay? I mean, you kind of wouldn't leave your room for days, and I was starting to get worried. Like actually worried—"

"Yes, I'm fine, Mom," I teased. "Now guess what?"

It was silent on the other end. I checked my screen to make sure the call was still active, and it was, so I held it back to my ear.

"Hello?"

"Call me Mom one more time, and I'll make you eat your teeth," Marie threatened.

There was the Marie I know and love. Believe it or not, that wasn't the first time she threatened to feed me my teeth.

"Great, okay, so guess what?"

"What, Kyle?"

"I don't need to do anger management!"

She went quiet again. I only heard her breathing on the other side. I rolled my eyes at her dramatic pauses.

"I'm confused," she said.

"My mom wanted to put me in anger management, but my dad stood up for me, saying I didn't need it, so now I don't need to go."

"Why did your mom want to put you in anger management?"

What's with all these questions?

"Because my therapist said I needed it—"

"What? I thought you said your therapy appointment went well?"

Crap.

I groaned, pulling the phone from my face to silently swear. I couldn't believe I just let that slip.

If I couldn't even hide this from Marie, how was I going to convince the police I wasn't with Nick?

"It was fine." I lied. "He just said—"

"Kyle Andrew Davis!"

"That's not my middle name—"

"I don't care! Don't lie to me!"

I clenched my jaw out of frustration. I wanted to hang up on her; I was so close to doing it too. But knowing Marie, she would have broken into my house and forced it out of me.

"Okay fine, I might have—"

I heard the door shut downstairs. There was a bunch of small noises following it. Marie was huffing on the phone, so I had to pull her away from my ear. I looked down the stairs to be faced with darkness.

"Hang on, Marie, I'll call you back."

"Kyle Andrew Davis, don't you dare hang up on—"

I pressed End Call and threw my phone onto the bed. I walked downstairs, turning one dim light on in the bathroom. A smell rose to my nose, making me feel sick. I tasted vomit in the back of my throat, threatening to come up. The smell was as if there was rotting meat with cheap perfume on. I gagged multiple times, walking toward the kitchen.

I heard thumping coming from Henry's room. His door was wide open, and I looked inside. At first, I was only met with nothing. Then I was able to make something out in the darkness.

I watched as a face stared at me, lying at the end of the stairs. His hands were raised behind him. I couldn't see who it was, but I realized that they were unmoving.

That's a dead body.

Is that Henry?

I wanted to scream, but no sound came out of my mouth. I fell backward, landing on my back. My feet kicked the door closed. Vomit poured out of my mouth and onto the hardwood floors. I quickly stood up, wiping my face, and ran into Mom's office. I locked the door behind me and started pacing.

Call the police!

My phone isn't on me.

As I was being hit with a million thoughts at once, a bone-chilling revelation came to mind.

Is that Luke trying to kill me?

Without hesitation, I ran over to Mom's desk and bent down, looking for the key. I finally found it and unlocked the drawer, grabbing the pistol. I took the safety off and held it in front of me, waiting for someone to walk through the door. I slowly made my way out of the office and down the hallway.

I felt stupid holding the gun; I had no idea how to use it other than the fact that I had to pull a trigger. I placed my fingers in position, ready to use it. I was shaking so badly; I could've pulled it too early.

I stood in front of Henry's door, sweating like a pig. I had never been more terrified in my life. Something was murdered on the other side of the door. I reached for the doorknob when the door slammed open.

Henry stood there, taken aback at my presence. "What, Kyle?" His eyes narrowed in on the barrel of the gun. He momentarily froze in place, then backed away. "Why do you have a gun?"

I held it to the ground, confused. "I saw a dead body! It was being dragged down the stairs."

Henry looked down his stairs before staring back at me. "My stairs?" I nodded. The gun was shaking violently; I couldn't control it. Henry grabbed my wrists to stop me from making a mistake. He flipped the safety back on, pushing me away from the stairs.

"I know what I saw!" I yelled. "I'm not crazy!"

Henry shushed me, pointing upstairs. I took a few breaths in, trying to relax.

"Kyle," Henry said in a calm voice. "I'm going to ask you a question, and I need you to be honest, okay?" I nodded.

I had never seen this side of Henry before. He normally hated me and never spoke to me like this. I was waiting for some kind of mean remark, but I could hear the concern in his voice.

He was either scared…

"Have you taken your medication like you should be?"

Or he cared.

I thought about the last time I took my medicine. I couldn't even remember when I had taken them. Henry took my silence as an answer.

"Kyle, you can't do that—"

"I know."

"That's dangerous! Look what happened; you could've shot me because of your hallucinations."

"I know!" I whispered, spitting everywhere. "You don't think I've heard this before? I'm so sick of having to take those pills."

Henry sighed, coming closer to me. "But it's for your safety and everyone around you. You thought you saw a dead body tonight, Kyle. Someone could've gotten seriously hurt."

I nodded, letting him scold me. To be honest, I was happy Henry cared so much. It was most likely because I held him at gunpoint. But it still felt nice to have an older brother again. I hadn't felt like I had one since Max died. That's when Henry became more distant and acted like he didn't care about me.

"Kyle, I need you to give me the gun now," Henry said, holding his hand out. He was all scratched up. He wasn't bleeding, so they weren't new, but it was strange how they were placed. I looked up at him, and his eyes reminded me of what happened a few nights ago.

I watched his head snap to the side. He wasn't smirking any more. His eyes were dark. I watched as he threw the water bottle to the side, the plastic breaking open and spilling water everywhere. Before I knew what was happening, he was standing in front of me with his hand wrapped around my throat. I could feel his grip getting tighter as I lost the ability to breathe. I tried to yell, but his hands were holding my vocal cords. All that came out of me were grunts. I watched as his eyes turned darker and darker. I could feel the color draining from my face. My eyes wanted to pop out of their sockets because of the pressure. Henry just grinned and tightened his grip on me.

I pried at his hands, trying to get them off me. But they wouldn't come loose. It felt like we were standing there like that for hours. I even tried kicking him, but I could only land them on his knees, which didn't affect him. He kept holding on to my throat, making my lungs beg for air.

I hope I pass out.

I backed away from him, fear resonating in my body. Henry's face fell, and he dropped his hand.

"Kyle, what's wrong?"

Don't trust him.

I swallowed, looking around the room. Everything was hazy. I felt sick. I tightened my grasp on the gun. Henry tilted his head to the side.

"Kyle, what's happening?"

I shook my head, trying my best to get away from him. I stumbled with the gun, falling onto the barrel. Henry lunged at me, grabbing for it. I couldn't figure out why, but I wasn't about to let him take it. I tumbled with him, trying to push the gun out of the way. Henry has longer arms and was able to reach it. He held it in his hands, standing up.

This is it.

He's trying to kill me.

I sat on the floor in a fetal position, waiting to hear the bullet. Waiting for the pain to come. Henry just stood above me, looking down at me like I was trash. I looked up to meet his eyes, and his expression softened.

"Did you think I was going to hurt you?"

23

Day Forty

I woke up the next morning with a huge headache, unsure of what the rest of the night consisted of. I came down the stairs to see Henry getting ready for work and making coffee. He wasn't talking to me, so I figured we went back to ignoring each other. Mom had already left for the day, and Dad was in the living room, grabbing his things to leave. He said goodbye to me and gave me money for an Uber to get to the police station.

Oh, that's today.

I sat at the dining table, unsure of what to do with just Henry and me in the house. He looked at the time, swearing, then started jogging around the house. I watched as he grabbed his keys, coffee, and then he ran to the bathroom. I started going on my phone, about to text Noelle to see what she was up to when something was placed in front of me. I looked up to see Henry walking out the door. Sitting on the table was my medication.

I guess this is happening now.

I quickly took my pills, putting the bottle back in the bathroom. I texted Noelle, asking what she was doing before getting ready to go to the police station. I wasn't sure what to wear, so I googled it. Not very many people had experienced going to the police for questioning, so I just dressed as if I were applying for a job because that was the only thing they had advice for. I wore a button-up with some of Dad's old khakis. I looked like a Boy Scout, but I figured that was better than my dark jeans and a hoodie covering most of my face.

I pocketed Dad's money and just walked to the station. People were staring at me, but not like they normally did. Most would look at me, then grab ahold of their children. Now, people seemed unbothered to walk past me.

Why do people judge so much?

I tried to push my nerves away, but they kept clawing at me the closer I got to my destination. I realized that this would be my last time going to the police station if I played my cards right. Unless someone else got murdered.

The station came into view, and I was ready to bounce. I could see myself turning and running and never coming back. But they would've found me. And running now would've looked suspicious. I kept walking.

The same lady was waiting at the desk as before. She smiled when she saw me and pointed in the direction of an officer. The officer had bright red curly hair that was flying everywhere. She was sitting down, typing on a computer. I walked over to her, noticing her nails. The actual nail part was unevenly cut, and lots of skin was pulled from around the finger. She probably bites her nails. She noticed me standing there and pointed to the seat in front of her desk. I sat down, folding my hands in my lap.

"One second, sweetheart," she said, not taking her eyes off the screen. "I just have to fill out a report." The sound of her nails clicking the keys was the only sound in the whole office. Her nails clicked the Enter button before she turned to me, smiling.

"Now, what can I do for you?"

"Um, I'm Kyle Davis," I told her. "I was called here to talk about Nick Walter."

She nodded, grabbing a notebook and coming around the desk. She leaned on the edge of it and took a pen from her cup. "We just have a few questions; it won't take long at all."

I nodded, shifting in my seat. It didn't seem like a proper investigation at all, and yet I felt my nerves taking total control over me.

Can she tell I'm sweating?

"When was the last time you saw Nick?"

"The day before he went missing. We hung out a little bit after school. Then the next day at school."

She wrote down everything I was saying. It seemed like word for word.

"Okay, and do you know anyone that would have had a reason for Nick being gone?"

What?

I shook my head. "No."

She nodded, flipping through her notebook. She took a breath in, standing up and walking back around to her desk. She started going through her drawers, searching for something.

Handcuffs?

I gulped, looking around the station. A lot of people were there. Some that weren't policemen too. Some in regular clothes, just talking to people. I couldn't tell whether they were reporting something or working out of their uniform.

"Aha!" the officer I was with said, startling me. I jumped a little in my seat, but she didn't notice. "Found it! Alright, so it says here that a little bit ago, you had an interview with two police officers at Westport Hospital that ended with a public disturbance. Care to explain?"

Oh god.

I coughed, trying to buy myself more time. The officer didn't even seem intimidating. She was smiling at me, waiting politely for an answer.

"Um, I have anger problems, but I'm seeing a therapist for it and going to anger management classes. I've gotten better."

It was a complete lie, and I had no way of proving it, but I thought it was worth a try. She had a blank expression on her face, writing it down.

"Well, I'm glad you are getting yourself help. Takes a real man to realize their problems and try to fix them."

"Thank you."

"Now, back to the previous question," she said, sitting down. Her eyes narrowed, and she tilted her head. "Listen, between you and me, this case is a goner."

A goner?

"Unless you can give me something. Anything! We have zero leads, and soon enough, this case will just be trashed."

I couldn't look her in the eye. I stared at the bridge of her nose, which had a slight crease in it. I wanted to confess everything. My whole body was burning with guilt. But I knew how much trouble I would've gotten in. I just shook my head.

"I'm sorry. I want this as much as you do, but I have no idea who would want to do this to Nick. I really wish I could help."

The last part wasn't a lie. I didn't know why someone would want to kill Nick, and I wanted to help. She just nodded, grabbing folders from her desk.

"Then that's all we needed. Thank you for your cooperation." She shook my hand before going back to her desk work. I left the station, breathing the air of freedom. I couldn't believe that I had done that so perfectly.

I bet I left a sweat stain in that chair.

I pretty much bolted home after that. I had all this built-up energy, waiting to burst inside me. I almost fell a couple of times, but I didn't care. I pushed past people and jumped over potholes. The world was just passing too slow for me. I needed to run. The air rushing against my face fed me energy, making me sprint faster. People stared and laughed. It just went in one ear and out the other. My feet were trying to keep up with my mind. I was in control.

I have the power.

I stopped when I got to my house; the heat and aching caught their way up to me. I fanned out my shirt, bringing a cool breeze to tickle my stomach. I walked inside to find an empty house. I noticed that Mom's office door was open, so I peeked inside.

Mom stood there on the phone, looking angry as hell. She hadn't noticed me, so I stood behind the door to listen. I heard her heels click against the floor as she walked around the room.

"What do you mean there's one missing?"

Missing? What's missing?

"I can't believe you are telling me that a dead body is gone."

Dead body?

"Obviously, something happened. Dead bodies don't just walk, Cassie!"

More heel clicking on the ground. I moved to walk away, which made the floor creak.

"Now I have to deal with the family suing the hospital!" A few moments of silence passed.

"The body didn't have a family? Can you ID it for me then?"

I took a few more steps out the door.

"How did this happen? We have so much security!"

I finally made it out of hearing range, ignoring the faint parts of the conversation I could still hear. I called Marie to tell her to meet me someplace. The phone was ringing, and she answered without saying a word.

"Marie?" I asked.

"I'm here."

I grabbed my book bag and slung it over my shoulders. "Okay, can you meet me at Luke's street?"

"Sure."

I closed the door behind me, clicking my tongue to the roof of my mouth. "Okay, great. Are you mad at me?"

"Oh yeah, I am." She was quiet after that. I could barely hear her breathing on the other side.

"Why?"

I walked down the sidewalk, holding the bag tightly.

"Because you never called me after you got spooked last night."

Oh, right.

I decided to spare her the details of the whole gun story because I didn't even know how it ended. I knew Marie wanted an explanation, so I made something up.

"Oh, it was just Henry getting home from work."

"Fine. I'll see you soon."

She hung up without another word.

~

I saw Marie there when I arrived. She stood by the sign with her arms crossed. When she saw me, she did not seem happy. She stomped over and flicked me in the head.

"Ow!" I yelled. "What the hell was that for?"

"For making me worry all day." She smiled. "Now, what are we doing?"

I reached into my book bag and pulled out sweatpants and hoodies. I threw a pair into Marie's arm, who was reluctant to take them. She held them out like they were dirty diapers. I placed mine on the ground before zipping the bag back up. She walked over to me, waving the clothes around.

"Okay, what the hell is going on?" she asked. She placed a hand on her hip like my mother did whenever I was in trouble.

"Put those on," I demanded. I was already unbuttoning my shirt, which got me a weird look from Marie. "Turn around!"

She threw her hands up in the air and faced the other direction.

"Yes, Kyle, because I am so interested in you." She spoke in a sarcastic tone. I laughed, throwing the hoodie over my body. "Also, I'm not changing in the middle of the street."

I hurriedly placed the sweatpants on and started to put my shoes back on. I looked around us and noticed a backyard shower in the neighbor's yard. "That's okay, you can change over there."

The shower was broken. Parts of the wood were chipped, showing the original color. The door swung open, and I was positive I saw a rat.

Marie looked in the direction I was pointing in and saw the little privacy stall. She shrugged her shoulders and ran over there. She had to climb this little fence, which she had no problem doing. She threw the clothes over and jumped. Can't say I wasn't impressed.

I stayed by the street while she changed. Cars passed by while the drivers gave me weird looks. I couldn't blame them. A teenage boy dressed in all black, holding a book bag? I'd be a little creeped out myself.

After a few minutes, she came back out in the hoodie and sweatpants I gave her. Her hair was pulled back into a ponytail, containing her curls as best as it could. She was holding her old clothes in her arms. She climbed back over the fence and smiled at me.

"Look, we match!" she exclaimed, pointing to our clothing. I rolled my eyes and held my hand out to grab her clothes. I kneeled, stuffing them into the bag.

She started to brush off the dirt from her hoodie that I hadn't realized was there. "Wait, so what are we doing?" she asked.

I smirked at her, standing back up. "I just happen to know that Luke, his mom, and Caroline are all out at a diner. This could be our only time to scope the room," I informed her. I watched her eyes grow, light glistening behind them. "We don't have too long, though. In and out as fast as we possibly can. Got it?"

"Got it." Before I knew it, Marie was sprinting off in the direction of the house. I have never seen that girl run faster than she did at that moment. She was on a mission, and she was ready to complete it.

I knew Marie was going to be excited about it, but I had no idea how excited. She looked like a kid that was just told they were going to Disney World. I realized that I didn't know much about Marie's childhood. I knew she lived with her grandparents, but I had no idea where her parents were. I knew she had a mom, but the only time I saw her was at the hospital.

I tried to catch up to her, but her boots were too fast. By the time I reached the house, the door was wide open, and Marie was standing there. I moved my head to the side, confused as to why it was already unlocked. Marie snaked her hand out from behind her back, holding up a key.

"How the hell—"

"I like to pickpocket." She then handed me my wallet.

"Marie!"

"Hey!" she yelled, backing up. "At least I returned it!"

I stuffed it back into the pocket of my sweatpants. She giggled, sticking her tongue out at me. I just rolled my eyes and went to take off my shoes, but Marie stopped me.

"No, we are doing this my way. Shoes stay on."

She walked into the house, her combat boots slapping the floor. I followed suit, knowing there was no point in arguing with her. Marie stared at the skull that we found last time and shuddered. I looked around the room, my attention zooming in on a tear on the wall. I made my way over there while Marie walked down the hall.

The tear was peeling the wallpaper. The pattern was flowers and trees, but the tear showed the gray behind it. I reached up to pull it back when I noticed something else. There was a string hanging out of the hole. I grabbed ahold of it. It was a plastic, clear piece of string. I yanked, then I heard glass shattering down the hall. I dropped everything and ran over to Marie. She was staring at a picture frame that was on the floor, with broken pieces surrounding it.

"I didn't see it!" she exclaimed, backing away from it. I rolled my eyes and quickly started to pick up the glass. Marie bent down to help, but I stopped her.

"No," I said. "I don't want you getting cut."

She rolled her eyes, bending down, and helped anyways. I picked up the frame and saw the photo hanging from it. It was

Luke, Nick, and me. We were on the swings in Luke's backyard. He got rid of the swing set a long time ago, so it wasn't there any more. Nick and I were messing with each other's hair while Luke was smiling giddily at the camera.

Is this why Luke would do this?

Was he jealous of Nick and mine's relationship?

Did he feel left out?

I threw all the pieces away, leaving the photo in a drawer. I silently prayed that they wouldn't notice the missing picture. Ms. Cloud's wall was filled with frames with different pictures, so I thought we had a good chance of getting away with it.

Marie and I went down the rest of the hallway, careful not to break anything else. We went into Luke's perfectly cleaned room, which got Marie scoffing.

"What?" I asked her, picking up some things from his desk and looking under them. I wasn't entirely sure what exactly I was looking for, but it just seemed too neat.

"Of course, Luke's room would look like this." she snarled. "Not a single thing out of place. I kind of want to ruin it."

I just laughed at her. She was right; nothing seemed out of place. His room looked like a serial killer's room. Which made sense if this was all his fault.

I should've seen this coming.

It was funny to think about at the time because I didn't think Luke would ever do something like that. Luke wasn't capable of murder. But after Mark and everything I went through, I had to be sure. Which is why I got Marie, and we were going to investigate his room. My gut was telling me that everything was fine, and I believed it. But I needed proof for myself.

"Okay, so what's the plan, captain?" I asked, looking at her scanning the room.

"Go through anything and everything."

Seemed like a good plan to me. Marie and I searched everything. It felt like we were on one of the crime shows Marie watched. We looked around his bed and under his pillows. Inside his closet was nothing but clothes. His perfectly neat desk was just that. We couldn't mess anything else up either, though, because then they would've known that we were here. All his books were perfectly placed in alphabetical order, which sort of creeped me out. When I was looking through his books, I realized a lot of them were about psychopaths and psychology.

What the hell?

I remember Luke telling me he had these books, but I didn't realize it was this many.

I started flipping through one and realized a lot of the things had been highlighted. Some pages were marked with sticky notes. I started to read some of the facts in my head.

Eighty-five percent of violent offenders are white males.

It was highlighted in blue with a yellow sticky note to the side. The note just had a star on it. Marie was huffing in the closet, going through his clothes. I turned to another page with a line that was pink.

Psychopaths tend to have a rough childhood involving absent parents or addicts as parents.

The sticky note next to that one read: *Dad leaving when six.*

Luke's dad did leave when he was only six, but because his mom was a lesbian. Of course, he didn't have to leave Luke, but I think he felt embarrassed. He was in a marriage that was a lie. When Ms. Cloud finally realized who she was, Mr. Cloud didn't want any part of it.

"Marie, come look at this," I said, waving her over. She walked from the closet and peered into the book over my shoulder. Her eyes widened, and she took the book from my hands.

"What?" she screeched. "This is kind of crazy."

I nodded. I started to get a sick feeling in my stomach. "He told me he was interested in this stuff, but I didn't know it was like this."

Marie eyed me, flipping through the book. "Yeah, these borderline weird."

She was right. My breath became heavy as I thought about what that could mean.

"Kyle, look at this."

She shoved the book back into my hands and pointed at a yellow highlighted fact. I followed where her finger was and read it to myself.

Sadists kill animals before moving on to humans.

I looked back up at Marie, who then pointed to the sticky note.

—Related to Davis?—

I threw the book out of instinct. Marie jumped back, staring at me. I swallowed the lump made of stone in my throat.

"Is that supposed to be about me?" I questioned, pacing the room. I had never killed an animal before. My mind raced with a million thoughts, all attacking me at once. I felt like I was trapped again, with nothing left to defend myself with.

"Did he know about the night with Nick?"

I stared at her. "Only if he did this to him."

We searched everything again. Looking for that damn gun was like trying to find a needle in a haystack. I never understood that expression before until now. Trying to find a gun in a psychopath's room was even harder.

We were looking for so long that Marie sat down on the ground after a while.

"We aren't going to find anything!"

I rolled my eyes. "Not with you sitting on the floor we aren't."

She went to stand up when there was a creak. I looked, and her hand pressed down on a wood panel on the floor. She looked up at me, grinning.

"What?" I asked, putting Luke's books back.

"Hold on," she said. "I saw this in a TV show before." She removed the wood and reached her hand inside.

I turned around to look around the room, throwing my hands up. I felt relieved that we didn't find anything. Her opening up the floorboard meant nothing to me. "There's nothing in here! Luke doesn't have the gun; let's just go."

"Kyle?"

"What?" I snapped, looking at Marie.

Marie sat there on her knees, with her eyes wide. My eyes shifted to what she held in her hands.

She had a revolver.

24

"Marie, be careful!" I yelled at the moron skipping to my house, wearing a backpack with a gun in it. We had taken the revolver from Luke's house and decided to bring it back to mine to figure out what to do. Plus, we needed proof. What if Luke had found out we knew about the gun? He would hide it or something.

"Relax, Kyle," she said, spinning. "The safety lock is on." She shook the bag to prove that she wasn't going to get shot. I went to grab it from her, but she turned away. We were almost at my house, and Marie insisted on holding the backpack. I was hesitant at first, but she assured me she would be careful.

Liar.

She slowed down and started keeping pace with me. I was lost in my thoughts, knowing what this meant. Marie wouldn't turn away from me; she just gave me a weird look.

"What?" I finally asked her.

"Whatcha thinking about?"

I paused, making her stop walking to look at me. I could tell my eyes were dark, staring into hers. Her facial expression dropped. I sighed before answering her.

"Just about how Luke is probably planning on killing us all."

I continued walking, hearing Marie's boots scrape against the concrete.

"You know," Marie said, "if Luke were to own a gun, it definitely would be a revolver. It just makes sense."

She's right.

Why does that make sense?

We came up to my house, and I noticed that there were no cars in the driveway. Everyone was still out even though it was late afternoon. I took the backpack from Marie, and we went into my room. I placed it on my bed, checking the time.

"Okay, Luke is probably already home," I told her, reaching for the revolver. "If he was planning to do anything tonight, he can't because we have his gun."

I pushed my dresser out, away from the wall. Marie was standing by the bag, watching me. She grabbed Nick's phone and the journal out from the bag, leaving it empty to put the revolver inside. She handed the backpack to me to hide behind my dresser. I placed the gun inside, and I put the bag in the far corner before pushing the piece of furniture back.

"What do we do?" Marie said. "We have his gun, but we can't go to the police."

"I know, Marie," I snapped. I was getting really frustrated. I started to pull at my hair. "I didn't think this far."

Marie started to pace around the room. She was starting to spiral. I could see it in her eyes. The door closed downstairs, footsteps marching around the house. I looked out the window to see Henry's car. A shaky breath escaped from my body. Marie was biting her nails, and tears were forming in her eyes. I grabbed ahold of her.

"You will be fine, Marie," I insisted. "We both will be."

I grabbed the bag from the dresser and gave it to Marie. She was violently shaking, fear written in her eyes. I think the realization of this all just hit her like a truck.

I took the revolver out and snapped the safety lock off. I placed it into her trembling hands and warned her.

"Stay here. Use it on anyone that comes into this room or house. My parents are not going to be home tonight, so if anyone comes in, you shoot them."

She nodded, grasping onto the gun. I told her that I was going to go deal with it and get the police.

"I don't care if I go to jail; we are going to be safe," I promised.

I grabbed onto Nick's phone, thinking it would be enough evidence. I ran down the stairs to be met with Henry about to come up.

"Hey, I was just looking for you," he called out.

"Yeah, listen," I told him, bringing him away from the stairs. "I need to go do something; can you do a favor for me?" Henry raised his eyebrows and crossed his arms. "Could you go out and just stay out for the night?"

"Why?"

"Um..." I tried to think of anything. My brain was racked

with multiple things I could say, but only one stuck.

"I have a girl coming over."

Henry stared at me; his mouth gaped open. He gulped, blinking his eyes as if he couldn't believe it. "Sure. I just need to grab something from my room. Then I'll go."

He went down the stairs, and I left the house. I didn't have time to wait to see him leave. I had to go to the police. I heard a buzzing coming from my pocket, and I took out my phone to see what it was. My screen was blank. I realized there was another phone in my back pocket.

Nick's phone.

I grabbed it with my convulsing hands, clicking the screen to open.

From: Luke
Kyle will see you soon, Nick.

I panicked. Everything that I thought I knew about this whole situation was right. Every gut feeling telling me something was off was right. I was next.

I should've gone to the police.

Horror shook every bone in my body. He was coming to kill me. I was next. I only had one option left.

I have to run.

I ran to the street, right in the middle of it. I heard faint yelling behind me, so I turned to see Luke sprinting toward me. He was far enough away for me to just barely know it was him, but not too far for me not to notice the shiny, glimmering metal object in his hand.

Oh god.

My feet acted first, running without me even realizing it. I stayed in the street in the hope of getting someone's attention, but there was no one. I was alone, being chased by someone who wanted me dead. I tried screaming for help, but it used too much of the energy that I needed to run. I knew Luke was right on my trail. I could hear him calling my name, getting louder and louder.

How is he catching up to me?

I realized that down the street was my school. I could go there and cause a scene. People would come out of their classrooms and help me. I could feel my heartbeat in my throat. My feet were burning from going so fast. But I couldn't stop.

I made it to the parking lot, panting. Luke was a little farther behind me, waving his hands. The knife he was holding kept reflecting in the sun, blinding me.

What is he trying to do?

I ran for the stairs to the building and went to pry open the doors. My hand reached the metal, and I pulled as hard as I could. They wouldn't budge. I tried again, but again they wouldn't move.

It's after hours.

No one is here.

I'm going to die.

<h1 style="text-align:center">25</h1>

I turned around to see Luke coming up to the bottom of the stairs. Blood was smeared across his face, and he looked beaten up. He held his hands out to me.

"Kyle, you've got to help me." His body was shaking; the knife almost dropped from his hands.

He's acting.

He just wants to hurt me.

"Help you?" I spat. "You killed Nick."

His eyes widened, and fear slapped him across his face. "No, Kyle, I would—"

"Get away from me!" I barked. I looked at the stairs we were on. The number of times I was on these stairs, waiting for my friends. The number of times I was by these stairs getting into fights.

"Kyle!" Nick's voice boomed. He ran up the stairs and hit me in the head. I was listening to music, so I took my earbuds out and slapped him across his shoulder.

"Don't hit me," I barked. Nick just laughed, sitting down next to me. People were walking past us to get into the school. Others stood in the parking lot, talking with their friends and hanging out. Nick pulled out a piece of paper and showed it to me.

"I'm going to give it to Noelle today." He grinned, shoving the note in my face.

I snorted, opening it up. I read it out loud.

"Noelle, would you want to go on a date? Circle yes or no." I looked at Nick, who was smiling ear to ear. He seemed pretty proud of his note.

I tore it up in front of him.

"What the hell, Kyle?" he complained, picking up the pieces.

"We aren't in middle school any more, Nick," I informed him, grabbing my bag. "Man up and ask her in person."

"Hey, guys!" Mark called out. He was waving us down, trying to catch up with us. "Want to meet at the diner after school today? I'm

trying to get that waitress to fall in love with me."

"Nick!" I yelled, freezing my butt off by the stairs. Snow was falling and sticking to my winter coat that wasn't keeping me warm whatsoever. Nick waved, a tall, geeky kid following him.

Luke?

I rolled my eyes and jumped down the stairs. I gave him a fake smile before turning to Nick.

"You are going to like me one day, Kyle," Luke challenged. "You'll see."

"Don't hold your breath," I muttered. Nick gave me a look before strutting up the stairs. He was gloating about how Noelle and he had a date the night before. He was practically jumping around like a kid. He started talking about the whole date and how well he thought it went.

"Then I walked her home, like the gentlemen I am." He patted himself on the back. Luke was beaming at him, looking as excited as Nick was for their relationship.

What a weirdo.

"Luke!" I yelled, waving the tall guy over. You could see him in any crowd. He saw me and smiled, grabbing someone's arm and pulling them alongside him. It was Noelle. She had to run to keep up with Luke's long strides that he called walking. She came up to me and slung an arm around my shoulder.

"Hey, Kyle!" She wrapped her other arm around me, giving me a quick hug. She let go after a second, still smiling. Her cheeks were rosy red and matching the tip of her nose. Luke grinned at me, messing with my hair. He was wearing a T-shirt that he got at the protest that weekend about seals.

"We stood in front of the office for hours holding signs —"

"And this is when I put my headphones on and pretend to be listening." I interrupted Luke, which made him pout. Noelle laughed, saying that she'd listen. I played some rock music while Luke was blabbing on about saving the seals. Nick came running up to us, kissing Noelle on the cheek when he reached us.

"Hey, guys, what did I miss?"

"Maybe I should kill you and then Nick when he comes here tomorrow alone," Mark muttered into my ears. My head snapped toward him, and he grinned knowing it bothered me.

If only he knew why…

Then he wouldn't bother me.

I wanted to fight him at that moment. I wanted to grab him by the head and smash him against my kneecap. Or throat punch him and watch him fall to the concrete. To watch as his eyes roll to the back of his head, and he was quiet. Then I looked at Noelle with fear in her eyes. I already saw myself as a monster; I couldn't let Noelle see me like that too.

Whatever expression I had on my face before, I wiped it off. Mark's grin fell, and his eyes glared into mine. I took my anger out on my hands as I closed them into tight fists. I felt the nails cut into my skin, and the blood started to drip. By the time I realized I was bleeding, Mark's fist came flying into my face. The impact landed right in my eye. I knew it was bruised and swelled immediately after. I let my body fall to the ground, and my head smashed into the pavement.

"Hey!" Luke complained. "Let him be! He didn't do anything!"

Luke was pleading with me. He looked so tired and weak. For a second, I let myself believe him. Maybe he was framed. Maybe he wasn't a murderer. I looked at his hands and noticed his fists were bloody and bruised.

Was he in a fight?

Did he win?

At that second, the sound of a gun exploded in my ear.

And I fell to the floor.

26

I didn't feel anything. There was no pain, no light, or any blood. I searched my body for the bullet hole, and I stopped when I saw the hole in Luke's head. Behind him stood Henry, holding Mom's pistol. His hands were shaking, and he dropped the gun. It went off a second time, from the impact, and shot Luke's lifeless body in the stomach.

I turned to the side and vomited. Henry appeared at my back, tapping it as if he were helping me. After a few minutes, Henry grabbed my waist, lifted me over his shoulder, and took off running. Everything was dizzy. I looked, and all of the stop signs were blurry, and passing cars were hard to see. But Henry kept going. I blacked out.

I woke up and we were in the forest. Henry was pacing back and forth, shaking his hands. I sat up, leaves sticking to my back.

"Oh god, I just killed someone," he whispered, not knowing I was awake. "I just shot the boy."

I stood up, and Henry noticed me. He wiped the expression of fear from his face and smiled at me. "Are you okay?"

I nodded, brushing off the leaves and dirt from my back. Henry walked over to me and wrapped his arms around me.

What is happening?

I thought of Luke's dead, unmoving body at the front of the school. I thought of what Ms. Cloud's reaction would be when she found out her son was shot with a gun. I wondered what her reaction would be when she found out he killed someone with a gun.

"I thought you hated me," I muttered in Henry's ear. He pulled away from me and shook his head.

"I don't like you at times, sure," Henry admitted, backing away from the hug. "But you're my brother. I couldn't lose another brother."

I noticed the backpack Henry was wearing, and I asked him what it was.

"Oh, just clothes and such. I grabbed it when you asked me to go out because I was going to go see a friend."

I nodded, then a thought ran through my head.

"Oh my god!" I yelled, walking away from the forest. "I need to get to Marie."

"No," Henry said, grabbing my wrists. "We need to go to the police."

I shook my head, prying my arm away from him. I remembered Marie's fragile state when I left. Her finger hovering over the trigger, ready to shoot at anything that moved.

"Marie is scared and alone."

Henry gulped. "Okay, how about this? We go to the police and tell them everything that just happened. I'll go home and get Marie."

I nodded, turning to walk, when Henry grabbed my shoulders. His face darkened, and he tightened his grasp on me.

"But Kyle, you need to tell the police you shot Luke."

~

Henry convinced me that he could go to jail because Luke wasn't attacking him. We created a story where Henry had the gun, but Luke tackled him, which made Henry drop it. I picked it up and shot Luke in the stomach, then again in the head when he tried to slash Henry with a knife.

We went to the police station and told them just that. The officer I was with the last time took me into a little investigation room. It seemed like we spent hours there.

"Alright, Kyle, can you tell me exactly what happened?"

I nodded, going through the whole thing with her. I started with coming out of my house, leaving out the part with the phone. I jumped to see Luke with a knife and running. I told them about being at the school and how I was yelling at him. Then the rest I just told them what Henry said to say.

"What kind of gun?"

"Pistol."

"You're sure?"

"Positive."

She didn't ask me any more questions and told me I was free

to go. Henry was already out, and they said that they were going to send someone for his mom and told us that I had to stay.

"He's a minor, and we need his parents here before he can go."

Henry nodded and sat down beside me. I turned to him, waiting for him to realize what he needed to do.

"Henry," I said. "Marie!"

"Oh right. I'll go get her," Henry said, standing up. He left the station and walked away. I watched him until I couldn't see him any more. I was waiting patiently for my parents or even Henry with Marie. I was starting to make friends with the lady behind the desk when I overheard something.

"You think they match up?" The officer that said this had a mustache that looked like a worm on his upper lip. The lady he was talking to was short with black hair.

"Yeah, except with this case," she said, pointing to one folder. "Cloud was killed with a pistol, according to the kid. The older boy brought in a revolver, which is what Walter was killed with."

What?

"You don't think they…"

"No, how stupid could they be to bring in the murder weapon of another case?" the lady asked, slapping him with the folders. "I think the kid doesn't know his guns."

But I do.

He had a pistol.

I thought about where Henry would've gotten a revolver. My breath got stuck in my throat as if someone just shut it off. I stood up and tried to walk out the door.

I need to get to Marie.

Tears streamed down my face as I screamed at the officer holding me back. He had ahold of both my arms, bringing me to the ground. Everything was happening slowly to me. I started begging for them to let me go, that my friend was in trouble. Whispers were exchanged, and the image of Marie dead on the floor in my room taunted me.

He killed her.

Epilogue

Henry's Room

There was no one with him. He was alone in the empty, broken home of his. Darkness surrounded him as he made his way down the stairs. Flicking the light on, he walked around his room. The walls were painted black with red dripping down them. His collection of weapons was expanding and seemed to overflow from the hiding spot under his bed. Guns and knives take up a lot of room; Henry was going to need to get a bigger spot to put them all. He couldn't imagine parting with even just one deadly weapon. The posters hung up on the walls contained things from a horror movie. People getting their skulls smashed in so hard that they looked like a broken, plastic doll. Another poster had a detached head placed next to a body. The eyes had bugs crawling out of them, peeling back the eyelids to escape from its mind.

Henry giggled, thinking about Kyle, who was most likely freaking out about the gun switch. Kyle had no idea that the revolver Henry turned in wasn't the actual one. He didn't have time to deal with the girl just yet.

"I have a girl coming over."

Henry stared at Kyle, unsure of what to say. Out of all the excuses he could've used, he picked that one?

"Sure. I just need to grab something from my room. Then I'll go."

Henry went down his stairs to his bedroom when the door from upstairs slammed shut. Henry knew Kyle's friend was waiting in his room with his gun. Her fingerprints getting all over the trigger button. He had followed them from Luke's, making sure his plan was going perfectly.

Henry grabbed Luke's phone from his desk and sent a text to Nick's phone.

To: Nick
Kyle will see you soon, Nick.

Those kids didn't even try to hide anything they were doing, Henry thought. Walking through the streets with a gun, yelling in Kyle's room. Henry saw them as amateurs. They were like ducks being hunted by a hunter. They had no clue what they were messing with.

Henry started up the stairs, going to Kyle's room. He could hear the panicked breathing from the girl inside; she was a terrible hider. Henry knew how easy it would be, how it wouldn't be as fun as the others. His hand traced the handle, the cool metal sending shocks up his back.

He went to open the door when a noise from downstairs echoed. Luke was early; he was too early. He wasn't supposed to be here for another five minutes. Henry quickly readjusted his plan and headed downstairs to deal with his problem.

"I'll come back for you."

Henry sat down on his broken chair, leaning his head on the desk. Blood splattered across his arm. He was unaware of who the blood belonged to. He turned to his closet where Mark Evans's dead body remained. When he heard of Mark dying at the hands of someone else, it made him boil with anger. So, he thought that if he couldn't kill him, he deserved to at least have the body.

Henry took out his key and unlocked the drawer beside him, pulling out a journal. He flipped through the pages until he landed on one with blood smeared all over it. Nick's name was written in black ink, crossed over with an X. Henry smiled to himself, remembering the night his plan took off.

He could hear the arguing of the teenage boys ahead. Henry peeked his head through the bushes, clutching the revolver to his chest tightly. As if it was a toy and some kid was going to steal it. He saw Nick push Kyle's chest. Henry knew the time was coming. Kyle couldn't control his anger, never mind his strength. Henry squatted down, aiming the gun at Nick's head. He was far enough away for them not to see him. Nick yelled something about lies, and Henry watched as Kyle's eyes turned red. He pushed Nick with both hands, resulting in Nick falling to the ground. Right before he hit his head, Henry pulled the trigger. He was aiming for his head, but it hit him in the back of his neck. Henry cursed silently, waiting for Kyle's next move. Henry observed as Kyle reached down, trying to clean up the blood. After a few minutes, Kyle took off running.

"Perfect," Henry muttered, stepping out of the bush he was hiding in. He walked to Nick, leaves crushing beneath his feet. He stood over the lifeless boy and watched the blood pour from his head. Henry realized that Kyle pushed him hard enough that it cracked his head open. Henry bent down and took some blood in his hands. He started smearing them on the trees and the ground, making it look like the kid struggled. He then wiped off any fingerprints Kyle might've left behind. He didn't want his brother to suffer at the hands of someone else. He grabbed the phone from Nick's pocket before grabbing him and throwing him over his shoulders. He knew exactly where to put him; he had picked out the spot the day before.

When Henry arrived home, he unlocked his drawer and crossed out Nick's name, smearing his blood on the page. Henry leaned back in his chair, wiping the sweat from his face. Then, he did something he hadn't done in an exceedingly long time.

He smiled.

Henry grinned, thinking about that night, how the fear rose in Kyle's eyes when he realized his best friend was dead. How crazy he went thinking it was him. He was even admitted into the psych ward because he started hallucinating.

Good, Henry thought to himself, turning the next couple of pages. The smell of rotting was in his room, but it never bothered Henry. Ever since he was little, he never minded the smell of corpses. Of plants, animals, or humans.

The next page spelled out Mark's name. Henry had crossed the name off with so much pressure and anger, he ripped through three pages. Good thing he had spaced them out so much, otherwise it would've been ruined. Underneath the name Henry had written.

Didn't get the chance.

He had everything planned out. The first time Mark got away because Henry let him. Letting him reconnect with Kyle was all part of his plan. At the hospital, he was going to replace Mark's IV drip with mercury. The IV bag was in a sleeve, so nobody would have noticed the difference until it was too late. However, when Henry got there, he was already dead. He came home that night to write up a new plan.

"Hold the door, please!" Henry yelled to the nurses up ahead. The nurses turned around to see him running at them. They all gave each other looks, and he smiled at them, holding up a brown paper bag.

"My mom is the chief, and she just called me to say that she forgot dinner, so I brought some to her," he explained, holding the edge of the door. "She told me to use this door because it's past visiting hours, so the front is closed."

The nurses smiled at him and moved out of the way so he could pass through. As Henry walked away from them, he heard their whispers, saying he was a good son. He moved through the halls swiftly, quick on his feet. He walked down many hallways and took a bunch of turns to go where he needed to.

Henry knew that Mark already had his autopsy, and the body was in the morgue. He found the door that he spent many hours at as a kid and walked inside. A doctor was standing in there, facing the metal boxes they kept the bodies in. Henry pulled out a rag that had chloroform on it. He walked behind the doctor as quietly as he could and gently placed the cloth over his mouth. A grunt came from the doctor, along with a bit of a struggle, but it wasn't long before he was on the ground. Henry searched through the morgue, looking for the body he so badly desired. He opened many coolers to find different dead people until Mark Evans's lifeless eyes stared back at him.

Now to get him out. Henry knew that the cameras right outside the door were broken. And all the ones down the hall to the exit were off for the shift change. It was the new way to stop the alarms that were set off by motion detectors. He bagged him up like a doll before leaving. He didn't want to run in case someone was nearby and saw him. He managed to escape the hospital without a single person seeing him.

He walked past a fenced-in house where he felt a tug on the bag. He realized that part of the fence was sticking out and hooked itself to the bag. Henry pulled on it, ripping the side of the body bag. Mark's arm fell out of the bag, dripping with blood. The fence must've gone through the skin as well. Henry quickly placed it back in the bag then held it from the side that was broken. He made it to his car and threw Mark into the back. Henry didn't even bother putting him in the trunk. When he got home, he lugged the bag over his shoulder, hoping it would keep the body from falling out. When he got to the front door, the bag had ripped even more, showcasing half of Mark's body. Henry grabbed Mark from the bag and threw the bag in the trash. The smell from Mark would spread throughout the house, but if Henry moved quickly enough, he would be fine. No one would notice, especially since it's so late. Henry dragged Mark's body into the house and down the stairs. When Henry was at the bottom of his stairs, tugging the dead body into his room, he heard a creek at the top of his stairs.

"Dammit." He breathed, using all his strength to pull Mark into his closet as fast as he could. He left the door open and ran up the stairs. He swung open the door to be greeted with an armed Kyle.

"What? Kyle?" Henry asked, his eyes narrowing on the pistol in his hands. "Why do you have a gun?"

Henry smirked, thinking of how he pulled off his greatest plan. His eyes moved to the jar placed by his bed. Seeing a tongue placed inside there made him grin with excitement. The tongue started to turn brown, so Henry had to figure out how to make it last longer. He didn't need his room smelling any worse. His attention shifted back to the book. He flipped through the next couple of pages, landing on Luke's name. His hand twitched for the pen to the side of him. He crossed the name off with a huge X. He wished he had the chance to grab the bullet from Luke's chest, but he couldn't because of Kyle. The pistol he killed him with would do as a souvenir for now.

Henry walked down the street with a backpack filled with his greatest goodies. Making a couple of turns, he finally made it to Luke's house. It was broad daylight, so there was no way in which he could sneak. So, he had to walk in. Luke was with Kyle, and Luke's mom was out with her girlfriend. Henry had been tracking which days she was out.

Henry pulled out a key he had swiped from Luke that day to unlock the door. He planned on putting it back if he made it back in time, so he was already wearing gloves to make sure his fingerprints weren't anywhere in the house. The door clicked open, and Henry made his way inside.

He kept his shoes on, pacing the floor. He climbed the stairs and made his way into Luke's room. He placed his bag down on the ground and pulled out his items: Nick's phone, a journal, and revolver. Henry placed Nick's phone in the drawer by his desk, leaving it the tiniest bit open. He placed the journal under Luke's mattress. Henry had to find a spot for the gun. He noticed a creaking in the floorboard below his feet, so he tore it open. Nothing was inside until Henry placed the revolver in there. He closed the board, clearing up his mess. He quickly left the house, leaving everything else as it was.

Everything was in place.

Henry had swiped Luke's phone a couple of days later. Long enough to know Kyle wouldn't be texting him, waiting for a response.

Henry placed the bullet in the journal, under Luke's name. He taped it and admired the bullet. His work was almost finished. His plan, which had taken years of development, was finally coming together. He stood up, closing his eyes to live through each kill. Each plan he made and him getting away with it.

A knife was sitting on his desk, which he wrapped his fingers around, picking it up. Kyle came to mind, which made Henry fume. He took the knife and stabbed it into the desk, cutting the wood. Henry sat back down, flipping through the pages before landing on a name that made him so angry he could kill. Which he did. He circled Kyle's name ten times. One for each time he wanted to run the knife through his body. Henry sighed, leaning back in his chair. He muttered something, only for his ears.

"For Max."

"Dad!" Kyle's voice screeched. "Something's wrong with Max!" Henry and his dad were sitting inside the sunroom. Henry had gotten sunburnt and didn't want to play outside any more, so his dad offered to play a card game. Kyle and Max were hanging by the pool, but they weren't allowed to go swimming because Max was too young. Neither one of them wanted to go inside, though, so their dad let them relax on the chairs.

"What's wrong, Kyle?" he asked, standing up. He placed his cards down, walking away. It was hard to hear what Kyle was saying from where they sat. It was something like, "I was…swimming." Henry had no idea what the middle part was, nor did he care. He reached

over and started peeking at what cards his dad had. There was a loud yell that echoed through Henry's ears.

He never liked things that were too loud.

Henry winced and scraped his chair back. He ran outside to see his father hunched over the side of the pool, reaching for something. Kyle stood behind him, shaking. His entire body looked like it was vibrating. Kyle turned to Henry with tears brimming in his eyes. Henry raced over to Kyle and his dad, his feet slapping against the burning concrete. His dad grabbed ahold of what looked like an ankle. He pulled on it, and a body came with it. He placed the body onto the cement and started pressing against his chest. Henry noticed that the face was all blue and it belonged to his little brother Max.

Kyle jumped onto his dad's back, screaming, "Stop! You're hurting him!"

His dad grunted, trying to keep up with the compressions while also fighting Kyle. Henry lunged forward, tackling Kyle to the ground. Both boys hit their heads with a loud smack against the ground. Henry tussled with Kyle, holding him to the floor.

"He's trying to save him, idiot!"

Henry's emotions fled wild. He couldn't control them. He had no idea what he was truly feeling. It was a mix of anger and sadness. And he didn't know what to do. He just looked back at his dead baby brother and cried. Kyle ran inside and dialed 911.

But he wasn't calling for Max.

He called the police on Henry for hurting his wrist.

Henry snapped the pen in half, thinking of what Kyle did. At the hospital, Kyle admitted that he was trying to teach Max how to swim. Henry knew then that he hated Kyle. He started to practice how to hunt and stalk his prey. All the feelings and urges Henry was told to suppress came tumbling out. There was no controlling them.

Henry stared up the stairs, picturing the trembling girl holding a gun. He laughed about how easy it was going to be. Although, he never made a page for her. He never thought Kyle would make another friend. He scribbled down the name: *Marie*.

Henry whispered under his breath, something that he had whispered three times before.

"I'm coming."